# When Angels Lie

## All hell is let loose and demons fly !

## by

# Richard L Gray

**Magpies Nest Publishing**

First Edition
Published by Magpies Nest Publishing 2004.
Printed and bound by BemroseBooth Limited, Derby.

Further copies may be ordered from:
Magpies Nest, 5 Old Hall Drive, Ulverston. LA12 7DG
www.magpiesnestpublishing.co.uk
email: angels@magpiesnestpublishing.co.uk

ISBN 0-9548885-1-0

# Acknowledgements

My thanks to all those who have helped and encouraged the writing of this book.

For now we see in a mirror dimly, but then face to face.
Now I know in part; then I shall understand fully, even
as I have been fully understood. So faith, hope, love
abide, these three; but the greatest of these is love.

1 Corinthians 13, vs 12-13.

# Prologue

Rita stood over Paul, looking at him accusingly. "You're a fool, Paul Stringer; can't you see what's happening? You're living a lie. It's become infectious and affecting your thinking. How can you minister to others when you need to be whole yourself?"

He jumped out of his chair and walked away from her, putting up a hand as if to ward her off. "Don't start again — I can't argue with you — I am what I am."

"You've given the Devil a foothold in your ministry," she shouted.

Angela stirred and mumbled, "Don't hurt me, Paul darling; I don't want you to hurt me." She moaned a little but was soon snoring again.

Rita frowned and looked at him closely. "Is there something you're not telling me, Paul?"

Paul groaned in frustration. He was about to explain when the doorbell rang followed by an urgent pounding of someone's fist. He hurried to the hall and opened the door. Kevin Raymond burst in cursing and swearing. Paul tried to hold him back but Kevin thumped him on the jaw, knocking him sideways.

Fury flashing in his narrow beady eyes, the churchwarden held up a little gold cross hanging from a fragile chain. "I found this on the chancel steps. The last time I saw it was round Angela's neck. I'll bloody kill her!"

He barged into the sitting room, pushing aside Rita who was trying to stop him. "Get out of the way — you're nothing but a bloody witch."

When he saw his daughter lying prostrate on the couch, he stopped as if unsure what to do next.

Angela began moaning again, "Paul, don't hurt me." Suddenly, she rolled from under her coat and off the sofa. Still muttering his name, she lay on the floor completely naked — trickles of blood staining her thighs and a little blue gem twinkling in her belly button.

"What the hell?" bellowed Kevin, rounding on Paul.

Paul, still shaken by the earlier assault, felt a painful blow to his stomach and then to his chin. The room swam around him....

# Chapter one

Spellbound, he sat listening to his liberal opponent, Canon Nick Palmer, conclude his address to the conference. It was a popular quotation from Saint Paul's letter to the Corinthians:

"If I speak in the tongues of men and of angels, but have not love, I am a noisy gong or a clanging cymbal ..."

Paul was completely captivated; partly by the words he'd heard that morning, but mostly by the messenger himself. Except for height and build, Nick Palmer was completely opposite in looks to himself. Nick's hair was short, fair and curly, his face a pleasant oval, his eyes blue and bright, his nose straight and his lips full and gently smiling. Although slim, his shoulders were broad — a living statue of Apollo.

For the first time in his life, Paul Samuel Stringer, the long-haired, tall, dark and handsome evangelical priest-in-charge of a deprived urban parish found himself to be in love. Impossible! It was against everything he believed in. In a state of utter confusion, he went to his room and took a cold shower.

Sitting with his therapist, Joy, two months later, Paul tried to get his thoughts together. His eyes roamed unseeingly around the comfortably furnished office with its shimmering French Impressionist prints on pale yellow walls. For a moment he focused on "Poplars on the Epte" by Monet, if indeed, focused was the right word. Like his present life, it seemed to consist of indistinct reality, and yet it held light and beauty impossible to describe in mere words. He thought of Nick and sighed deeply. He brought his mind back to his counselling session. He'd already told Joy about the conference where he'd met Nick Palmer; now he was determined to open up and admit to falling in love with the man.

"You're in the driving seat, Paul," Joy said placidly, "take your time."

He felt a need to justify his homosexuality. "I was confused by my attraction to Nick. I tried hard to avoid the slightest contact with him — not as easy as it sounds." He smiled to himself, thinking of the drastic lengths he'd gone to. "Then fate took a hand — or was it God? We literally bumped into each other. It was a moment I'll never forget." He paused to relive the experience. "You know how these things stand out in your mind."

"Perhaps you might like to share it with me," Joy said encouragingly.

Paul looked at his therapist's friendly lined face with its gentle eyes and passive smile. He warmed to her receptive posture — she made him feel at ease. Yes, he could tell her; she was a good listener. He began again.

"I was carrying books and nearly dropped them. Nick caught hold of my arms to steady me. You've no idea what that did to me — I was utterly thrilled. We looked into each other's eyes, muttering conventional apologies. My eyes were drawn to those smilinglips — mm, yes. I couldn't help it, you see."

Paul frowned. "I couldn't understand what was happening to me; it was against everything I believed in. Can't tell you how I felt about it really." He gave a deep sigh. "I guess Nick was kind of surprised too. He wanted to talk in private. He gave me his key and asked me to go to his room; said he needed to have a word with his wife Lucy first. She was waiting for him downstairs. That was a bit of a shock — I didn't know he was married."

He paused and looked at Joy; she was nodding in empathy.

"Waiting for Nick was absolute agony. What on earth did I think I was doing in another man's bedroom — a married man at that? But of course, I knew why I was there; I just couldn't admit it to myself. I paced the floor, utterly disgusted — part of me wanting to get the hell out of there. The door opened and Nick came in. When he closed the door behind him, I was visibly shaking. Nick noticed — he kept his distance. 'I only want to talk to you for a minute or two,' he told me, smiling that lovely smile of his."

Paul took a moment to recall his first intimate moments with his lover.

"I can see him now: leaning against the wall by the window, sunlight catching his hair and turning it to burnished gold; his eyes, the colour of the sea on a perfect day." He grinned at Joy. "Sounds corny, doesn't it?"

She smiled benignly. "I would say romantic, delightfully romantic."

"He said his marriage to Lucy was in name only. He told me

he was gay but had been celibate for a number of years. I was surprised at his openness and said so. He looked me straight in the eye. 'I know you won't betray me,' he said with utter confidence. I was flattered. 'How can you be so certain?' I asked him."

Paul hesitated, unsure whether to elaborate. "Perhaps I should tell you I was wearing tight jeans, and, well — I guess you get the picture."

Joy was nodding. Yes, she understood — good.

"You can imagine; I was so embarrassed I dropped the books I was carrying. Nick smiled at me, in an understanding sort of way. He helped me pick them up. 'You're the same as me — that's why,' he said, quite casual like. I tried to deny it but of course he was right; Nick's right about everything. When he held me in his arms, I didn't resist — I just couldn't help myself. Then he kissed me. I had never felt such sensuous pleasure. For the first time in my life, I came alive to what I am."

After a moment, Joy said, "I can feel it in your voice, Paul, and see it in your eyes — you're obviously a man in love."

He wrestled within himself. Dare he make his final confession, that he'd broken the Church's taboo? He must — confession was good for the soul. "Since then we've become lovers. I'm now a practising homosexual."

Joy smiled and nodded in simple acceptance of his sexuality.

A weight seemed to lift from his mind. He could now tell her how dramatically his life had changed. "I no longer feel those black and white certainties that I once did. Nick's opened up my mind, you see. He's incredibly wise and knowledgeable — spiritual too. Some people can't stand his liberal attitudes, but even his critics admire him. We're quite opposites you know. Nick follows High Church tradition; I've always been Conservative Evangelical. I'm emotional; Nick's the strong one."

"Mm; sounds as if Nick's helping you grow."

"Yes, I think he is. Walking and talking together, hearing him play the organ in his beautiful old church — that sort of thing, I can see things differently now. I've had to question what I truly believe. But you know, after my zealous anti-gay preaching I feel a hypocrite of the worse kind. I may have changed the emphasis of my teaching but I'm not free to come out."

"I can understand that," Joy said, nodding in empathy.

"Of one thing I'm certain, I must leave my present parish — perhaps leave the Ministry altogether. I can't talk to my rural dean because he's homophobic. That's why I approached my bishop. As you know, he suggested I see you before I make irrevocable decisions. But I don't seem to be getting very far."

"Paul, I know you want guidance, but I want you to realise the depth of your own resources; the God within you as some might say. I would like you to make a journey into your imagination — a journey of self-discovery. It might help you find direction as to where you're going. Where God is guiding you, if you prefer to think of it that way."

"But I don't know what God wants of me anymore; if indeed he still wants me to serve him."

"You're still the same person as when you were ordained. Now you know more about yourself, that's all. I think what we're about to do might clarify your thoughts and feelings. Anyway, are you willing to try?"

Paul closed his eyes a moment. How he wished he could have writing on the wall and a voice from heaven — something to give him the kind of certainty he'd always felt about his vocation. But yes, he had to travel the road set before him. He could only trust it would lead him back to God and to the security of knowing his ordination was indeed genuine.

"Yes. I am willing," he said, quietly but firmly.

"I'm going to give you the bare bones of the journey. You let your imagination fill in the details. I will take it very slowly. If you drift away from what I'm saying, don't let it bother you — this is your journey."

Paul lowered his head and whispered a quiet prayer asking for enlightenment.

Joy began: "You're at the foot of a low mountain. It's getting dark but there is a bright moon. You look upwards and know that somehow you must get to the top. You find a path leading in the right direction...."

Paul sat listening as Joy slowly gave him the story outline. His imagination was fully at work. As the story came to an end, he found himself in tears.

"If you would like to talk about it," Joy said softly, "I'm ready to listen."

Taking out a handkerchief to wipe the wetness from his cheeks, Paul nodded. "Yes, I would like to."

"Give yourself a moment — there's no hurry."

"Such a very bright moon and a cloudless sky. The path is smooth and well lit. I know where I'm going and I'm jogging along. The way gets steeper — I have to watch my step. A few rough stones appear — I kick them out of the way. I'm strong and I can do anything. Small boulders roll in front of me — I leap over them. Huge rocks block my way but I scramble over them. I'm filled with power. Nothing can stop me!"

His voice changed as his journey took a sudden turn. Elation turned to despair.

"The moon has disappeared. All is darkness. I'm tripping over." He put his hands to his face and moaned, "There's no light to guide me. I'm stumbling in the dark. I don't know where I'm going. I'm lost."

He heard Joy's voice from far away: "Take your time. There's no hurry; take your time. Stay with it; you're coming through."

"I'm stumbling upwards, bumping into things. Suddenly I see the light of a fire ahead. It draws me like a magnet. Someone is sitting by the fire. He is the Ancient of Days — he always has been and always will be. He points for me to sit opposite him. I ask him, 'What do you want from me?' He doesn't answer. I plead with him, 'Tell me what you want me to do? Please, please, tell me!' But he doesn't answer.

"I look at his face. How strange — it's young, not old. I look into his eyes but all I see are two deep dark pools. They're sucking me in — deeper — deeper. I'm trying to resist — I can't, I can't! They're pulling me into him — I have to let go. I become part of him."

He stopped for a moment, savouring the comfort of peace and tranquility after the emotional storm.

"It feels good and I want to stay. I'm safe and secure. I open my eyes and I see myself sitting there — in front of me. I hear the question I asked and see the pain on my face and suddenly I'm back inside myself.

"The old man gets up and walks away. I can't see him. Now he comes back to the fire. He's handing me something. I know what it is even before I look at it. It's an old Bible, thumbed through thousands of times and worn at the edges. The book falls open at John's gospel — light flows outward from deep within the pages. I feel completely overwhelmed with love."

Tears came to Paul's eyes. They were tears of joy and, not wanting the beautiful holy feelings to stop, he let them flow. After a few minutes, he continued with his story.

"I tell him that the gift is too precious to take from him. He pushes it firmly into my hands. He doesn't speak but somehow he communicates. I must go back into the world and share my gift with others — all who will receive it. I walk down the path; the light of my gift is showing me the way. I reach the bottom of the mountain. I open the Bible and a strong beam of light stretches out into the darkness. A voice is telling me to trust the light and take it into the dark places. All will be revealed."

Joy gave him a few moments before speaking. "That's quite a journey, Paul. Perhaps you would like to share your feelings about it."

"I think perhaps God is calling me to the mission field but I'm not sure what kind. There are so many dark places in need of God's love. I can't stay where I am — my work there is done anyway. I will have to see Bishop Lionel and get his advice. But what of my lover? I can't leave him now that God has brought us together."

Joy gently touched his arm. "It's been a very emotional time for you. Don't rush into anything. Perhaps you should talk over this experience with your partner and tell him how you feel."

He took hold of Joy's hands and looked into her soft eyes. "Thank you for everything. If I feel the need, will you see me again?"

"Of course, but somehow I don't think you'll need to come back. Give me a ring if you want an appointment." She rose from her chair, indicating the session was over.

As soon as Paul sat in his car, he rang Nick on his mobile to ask him if he had an hour to spare that afternoon; he needed to talk to him. Nick said he was about to begin a meeting with Bishop Lionel and the vocations advisers. He told Paul that he had a funeral mid-afternoon but would be pleased to see him any time after four. "Would you like to join Lucy and me for a meal and stay for

Evening Prayer? I can't see you afterwards, we have a Parochial Church Meeting to attend."

"That's great; I have to get back this evening anyway. I really appreciate this, Nick. Bye — see you."

He drove back to his modern, featureless red brick, vicarage home in a bit of a daze. He felt excited by his experience and aglow with love. It was hard to settle down his emotions but he had work to do. Trying to blank out the morning's activity, he shuffled through the untidy piles of paper on his desk, and dealt with correspondence for the next two hours.

As usual, he had frequent interruptions from telephone calls and people at the door. He dealt with each enquirer with his customary patience but with an extra dose of charity. While typing, he ate a hurriedly-made cheese sandwich for his lunch, carelessly dropping crumbs on his computer keyboard. He was picking out crumbled Stilton from between the keys when the doorbell rang. An anxious teenage mother had arrived to see about getting her baby baptised. She was thin and pale, so Paul fed her with milky coffee and gave her the last of his cake, baked for him by a motherly parishioner. He drank his coffee black and shared the last of his biscuits with the young mother — her need was greater than his. As soon as the girl, replete with the milk of human kindness and armed with a booklet on baptism, had left his vicarage, he set off to see Nick before someone else turned up on his doorstep. He might live alone but, apart from bedtime, he seldom had much time to himself.

While he was driving the fifty miles to Nick's place, he tried to think about his next sermon, but Nick clouded his mind. Where did his lover fit in with his own journey? Well, at least being the Director of Ordinands, he would have a very good idea of what mission work might be available in the diocese. A motorcyclist suddenly swerved in front of him causing him to brake hard. It was a sober reminder to him of other road users and of the need for vigilance. Like travelling his new path of life, without due care people could be hurt — especially his loved ones. He glanced in his mirror and automatically adjusted his gears, praying for clear vision and foresight in all things.

When he arrived at St John's Rectory, Nick, although pleased to see him, had only just returned from the local crematorium and was looking a little strained. Lucy made the three of them a cup of tea but left the men to talk on their own. "I have work to do," she said cheerfully. "If the phone rings, you ignore it, I'll answer it in my study."

"Great," called Nick after her. "I'll prepare the meal in half an hour or so. Paul can give me hand."

The two men smiled at each other. Paul knew Nick was holding back; they both were. They had agreed to be utterly discrete and keep their love life entirely separate and at appointed times, but it wasn't easy. Love pulled him like a magnet; he wanted to be near Nick, to touch and hold him, and feel the blending of their souls and bodies. How could he possibly leave the man he loved to minister at some far off place?

"You sounded desperate, are you going to tell me why you are here?" asked Nick. "As much as I adore gazing at your handsome rugged face, either we had better get chatting or move upstairs. We don't have long," he added, his blue eyes twinkling with good humour.

"Now that's an unfair choice," Paul told him grinning. "Actually, I want to talk to you officially as well as personally."

He told Nick all that had happened with his counsellor that morning. Once again his emotions were touched in the telling of the story. Nick came over to him and put a hand on his shoulder.

"A very moving experience," he said gently. "What have you decided? How can I help you?"

"I'm leaving my parish — that is certain." Paul paused a moment. "I think I'm being called to the mission field. Do you think you can advise me? I couldn't bear to be far away from you; can there be anything for me in this diocese?"

Nick was silent for a while. When he spoke again, it was with the voice of his office. "I think you're right to leave your parish; too much has happened for you to be comfortable there. But ring Bishop Lionel; let him know about your decision before you start looking around."

Paul nodded. "You're right of course."

"Now come into the kitchen," Nick said smiling. "We can play happy partners."

Paul normally spent as little time in the kitchen as he could. His meals were always quick and easy; he never had time to waste on food preparation. Pots tended to be left in the sink until needed, and clothes left hanging about waiting to be washed or ironed by his fortnightly cleaner. But with Nick beside him, domestic chores were a joy. They sang joyful hymns together in their rich tenor voices, and laughed at the absurdity of dog collared Paul dressed in an apron printed with the body of a semi-naked lusty male.

When the food was ready, Lucy joined them. The conversation was light and happy. Lucy's presence and tinkling laughter brought radiance to the table. As she talked about her youth work and input into the local school Religious Education programme, Paul could see what an asset she was to the parish as well as to Nick. They obviously worked well together; for a young priest, Nick had given her a lot of responsibility, including oversight of the daughter church with its council estate congregation.

Paul was loath to return home but it had to be done. After Evening Prayer, Nick walked with him to his car parked in the rectory drive. Suddenly, Nick took his arm and walked him back into the house, shut the door and locked it. "Come into the study a moment; I have to speak to you."

They sat in chairs facing each other. Nick took hold of Paul's hand. "I wasn't going to tell you this until you had explored with Bishop Lionel your desire to be engaged in the field of mission. You see; it might be possible for you to work alongside the Church Army on their Bus Project — they have just lost one of their officers. I know the bishop has a high regard for your work among youth and your evangelical zeal is beyond question."

Paul's face lit up. "Do you think that's where God is leading me?" Then a frown drew his heavy brows together. "What about us, Nick?"

"There is an alternative but I'm afraid to tell you about it — it might sway you away from your ideals." Nick tightened his grip of Paul's hand and then released it. He sat back in his chair. "I shouldn't be telling you this, it's the bishop's job. But I'm afraid my selfish desire to have you near me is clouding my judgement about everything." He looked at Paul closely. "It may be that what I was told by Bishop Lionel this morning is the way forward for both of us."

Paul was intrigued. "I don't want you to break any confidences, but it would make my mind much easier if I had that information before I see the bishop."

Nick spread out his hands in an open gesture. "Well first, I'm to be the new rural dean for this area — at least, I've been offered the position; I haven't formally accepted it yet."

"That's great!"

"Before we get diverted," Nick said quickly, "it's the other piece of news that really concerns you. I only hope I'm right in telling you this now." He closed his eyes a moment as though sending up a silent prayer. "Bishop Lionel talked to me this morning about you. Knowing my views, which he shares, he thought I would be sympathetic to your problem and would give you any necessary support. Of course, he doesn't know about us; as far as the bishop's concerned I'm a conventional married man." He paused again, this time looking at Paul and smiling broadly.

Paul was growing tense with excitement. "And? Come on, Nick — get on with it."

"The bishop has something in mind for you. The parish adjoining this one, the Benefice of Longdale, Penningly and Bradmire, has become vacant; their vicar gave up the struggle and decided to retire. Since the three parishes were joined up, it became too much of a strain dealing with the malcontents. While the future of the benefice is uncertain, Bishop Lionel has suspended the patronage and wants to appoint a priest-in-charge with plenty of energy; one who can draw the people together, and is good with young people. Two new housing estates have been built over the last few years, and a large primary school between Longdale and Penningly has just been opened."

Paul couldn't believe what he was hearing. But before he could say anything, Nick put up his hand as though in warning and went on speaking.

"The closing of the small village schools, and the influence of middle-class townies have been the cause of a lot of friction. Money is a pressing problem. The wealthiest church, St Michael's at Longdale, objects to supporting the other two congregations. There's a clash of churchmanship too. If the three churches are to stay open, a lot of work needs to be done."

"With God's help, I can do it," said Paul with confidence, utterly elated at the prospect of working so close to Nick.

"There's more," said Nick, sitting back in his chair and smiling. "There are plans, held up due to objectors, to bring that benefice in with this one and run a Team Ministry. It makes sense. It's a very large area but it would be a sharing of gifts and skills and everyone would benefit. We have a comprehensive school in this parish and the children from the villages come here. The prospect for youth work—"

Nick stopped talking. The bell was ringing at the back door.

Paul jumped up. "Gosh, look at the time. I'm dreadfully sorry; I've kept you from your meeting. They've probably come for you. I'll go." He stood a moment, not wanting to go but knowing he must. "Nick, what can I say? Thanks for everything."

They stood looking at each other and then embraced. The feel, warmth and scent of Nick's body completely overwhelmed him with desires for closer intimacy. But the bell was ringing again. They parted and quickly walked to the front door.

"I love you, Paul," Nick said quietly. "Of course, it would be great to work more closely together but it has its dangers. You must follow your own guidance."

Driving home, Paul had much to think about. Now that leaving his present parish was certain, he was feeling the inevitable sadness of parting from those he had come to love, especially the ones he had seen converted and nurtured in the faith of Jesus Christ. He knew his departure would sadden his flock, but it had to be. Some of his congregation had very strong views on homosexuality; their reaction to his more recent teaching when trying to redress his own previous hard line, had convinced him that he would do more harm by staying than by leaving. They could well throw out the baby with, what they might consider to be, the stinking bath water.

# Chapter two

"Well, what have you decided?" Lucy asked Paul, her face bright with expectation.

Paul had just returned to St John's Rectory where he'd spent the previous evening in readiness for his interview with the representatives of the Longdale, Penningly and Bradmire churches.

"I'm still not sure," he answered frowning. "They all appeared to be keen. Well, not quite all; St Michael's churchwarden, Kevin Raymond, seems to think every young vicar is after his wife and daughter."

Nick laughed. "I know what you mean; every time I've taken a service at St Michael's, and I've done a lot of them this past year, Kevin's been watching out for hanky-panky. But then, his womenfolk do tend to make a fuss of the clergy."

"Especially good-looking ones!" Lucy interjected with a grin. "It's no different for me you know. Wives can get quite jealous if their husbands are keen to help me out. Quite honestly, I think most of the objections about women priests stem from deep-seated fears that we are all Jezebels out to lure men from the straight and narrow."

Paul smiled at his thoughts. "That's rather ironic considering the circumstances," he told her.

"You mean because Nick is gay, and you think we married so that he would be seen as a respectable cleric?" asked Lucy. "We do love each other you know, even if we never sleep together."

"Never?" Paul asked. He already knew the answer to his question but there were times when he needed to be reassured. It was a big step — his taking over Nick's neighbouring parish so he could be near his lover. He was now having doubts about the rightness of it. Was he being tested? He wanted a sign; something to tell him to accept or reject the post he knew would be offered him. The interview with the representatives of the three churches had gone far too well. If they didn't accept him, the interregnum they were in could go on for ages. In a way they had little choice, but he'd been inundated with offers from parishes that knew of his reputation.

Nick was clearly pained by his lover's suggestive question. "What's the matter, Paul? Didn't last night convince you how much

I love you — need you?"

Lucy was looking embarrassed. She quickly rose from her chair. "I'll go prepare lunch; you two can kiss and make up," she said, smiling uneasily as she left the room.

Paul left his chair and walked to the window. The old rectory garden looked fresh and peaceful after the light summer rain. Trees were glistening with raindrops from the recent shower, flowers were bright in the borders and the neatly-mown lawn was the greenest he had ever seen. All so very different from his own place where the kids used his garden as an adventure playground. Beyond the wall, St John's Church, where Nick ministered, was silhouetted against a cloudless sky.

Looking out, he realised it was the same view, only from lower down, as he'd seen early that morning after sharing Nick's bed. It was the first time they had spent a whole night together: kissing and caressing, bodies entwined, twisting and turning in a dance of erotic desire until the heat of passion was spent. It had been a wonderful, magical experience and their time together afterwards, saying Morning Prayer in the Lady chapel, had somehow put a seal to their love. He sighed heavily before answering Nick's question.

"I guess I'm feeling guilty and looking for an excuse not to come here," he said despondently. He was observing a rook cawing loudly in an oak tree and thinking it not unlike the black-robed preacher he'd heard denouncing homosexuality as a sin — a creeping evil within society — and all those who practised it as either sick or unrepentant sinners far from God.

"Guilty? Of what? Falling in love?" Nick almost barked at him. "Don't we believe that God draws souls together? Were it not for man's prejudice, we could live together openly and demonstrate what true committed love really means. But we've been over this many times." His tetchiness turned to anger. "Why did you draw Lucy into it?"

Paul felt the sting of Nick's rebuke. It was the first time he'd heard Nick raise his voice to anyone and it pained him considerably. He kept his eyes fixed on the rook, not wanting his lover to see how much he was hurting. "I guess it's because you've made a commitment before God — it must mean something to you. You even look the perfect couple. Perhaps I'm jealous; I just don't know."

Nick took hold of Paul's shoulders and turned him around to face him. "Why should I have to keep telling you this? You know I love Lucy. Yes, we both made vows before God and we will keep our vows to love and to cherish. We enjoy living together and it's very convenient for both of us. She's an excellent curate as well as being my wife." He softened his voice. "Lucy is a godsend to both of us. Don't you accept that?"

Paul considered Nick's statement. "I don't know about that, Nick. Suppose Lucy meets some nice guy and wants to marry him — or live with him?"

"You know as well as I do, the divorce rate among clerics is little different to the rest of the population, but it won't come to that. We both knew what we were doing and meant what we said. The only thing different to normal marriage is that we don't have sex with each other. We don't want to and don't need to."

Paul was silent, feeling ashamed of his doubts. Nick continued:

"Lucy won't mind me telling you this; she's quite capable of satisfying herself without me. She says her heart belongs to Jesus. Marrying a priest without giving him her heart or body gives her room to love God without being pestered by men."

"I understand. I'm sorry, Nick, really sorry. It's still so new, my emotions run away with me." Ashamed of his doubts, he turned his eyes away from Nick's penetrating gaze. "I want to be near you and I have to restrain myself. It isn't easy. Accepting the new post would be ideal but it all seems to be going too smoothly. The Christian path isn't meant to be so easy."

"Paul, ask yourself how you would take it if nothing but obstacles barred your way. Surely you would be saying that it wasn't meant to be! Believe me, whatever impression they gave at your interview this morning, the job isn't easy — it broke Jim Smithson. Apart from notable exceptions, they're all renegades determined to get their own way. Sure, they want to keep the act going but they'll soon let you know who's paying the piper. Believe me, it's going to be no picnic!"

Paul sighed. "Now I feel quite inadequate."

Nick slapped Paul's shoulders and laughed. "Cheer up. Smile! The Christian path isn't meant to be smooth, or so you tell me. Don't forget, as rural dean, I'll be here to support you."

Paul decided to go to Longdale after lunch and take another look at St Michael's. He wanted to get a feel for the place on his own. Nick, who was overseeing the parish during the interregnum, said he had a key and, since he was visiting a bereaved family nearby, would drive him there.

"I'll leave you at St Michael's and pick you up later," he told Paul "You can have the key to the vicarage too. Be sure that is where you want to live. Penningly had a new vicarage built a few years ago. When the parishes were joined they expected their new vicar to live there. Jim Smithson refused to move from Longdale. Since the new house is only rented out, you could move in there pretty soon. Being smaller than the old vicarage, it's more convenient for a single man."

"Won't that upset the people of Longdale?"

"Whatever you do, you'll upset someone," replied Nick solemnly. "Be clear from the start, you won't be pushed around. If you are united in your own self, it will help the three congregations to come together."

Paul looked at Nick in total admiration. The man had a strong air of authority about him, and yet he could be so very understanding and gentle. No wonder he was on a number of important Diocesan Boards and Committees.

It was but a short drive to Longdale from Nick's rectory at Glenton. Paul said very little during the few minutes they were together; he just wanted to rest in the warmth of Nick's presence. In a few months they would be neighbours. It was a thrilling prospect but he knew their times of being together would still be limited.

When Nick stopped the car, he handed Paul the keys to the church and vicarage doors. With deep emotion, he pressed them into his hand. "Be alone with God. Get the feel of the place. You'll know if it's right for you."

Paul watched Nick drive away and then, with determination, walked up the wide path bordered by yew trees. He reached the porch of St Michael's Church and turned the key in the lock. Somehow the interior of the building seemed different to when he'd been taken there that morning.

He walked silently around the carpeted nave, slowly drifting up to the chancel where he sat and knelt in the vicar's stall. In spite of it being much more ornate than what he was used to, somehow it felt familiar. He walked to the sanctuary and looked at the beautiful gold-embroidered cloth that fronted the altar — magnificent! He admired the fine carved reredos. He smiled at the enormous brass cross and the gleaming polished candlesticks — such items were not used in his present church.

He had a simple oak altar, placed where the people could gather round to share in the bread and wine — passed around the circle to his brothers and sisters in Christ. His altar was unadorned, save for a simple wooden cross and a white linen cloth during Communion. But he did have bright banners, designed and made by the youngsters, hanging around the otherwise plain walls. St Michael's had an exquisite wall-hanging of St Michael surrounded by angels, but no children's work — that was something he would definitely have to remedy.

Except for when the sun occasionally streamed in through the stained glass windows, it was fairly dim in the church. He didn't care much for the ornate marble plaques and expensive memorials to past patrons, and the effigy of a notable offended his evangelical sensibilities. A gaudy statue of the Virgin Mary, standing by the MU banner, suddenly tensed his stomach muscles. These were things he would have to live with — but could he?

He walked around, getting the feel of what it would be like to be fully robed and taking a service with revered ceremony. He was happy about it when he'd taken part in a service at St John's with Nick by his side, but now he was feeling nervous, as if he were about to betray everything he had always believed in.

He was accustomed to a lively music group and singing of choruses so popular with the youth, as well as the usual popular hymns accompanied on an electric organ. Could he adapt his style of ministry to embrace the formality of organ music and robed choir?

Paul was beginning to waver again. The people may want him because of his reputation for filling pews and bringing in young people, but how will they feel about his methods? The interviewers had failed to get to grips with that aspect of renewal; they were more concerned with discussing results. When he'd talked of changed lives, they had smiled benignly. Did they just want him there to put bums on seats? And by doing it their way? Impossible!

He sighed heavily and made his way to the pulpit. He walked up the steps and looked around as though addressing a congregation. He wasn't used to being so elevated above the people but he realised, until they had a sound system put in, he needed the height. He knelt in prayer for a few moments, agonising over his situation and begging God to clear his vision.

"Jesus, my Lord, give me light so I can see into the unknown," he pleaded.

When he rose from his knees, his eyes rested on the words embroidered on the handsome green and gold pulpit-cloth in front of him. As he read the verse, copied from Psalm 119, the hairs of his neck stood on end and his whole body trembled. He fell to his knees, his mountain journey vivid in his mind. He could see the gift in his hands and the light beaming out of it. Elated, he stood up; resolved never to doubt again. He took deep breaths to control his emotions and then read out the words on the pulpit cloth, as though to his congregation. His voice was clear and strong, and full of conviction.

"Thy word is a lamp to my feet and a light to my path."

As the words reached out into the dimness of the church, for a moment the whole building seemed to come alive. The sun had come from behind a cloud, illuminating the building with a blaze of light and colour. It was as if the church was filled with a crowd of witnesses: men and women from the past who had prayed, hoped, praised and fed from the Body of Christ in that ancient consecrated building.

Paul was jubilant. He had asked for a sign — surely this must be it! God had spoken to him. He was in the right place. No more doubts and no more fears; he was in the will of God and all would be well. Ecstatic, he lifted up his eyes and flung his arms wide.

"Alleluia! Praise the Lord!" he yelled. And then his eyes glazed over with tears of joy as he sang, "How great thou art", in his powerful tenor voice.

As he came down to earth, he breathed in deeply. He'd been in heaven singing with the angels; now he had work to do.

From the back of the church came a sweet youthful voice. "Hello; are you our new vicar?"

Paul looked down the nave of the building. A girl dressed in white had come quietly into the church with a bunch of flowers. She was framed against the open door, and a trick of sunlight from a porch window gave her pale golden hair a glowing halo. He was taken aback. How long had she been standing there?

"Hello," he said cheerfully, covering up his embarrassment, "it seems an angel has caught me out."

The girl laughed. "Actually, I'm Angela Raymond. My father is one of the churchwardens here."

"Well, I can't answer your question, Angela. You probably know I came this morning to see your father and others, but we have to wait and see the outcome. There is much to consider."

"I know you're coming here. I just know it," said Angela forcefully. She laughed merrily. "Everyone knows angels don't lie."

Paul smiled. "Is that so? I suppose you've heard your dad talking. I have to be certain about coming here too, you know."

"But you will, I know you will. I asked God to send us a nice young vicar, not some old codger like Smithson — ready to push up the daisies in the churchyard."

"Really, Angela, that's not a nice way to talk about a servant of God," said Paul sternly, as he made his way down the steps. "Jim Smithson had a hard job to do and he gave of his best." He looked at her and smiled; now was not the time to argue Christian charity. "We'll leave it at that, shall we?"

"You're Paul Stringer. My sister said you were good-looking. She's right. Are you married?"

"Gosh, what a nosy child. It's none of your business," Paul told her, shaking his head sternly to hide his amusement.

"I'm not a child," Angela retorted, pouting her lips. "I'm eighteen," she said defiantly.

Paul looked at her more closely. She had put down the flowers and was standing with her arms akimbo. Her shoulders were pulled back, forcing her ample breasts to push at the fabric of her low-necked shirt. His eyes were drawn to a glittering blue jewel that was attached to her belly button, revealed in a gap between her top and her skimpy white leather skirt. She was short to medium in height, chubby but shapely with it. Lovely blonde hair framed her round pretty face and she was glowing with youth and vitality. Her light-blue eyes were sparkling as she saw him looking her over.

He could now understand Kevin Raymond's worry concerning his daughter.

"Eighteen? Really?" said Paul, thinking her to be more likely fifteen, or possibly sixteen.

"Well nearly. I've left school though, " she told him, still pouting her pretty full lips.

"And I thought you said angels don't lie!" Paul replied, smiling at this forward young woman. She wasn't multi-pierced and made up heavily like some of his own flock but he suspected that was only because her parents kept a close eye on her.

"It was only a teeny one," she answered, relaxing her stance. "I'm starting college soon. I want to be a secretary."

"Just as well. You might find being an angel a tough occupation," he told her grinning.

She pulled a face at him. "You didn't answer my question."

"What was it?"

"Are you married?"

"I'm married to my vocation," he told her, turning to leave the building.

She shouted after him, "Catholic priests say that and we all know what they get up to."

Paul turned back. He wasn't shocked; he was used to much worse statements from teenagers. At least, she wasn't using the type of language he'd often heard.

"I'm being serious, Angela. But you know, you shouldn't believe everything you read or hear."

"Oh, yes? Well my dad says they should have it chopped off!"

"I'll disregard that remark. Perhaps your next priest will open up discussions on the meaning of vocation. Maybe on love and loving too." He made his way to the door; "Well, it's nice to have met you, Angela, but I have to go now."

"I'll see you again soon," she said, picking up her flowers and moving up the aisle.

Paul turned as he went through the heavy oak door into the bright sunshine. Angela was standing watching him with her flowers in her hands — just like a bride. She smiled and gave him a little wave. He waved back.

He was about to go through the gate to the vicarage garden when he realised that he'd left the church door open for anyone to walk through, or birds to fly inside the building. And did Angela have a key to lock up after her? He retraced his steps.

He was amazed by what he saw and heard. Verdi's Chorus of Hebrew Slaves, coming from a disc-player, met him at the door. Angela had taken off her trainers and was dancing to the music in the chancel. Paul slipped inside and sat on a back pew watching her. He was utterly enchanted by her graceful movements and interpretation of the music. The sound changed to an upbeat love song and with it the movement of her dancing. Clearly, she had a wonderful gift to offer the Church. He smiled at his thoughts: his little angel's talent could be the cornerstone of a youth dance group, just like he had in his present parish.

He was loath to stop her and decided to creep outside again. She must have come expecting the door to be locked and probably had her father's key. He decided to do a quickie of the vicarage and return to check. As he was about to go down the path, Kevin Raymond appeared. He looked at Paul in surprise. "Come to have another look?" he asked abruptly.

"Yes. I hope you don't mind. Canon Palmer gave me the key."

Raymond shrugged his shoulders. "Why should I mind?"

"Your daughter is inside. Does she have a key to lock up?"

"No, but I have. She's supposed to be meeting me outside. They'll be others here shortly. There's a funeral in church tomorrow morning. The rural dean will be taking it. They don't want the organ. They're playing bloody tapes, or something or other. Don't know what the Church is coming to. Before long they'll want bloody dancing in the aisles! Anyway, I must go and see if the grave's ready." He walked off to the side of the church and was soon lost among the gravestones and trees.

Paul smiled but said nothing. Kevin Raymond was only one of the congregation and, with God, all things were possible.

He walked to the vicarage and had a look around. It certainly did not have the grace of Glenton's eighteenth century rectory, but the Victorians had made good provision for a cleric of reasonable means and with a big family. He liked the feel of the place: the rooms were large and airy with tall windows letting in the light.

The largest reception room was big enough for good-sized meetings — lots of possibilities there. Since the nearest hall was at Penningly, maybe they could do something at the vicarage for local children. He walked up the wide staircase to the bedrooms. Lots more possibilities. He looked out of the windows. The huge garden with its large patch of level lawn was fantastic for kids. He could already see himself playing football with the lads. His imagination ran riot. He could get indoor toys and outdoor playthings for young children and invite young mothers to come together for a simple ten-minute service, followed by a chat over coffee. Oh, yes! And they must have a crèche. Plenty of room for everything and everyone. His head buzzed with ideas. He made his mind up. Surely, this was where God wanted him to be.

He walked out, locking the door behind him, and made his way back to the church through the garden and along the churchyard path that ran amongst the oldest of the tombstones, to wait for Nick. He was just in time to see Angela run out of the church and go into the trees. She was crying and holding her hand to her face. He sought her out, but she saw him coming and dodged away. Clearly, she didn't want to be seen and so he didn't follow her. Had her father caught her dancing and they'd had a row? Surely he hadn't slapped her? He sighed; Kevin Raymond might well turn out to be his biggest obstacle to renewal.

As Paul turned towards the gate, he stopped. Just in front of his feet, a small object was catching the sunlight filtering through the trees. He thought he knew what it was — Angela's glittering blue jewel. He picked it up, almost reverently, from amongst the pebbles and odd bits of confetti, and slipped it into his pocket. Had her father told her off about that too?

Nick's blue Mondeo drew up at the gate. Paul jumped inside and began talking excitedly about his experience in the church. Nick listened most of the time in silence, occasionally smiling and nodding. He gave a little laugh when Paul mentioned the things said by Angela. He smiled appreciatively at her dancing and Paul's plans for her, but his face clouded over when told about what had just happened.

"It would have been Kevin — no doubt about it. Not the first time either. It will be a happy day when he gets voted out of office," Nick said, his face taught with anger.

"Or when he gets converted?"

Nick smiled. "You're right. He wouldn't be the first hard case to have a change of heart."

Paul laughed, but suddenly he became serious. "No indeed. The pity is, I can easily confess my love for God but I can't openly confess my love for you."

The Mondeo turned into the rectory drive — a long stretch of yellow-gritted asphalt bordered by a variety of flowering shrubs. Not given to gardening, Paul could only recognise azaleas and rhododendrons.

"Maybe one day," Nick said, breaking the brief silence. The car slowed to a halt. "We just have time for a drink before Evening Prayer. Lucy's expecting you to stay for supper; all right by you?"

"Well, my lot will have to get used to not having me around. "I'll phone Phyllis, our reader, and ask her to take the baptism preparation class on her own tonight."

Nick pulled on the brake. "Good. But I have a meeting tonight. Want to stay over for breakfast?"

Paul looked at Nick. He saw the same desire burning in his eyes that he too was feeling. "Yes. I do."

Nick squeezed his hand but quickly released it. He left the car and headed for the door. Paul followed slowly behind him; his emotions were roused and he needed to calm himself. He drifted into the kitchen and stared unseeingly out of the window while Nick made them some tea. Sudden squabbling of birds, vying for food thrown on the grass, snapped him out of his dreaming. He turned from the pleasant view of lawn and orchard and joined Nick at the round breakfast table.

On a blue floral cloth, which matched the kitchen seat cushions and curtains — tell-tale signs of a woman's touch — Nick had placed a plate of Lucy's cookies and a pot of tea. Humming softly, Nick poured golden liquid into china cups. They helped themselves to milk; neither took sugar. Drinking tea, they sat in silence for a few moments before Paul quietly voiced his thoughts.

"I've never asked you, Nick, were there many others before me?"

"No, only one."

"Was the relationship important to you?"

Nick smiled ironically. "Yes, very. We both said there would never be anyone else. We had a small private ceremony and made vows to each other. Of course, we never expected to live together as partners."

"What happened? Or is it too painful to speak about it?"

"He became a bishop. He was right for the position; no one ever doubted it." He gave a deep sigh. "We both knew he had no choice but to become celibate — he was too much in the public eye. After much prayer, I decided to do the same. You see, that way neither of us would break the promise we'd made to each other. To be truthful, I didn't want anyone else — not ever. I came here to minister. Sometime later, Lucy came to be my curate. We got on well. One night I was feeling lonely and broken. I confessed to her that I was gay. A year later we were married." Nick paused a moment, his gentle blue eyes fixed on Paul. His voice softened to a tender whisper. "Then God sent you into my life."

In truth, Paul was jealous of the lover who'd meant so much to Nick. But he was overwhelmed that such an upright, deeply spiritual priest had broken a vow for love of him. He looked into Nick's eyes as passion swelled in his heart. But what he had to say could wait; they had a whole night to spend together.

# Chapter three

The licensing of Paul Samuel Stringer to Longdale, Penningly and Bradmire took place in September on the Feast of St Michael and All Angels. More than two coach-loads of his former parishioners, plus friends and family, joined the congregation and made sure that not a seat was left unoccupied; chairs and a couple of benches had to be brought in to avoid standing. The choir was crammed together in stalls on one side of the chancel while invited clergy and readers filled the seats on the other side, spilling out on to chairs placed in every space big enough to take one.

Considering the differences between the churches, and the wrangling and bitter disputes they constantly engaged in, the occasion appeared to be a joyful and harmonious event in the life of the community. The three Mothers' Union groups pulled together to produce a very handsome feast; nothing was lacking and, like the Feeding of the Five Thousand, a considerable amount of food was collected afterwards. It seemed that most people wanted to be involved one way or another and Paul found the response very heartening; surely it augured well for the future?

Much to Paul's joy, the choir of St Michael's was joined by the struggling remnants of the other two churches, and for once they all had an opportunity to sing out their voices together and to good effect. With the powerful playing of the organ, the rich voices of most of the clergy, and the congregation's joyful singing of the hymns Paul had chosen, it was indeed an occasion to remember.

Bishop Lionel's address made it even more so. He spoke in no uncertain terms of the need for tolerance, and the strength achieved by pulling together. "You have been given a rare opportunity to receive, as your minister, a young energetic priest. One who is known to be a popular preacher, a pastoral counsellor and a keen worker among the young. It is my hope, and my fervent prayer, that you will nourish and care for him, so that together you will seek to expand God's Kingdom in this place."

During the reception, the youngsters from his previous parish crowded around Paul. From the comments made to him afterwards, this youthful adulation gave his new parishioners hopes for their own young people who were presently alienated from the Church. After the coaches had left, Paul had a better chance to meet the locals and those clergy still at the reception. A few of his fellow ministers were sceptical of Paul's chances of repeating the success of his former parish. They were not afraid to say so.

Robert Black, an elderly priest-in-charge of St Jude's in the neighbouring parish of Oaklee, was exceedingly pessimistic. "This parish isn't too bad but didn't Nick Palmer warn you about the other two? Jim Smithson wanted to close Bradmire, St Mary's. He was lucky to get half a dozen there some Sundays, and that included the churchwardens and organist. He tried a youth group and the locals complained; they didn't like the noise and the kids turning the churchyard into an obstacle course. Rude letters were put through his letterbox after the meeting to discuss turning St Mary's into a chapel of ease."

George King, Black's far neighbour, chipped in, "Haven't you said enough, Robert? Paul will be resigning before he's begun and we'll be back helping out here!" He turned to Paul. "Anyway, if you need a shoulder to cry on, give me a ring." He grinned and added, "I'll have to watch you with my dear wife though; Linda's taken a real fancy to you."

"Yes," said Robert. "If you haven't got a woman already, best to get on with it. All the mothers will be out to catch you for their daughters, and the dads will be after you with their shotguns!"

"Now are you two trying to get rid of our new priest before he puts you in the shade?" said a woman's voice from behind them. "But, I must admit, I don't envy you, Paul."

Paul turned and saw a slim, attractive young woman in a blue dress. She smiled at Paul and introduced herself as Rita Lee, St Michael's organist.

"I'm really pleased you've come, we need some young blood. We'll do everything we can to help; some of us are quite excited at getting things moving again. This was a vibrant parish a few years ago — touched by charismatic renewal. If we could get certain folk out of office, it could be again."

She gave him a beaming smile and then made way for Bishop Lionel who was approaching, apparently to say his farewells.

An hour later, most people had gone from the Penningly Church hall, the tables had been cleared and the dishes washed. Paul made a point of personally thanking the ladies left behind for their work and welcome. Accompanied by Nick and Lucy, he waved a last farewell and made his departure, feeling tired but elated. In near silence, he drove to Longdale vicarage where the Mondeo was parked.

After spending most of the week moving furniture around his vicarage, hanging curtains and laying old but serviceable carpets, Paul was ready for bed and a good night's sleep. Lucy tried to persuade him to go back with them and stay the night.

Paul thought a moment before deciding. "Thanks, I really appreciate the offer, but now my ministry has begun in this place I feel I have to be here tonight."

Nick nodded. "As much as I would like you to take up Lucy's invitation, I have to agree with you. A wise decision, Paul."

They jumped out of Paul's Land Rover Discovery and walked over to Nick's car. When they reached the blue Mondeo, Paul said to Lucy, "Thanks for asking the parishes to donate furniture and carpets for the house. I've had jolly good stuff brought round — very useful. It's been grand to meet some of the folk too. My cupboards are full of tins of cakes and biscuits baked by the ladies. It's unbelievable that the folk here have such a bad reputation."

"Honeymoon days, Paul. You haven't had chance to upset anyone yet," said Nick. "They see a keen energetic young man itching to get on with the job. They'll soon be letting you know when your enthusiasm fails to live up to their expectations. Anyway, enjoy it while it lasts."

Paul embraced Lucy in a brotherly fashion. He turned to Nick and offered him his hand: "Thanks for everything; I'll see you in the morning."

Nick grasped hold of Paul's hand. In the light coming from the vicarage windows, he looked into his eyes. "God has brought you here, Paul; never doubt it. I'll support you every step of the way, and so will Lucy. It's good she's taking our services on Sunday so I can give you a hand with your first Eucharist here. I feel the sharing to be very symbolic of things to come."

Paul felt Nick's love flowing into him. "I'm looking forward to it too." Pressing his hand before releasing it, he added joyfully, "I'm so pleased you persuaded the other two congregations to give up their services and come here. It will be quite a united occasion."

Nick shook his head. "Believe me, they were not happy about it. Each of them wanted to have their own services. But, you are right, it will be a blessed occasion for bringing unity out of division."

Nick slipped into his car and sat beside Lucy who was in the driver's seat. Paul waved them off until the car turned the corner of the lane. He suddenly felt very alone. Excitement of the day's events having worn away, he was only too aware of the monumental task that lay before him. Before he could rest, he knew what had to be done.

Collecting the church key from the vicarage, he took the garden path that led to St Michael's. A lamp in the nearby lane lit his way but he wished he'd brought a torch; the church was in darkness and trees cast too many shadows to see properly. As he neared the porch, he heard voices; one he recognised as Angela's.

"Gerroff, Mark! I don't want to."

"You can't be a virgin for ever."

"Who said I wanted to be?"

"Well then — come on. You like what we've done so far."

"That's different."

"Not much. Come on, Angie, get 'em off — they get in the way."

There were sounds of scuffling and Angela yelling, "No! Gerroff! I'm going."

"Oh, no, you're not!"

"Just try and stop me!"

"You're always teasing."

"Huh!"

"Come on, Angie — please?"

"No! I keep telling you, I'm saving myself."

"Who for? That new vicar you're always talking about? Come out of the clouds and get real; he won't marry a kid like you."

"Kid? Thanks very much! I'm off."

"You're not going anywhere! I'm sick of you having me on. After all the things I've given you, it's pay-back time!"

Paul decided it had gone far enough. He walked quietly back down the path and then started whistling as he once more made his way to the porch. Sounds of scuffling met his ears. Angela came out of the darkness.

"Hello, it's you, Angela," Paul remarked casually. "I thought I heard someone shouting. Are you all right?"

"It must have been kids, Mr Stringer; they're always messing about in the graveyard," she answered nonchalantly. "They often come in the porch to smoke. My dad says we should have gates to keep them out."

Paul could sense, rather than see and hear, the boyfriend adjusting his clothing. "Do you have someone with you, Angela?"

"I'm here," said Mark stepping out of the blackness. "We're going."

"I don't think we've met," said Paul, sweeping his eyes over the young man and noticing his appearance not unlike his used to be. Since his association with Nick, Paul had smartened himself up. Now he only wore jeans when doing scruffy jobs and, not wanting to look girlie, he kept his hair much shorter than before.

"He's Mark," said Angela.

"Angie's boyfriend," said Mark with emphasis.

"Huh! Not any more."

"We'll see about that," snapped Mark, and started to walk off.

Paul felt like giving him a good thrashing. He watched him pull a bike from behind a tree and pedal off down the path and through the open gate.

Angela was saying, "He's dumb. Can't take no for an answer."

Paul turned to her in the semi-darkness. "Are you really all right, Angela?"

"Of course I am. Anyone messing with me knows what he'll get."

Tough talk, thought Paul. He'd heard it many times and he knew it often masked nasty incidents and near misses. Girls often dressed for attention but not all of them were happy when they got it. Not one girl, however scantily dressed, adorned with make-up, or bolstered with breast implants had ever turned him on. He could only use his imagination as to how most boys felt and reacted.

"I think I'd better take you home," he said, as he walked Angela down the path.

"I've got my bike," she answered, sounding disappointed.

"No problem. It'll go in the back of the Discovery."

"That's a big car for a vicar," she said, causing Paul to grin.

"It's getting on a bit. I had it converted to gas so it's not too bad on running costs. It was jolly useful in my last parish for taking small groups places. We did a bit of green-laning as well. I like to get off the beaten track and take to the hills. I do a bit of walking up there."

"I wouldn't mind coming sometime," Angela told him but Paul just ignored her remark and walked to his vehicle.

She collected her bicycle. Paul put in the back of the Discovery while she stepped up into the front passenger seat. They hadn't driven far along the lane, when they passed Mark standing with his bike under a tree.

"Cheek! He was hoping to get me on the way home," said Angela angrily. She turned in her seat to watch him until he was out of sight. "I don't think he noticed it was us." She started laughing gleefully. "Serve him right if he's waiting all night!"

A few minutes later, Paul was lifting Angela's bike out of his Discovery. As he drove off, curtains parted in the front room of her house and a face peered out. Perhaps he should have stopped to explain. It was too late now. On the way back, he saw Mark still waiting. He slowed down and gave the young man a wave as he passed him by. In his mirror, he saw him get on his bike and cycle off.

Paul parked at the church and went inside, sitting in near darkness. He prayed for understanding, wisdom and unconditional love for his flock. He then settled into contemplative silence that was beyond words. After thirty minutes, spiritually refreshed, he went home to bed, tired but at peace within himself.

When he arrived at the church on Sunday morning, a number of people were already busy. In the vestry, Kevin Raymond was unlocking the safe for the sacristan to retrieve the silver vessels for the Communion. The churchwarden looked up, greeted Paul with a nod of his head and a gruff, "Good morning," then took out the register and prepared it for signing.

There was little for Paul to do. Someone had ironed his alb and put out his chasuble ready for him to wear. Since Kevin did not appear to want to chat or discuss anything, he left him to his self-appointed tasks.

Walking through into the church, he saw Diana Raymond, Kevin's wife, watering the flowers and replacing the ones that had faded. People at the back were getting out hymn and service books, while others were putting out the plates and wafers ready for the offerings to be taken up. Paul felt a warm glow come over him. He may be unfamiliar with many aspects of High Church ceremony but some things were the same and the people knew what they were doing.

Rita Lee was up in the organ loft practising the processional hymn with a lively beat, and as he returned to the vestry, he could hear Kevin Raymond grumbling that it should be more solemn. A few choir members from the other two churches had arrived in the robing room; they were complaining at yet another service at St Michael's. When they turned and saw Paul through the open doorway, they smiled and almost like a chorus from a Gilbert and Sullivan opera, said, "Good morning, Vicar."

Paul smiled and greeted them in return but he was now seeing for himself some of the stirrings beneath the placid surface of his pond. He walked to the sanctuary and knelt in prayer, as much to quieten his nerves as to ask for the Almighty's help; he'd already done that aplenty before leaving the vicarage.

When he returned to the vestry, most of the choir seemed to have arrived and the crowded robing room sounded more like a rookery. The door opened and the rural dean stepped inside, his robes over his arm. He was greeted with, "Good morning, Canon Palmer," by all who saw him, and was given beaming smiles by the ladies of the choir.

When Nick saw Paul, he smiled and went over to him. "Good morning, Paul, shall we go to the sanctuary and have a word about the service?"

Paul knew it wasn't the service that his lover wanted to discuss, they had already been over it a couple of times; he wanted a quiet moment of communion together. Nick put his hand on his shoulder while they looked at the altar, now aglow with lighted candles and sparkling silver candlesticks caught in the beam of the altar spotlight. "This is the beginning of a new stage in your life, Paul," Nick whispered, "I feel greatly privileged to be sharing it with you." They both knelt for a moment of spiritual unity.

As Paul and Nick were robing, the vestry door opened and

Angela came in with Mark rushing up behind her. Kevin glanced at her with anger in his eyes. She apologised for being late but Mark just mumbled an excuse. They both hurried away to put on their robes.

"Be quick about it, Mark," said Kevin. "The service is about to start; you should have been here ages ago. If you left the bloody girls alone, maybe you'd get here on time!"

Paul was surprised to find that Angela and Mark were acolytes that morning and would be carrying candles in the procession. Kevin told him that the few young people they had in the church took it in turns to assist in the sanctuary. Sometimes, just one or two turned up. This was a special occasion and he'd made sure there would be a good turnout.

The procession was formed. Angela and Mark hurriedly joined it with their candles. After a moment's silence, Paul said a prayer and someone nodded to the organist to bring her playing to a close. The processional hymn was announced; the people stood, and the crucifer led the choir, thurifer, acolytes and clergy around the aisles and finally into their places.

When the service was over, Paul stood at the door speaking to those who were going home and then he went back inside to talk to those who'd stayed for coffee and biscuits. Nick was there listening to Paul's parents. He heard snippets of the conversation.

"It's time our Paul had a wife. He needs someone to keep him company and give him a hand in that big vicarage," his mother was saying.

"You're at it again; he'll find a girl when he's ready," Mr Stringer playfully scolded. "Anyway, leave Canon Palmer to talk to the others, we can discuss our son's love-life later."

Paul smiled at Nick. "I'm sure our rural dean has more interesting things to talk about."

"Oh, I don't know about that," laughed Nick. "But I must go now and give Lucy a hand. I'll see you both later."

"What a lovely man, Paul. You can learn a lot from him," said his mother.

"Yes indeed. I must talk to others, Mum; will you excuse me? We'll have plenty of time at Nick's."

"Of course," his father answered. "You go and do your job."

"I must find Ann and Brian. Have you seen them?" asked Paul. "They'll be off home soon."

"Your sister's looking at the flowers," came a voice from behind him. He turned to see Rita Lee smiling at him.

"Thanks; and thanks to for the magnificent playing this morning. We must get together and explore possibilities for the future," said Paul.

His mother piped in, "He likes to get young people involved. In his last parish they had a lively music group; it brought hundreds into the church. Paul can play a guitar you know, and he's fantastic with his drums. He can play the piano too."

"Thanks, Mum, but I'll be discussing these things later." Turning to Rita again, he muttered, "Enthusiastic mothers; they all think their own son's a genius."

He turned to speak to the others milling around him, but not before he caught his mother saying to Rita, "I see you're not married."

An hour later, when Paul, his parents, and the Palmers were sitting down to lunch in the rectory's dining room — so very elegant with its Adam's fireplace, tall draped windows, and Hepplewhite furniture — Rita Lee was the subject of Mrs Stringer's conversation.

"She's a very talented lady. You're lucky to have her, Paul. She's a real asset, and she's very good-looking, don't you think?"

"I can't see her looks have anything to do with her playing, but she's certainly an excellent organist," he agreed.

"She's head of music at the school here," Lucy informed them. "We get together sometimes to put on assemblies."

"That's useful to know," said Paul. His mind was already working on the possibility of reaching the youngsters in his own parish through the school they attended in Nick's area.

"She's done well to get to be a head of department," said Mrs Stringer. "She can't be more than thirty. Only two years older than you, Paul. Good-looking and talented, and not even engaged."

"Not everyone wants to get married mother."

"Well, she doesn't look the promiscuous sort. She's a lovely girl," his mother persisted. "She'll make an ambitious young man a lovely wife."

Paul wished he could tell his mother the truth about his sexuality but he knew it would crush her. His sister and Brian were having IVF treatment but the possibilities of Ann conceiving were beginning to fade. Hopes for grandchildren were now pinned entirely on him. It was a burden hard for him to bear, but to tell them the truth would be a double whammy!

Lucy put in cheerfully, "With all those handsome teachers she works with, I'm sure one of us will be marrying her off in the not-too-distant future. But you know, Janet, some women prefer to be celibate — as do some men."

"And some folk prefer their own sex," said Paul's father. "It doesn't seem natural to me. Biologically, that is. What do you think, Canon Palmer?"

Before Nick could answer, Paul's mother intervened. "Jack, please don't bring that up again — not here," she said anxiously.

"It's just the right place," her husband retorted. "We have two priests here." He turned to Lucy. "I'm sorry, Mrs Palmer, I accept you have a great ministry as the Canon's wife, but women can't be priests." He looked back at his embarrassed wife. "And neither can gay men. Our church wants to accept a gay curate. It's ridiculous! Homosexuals cannot be priests."

"He says he's celibate," said Mrs Stringer nervously.

Her husband gave a brief guffaw. "What a person says and what a person does, may be quite different. Will our youth be safe? That's what's important."

It was more of a statement than a question but Nick was not prepared to let it go.

"As safe as any young people are nowadays, Jack. A person's sexuality is his own affair. This priest you speak of, has been open about his sexuality. That was a very brave thing for him to do. If he brought the ministry into disrepute through licentious living, that would be a different matter. But the same thing applies to straight clergy. You're more likely to get a vicar running off with the treasurer's wife than with the treasurer. I have no doubt that this curate has been thoroughly vetted, possibly by me if he's in this diocese, and I can assure you the safety of young people is always uppermost in the screening procedure."

"Are you saying, you would accept such a man in your deanery?"

said Jack surprised by what he was hearing.

"I would accept him in this parish. I'm more concerned with a person's gifts and talents, not their sexuality."

Paul looked across at Nick and smiled.

His father obviously noticed. "You surely don't agree with him? Not long ago you were against the ordination of gay men; you told me so yourself."

"That was before I heard Nick speak on the subject. He's a very wise and understanding man, which is why the bishop made him Diocesan Director of Ordinands, and how he got to be rural dean. I trust his judgement."

"Well, I'd take a hell of a lot of convincing!" Jack Stringer said. "I find the whole idea disgusting. The men, if you can call them that, must be sick or depraved. I blame the parents."

"Do you have someone to help you with that big garden, Paul?" Janet said brightly — too brightly. "Isn't it a lovely big lawn? Big enough for tennis I should think. And you have an orchard too with a swing. I saw a see-saw near a big patch of rhubarb, and a splendid Wendy-house under that big oak. Did the last vicar have a large family?"

Paul looked at his mother with genuine concern. Clearly, she was very unhappy with the way the conversation had been going; it showed in her wrinkled brow and false smile. He wanted to hug her, to tell her he loved her, but he also wanted her to know the truth about his sexuality, and that it was okay to be gay. It seemed cruel for her to go on with false hopes of him marrying and producing children. He smiled and looked into her worried eyes.

"Actually, I put those toys there. Sorry, Mum, not for a future family of my own but for the village kids. I saw them for sale on the church notice-board last week. I'm hoping to get a mother and toddler group going, a pram service and other activities involving children."

"I wish I lived near. I'd love to help," his mother told him. "But from what we've seen of the people here, I'm sure you'll get everything you need. Rita seems very supportive and there must be many others like her."

"With his looks, he'll be fighting off volunteers," his father said laughing.

The conversation continued with Paul outlining his many plans and ideas for the future. He felt his zeal building up the more he explained. Lucy and Nick served the food and cleared away dishes but Paul offered to make the coffee. Leaving the others to chat, he went off to the kitchen but he deliberately left the doors open so that he could hear the ongoing conversation.

"I'm sorry for sounding off, Canon Palmer," his father was saying; "especially in your own home; it was unforgivable."

"Not unforgivable, of that I can assure you," Nick replied graciously.

"Our son's lucky to have you two. I know he's always surrounded by folk, but I think he's been pretty lonely living by himself all these years. He doesn't say so of course but—"

Paul heard his mother cut in. "We haven't seen much of him for the last six months. He used to come home sometimes on his day off; said he needed to get away or he'd never have a break. We thought perhaps he had a girl but it seems not. Don't let him work too hard will you? You'd think there was enough work for him to do without all this extra he's planning on."

"That's what keeps him going. Paul isn't the sort to let things stagnate. Bishop Lionel has every confidence in him, and so do I."

"If only he had a wife to support and help him."

"I shouldn't push it Mrs Stringer; not all clergy marriages work and...."

The percolator started gurgling, drowning out all other sounds. Paul was alone with his own thoughts. As far as his parents were concerned, he would always be alone.

# Chapter four

The Saturday after Christmas, Paul was pondering the theme of his sermon for the following morning. He'd already prayed about it but nothing specific had emerged to inspire him. So after fiddling with his pen for a few minutes, he decided to take stock of his progress in each of the three churches within his parish.

On the surface things had gone well at St Michael's. The churchwardens and PCC had responded well to his suggestions to involve mothers and young children. There was no shortage of help for the crèche, pram service or the mothers and toddlers groups. Baptism classes had been started and a few communicants, women in their thirties and forties, had volunteered to assist.

He soon found out that they, and some of the other helpers, had been moved by the charismatic preaching they had received quite a few years earlier. Evidently, the vicar at that time, Peter Millar, had been to a charismatic conference and had come back a changed man. At first there had been a lot of scepticism but after St Michael's hosted visiting charismatic preachers and teams, the congregation had been bowled over — sometimes literally.

During Peter's ministry, there had been a huge increase in church attendance and lay involvement. But in spite of sacrificial giving, and the flocking in of young people from miles around to the special youth services, not everyone was happy. Kevin Raymond led a group of anti-charismatics determined to get their church back to normal.

Rita Lee, who was at the vicarage to discuss music two weeks before Christmas, told him, "Kevin's wife, Diana, got caught up in it. She was baptised in the Spirit. As often happens, she fell over backwards when she had the laying on of hands. She received the gift of tongues at the same time. But then, a lot of people did. It was sort of expected."

Paul asked her if Kevin had been suspicious because he hadn't shared in his wife's blessing.

"Worse than that," said Rita. "They'd been trying for a baby for years. Eventually they adopted a little girl, Angela's sister. But Diana still wanted to have a baby of her own and she asked for prayer. She went to see Peter and he, and others, prayed with her.

Someone spoke with the gift of prophecy saying that her prayer would be answered. Well, you can imagine how pleased Diana was; she started hugging people in church. I think I should tell you, our services were happy-clappy in those days and quite a few of the older people didn't like it one bit. They said it was unholy and people should be more respectful in church."

"And Kevin was one of them?"

"He certainly was. That year was the first time he'd been voted churchwarden and he was taking it very seriously. He wrote to the rural dean, the archdeacon and both of the bishops, but without the full backing of the PCC Kevin was fighting a losing battle. Things were getting pretty bad between him and his wife. Then two or three months after the special prayers, Diana said she was pregnant. Kevin doesn't believe in miracles; if he did, he would have been rejoicing like Diana was."

Paul now had an understanding of the man's attitude towards his daughter.

Rita told him, "Some time before the baby was born, Peter announced that he'd been called to another parish at the other end of the country. A coincidence don't you think? But Diana has always maintained that her daughter is a miracle granted to her by God; that's why she called her Angela."

Paul had seen Peter Millar's photograph in the vestry, in line with those of other past vicars of St Michael's Church. He could easily have been Angela's father. The bullet-headed, beady-eyed, short and stocky Kevin had no features in common with his daughter. Now Paul understood the churchwarden's attitude towards enthusiastic young priests.

According to Rita, the young folk of those days weren't happy to see Peter go. His ministry was exciting and wonderful things happened, especially at the services. Whether young Angela was a miracle or not, some people found healing and a kind of wholeness.

Rita told him, "Jenny Lang had a stammer but by the time Peter left she spoke perfectly. Some of the lads had been on drugs but they came off them and gave their lives to Jesus. The music was great and we had a dance group that performed in church. Special evening services catered for us teenagers and the church was full of lively, happy people who came from miles around."

"What happened to the young folk when Peter left?" Paul asked.

"The youth leaders did their best, but without a spiritual guide to hold them together, and with the antagonism of certain people who deliberately put stumbling blocks in their way, the young people drifted.

"Of course, some remain and you'll soon find out who they are. If they don't hold positions in the church, they're working behind the scenes. We wait for the time when the church will start to live again. I think perhaps our waiting will soon be over, but I don't envy you the task."

As Paul recalled Rita's words, he had a picture of her in his mind. She was looking up at him through her dark-rimmed glasses, her hazel eyes bright with expectation of good things to come. Her smooth dark reddish-brown hair was framing her pleasant square-jawed face and her lips were constantly smiling at him. He recalled her strolling beside him in the vicarage garden. In a way, they were the perfect couple. Both of them were slim and with her being only a little shorter than him, they walked and talked comfortably together. Bill Briggs, the husband of Doreen the verger, was working in the garden and he'd given them a wink. Rita had blushed and looked down at her feet. Paul hoped she wasn't falling in love with him.

Paul brought his mind back to reviewing his ministry. He intended eventually to print out the Sunday services on sheets like many parishes did, and to include notices and general information. The service sheets for the extra Christmas services had gone down well; so had the services themselves. For the first time he had the children from the local Primary School involved in a Nativity play during a church service.

His being involved in the school assembly once a week had brought many benefits. The children obviously enjoyed his visits and the staff liked having him there. Cooperation was excellent. They put together a Christingle service for Bradmire St Mary's. He'd used his puppets and got the children and parents involved in every aspect of the service; the place was packed. The moribund church had come to life!

Certainly, his ministry was going well but he was still unhappy about the spiritual life of his parish. And he had a deep concern for the disaffected youth who hung about the villages getting into trouble.

He was dwelling on the way ahead when the ringing of the doorbell interrupted his thoughts. Rita Lee had arrived to discuss Sunday's hymns. Paul took her into the only homely room in his vicarage — the kitchen. It was big and old fashioned with a central heavy oak table, a few chairs to match and an assortment of cupboards around the walls with the usual necessities for modern living; the fridge and microwave oven being the ones most used. A couple of comfortable armchairs were in front of a log-burning stove and Paul ushered his visitor into one of them. While Rita, dressed in a smart long-skirted brown suit and cream jumper, took off her long fashionable camel coat, Paul apologised for the informality.

"The central heating's on but this is the only warm room. My study's a bit on the cool side and I haven't lit a fire in the sitting room. Will you have a coffee and mince pie? My tins are full of the things. I guess the kindly ladies here think I need the calories."

"Or maybe a wife," said Rita laughing. "Thanks, I'd love a coffee but I'll give the pies a miss."

He poured out some coffee. "Help yourself to sugar and cream."

"Just black, thanks. You know, there's quite a bit of speculation going on. All the old biddies are either watching the comings and goings at this place, or choosing a wife for you. Most of your parishioners think you should be married."

"Possibly. But it won't happen. I'm married to my work." Paul told her smiling, not the least offended.

As Rita, crossing her long legs, settled back in her chair, she asked, "Does that mean you're celibate?"

Paul looked her in the eye. He would like to tell her the truth and he certainly didn't want to lie, but the question should not have been asked. Was she fishing to know where she stood? Her eyes gave nothing away.

Rita broke into his thoughts. "I'm so sorry. It was impertinent of me. I've offended you. Of course you are. Oh, I'm sorry, I'm doing it again. Your sex life is your own business."

Paul smiled. "Suppose we discuss the hymns for tomorrow?"

"I'm more concerned about our youth, and the spiritual needs of the parish."

She instantly had his attention. "Those issues are very much on my own heart too."

"That's wonderful," she said, her eyes lighting up.

"When I came here, you invited me to the prayer group that meets in Longdale. I'm sorry I haven't managed to get to a meeting yet."

Rita shrugged her shoulders but said nothing.

He continued: "It seems a poor excuse to say that you meet on my day off, especially since I took a funeral on one of the days, but with all the extra activities recently I just need to get out of the parish. When I'm at home, I'm constantly bombarded with visitors."

"I'm so sorry. Have I disturbed you? I could easily have phoned the hymns for tomorrow. You were probably busy with your sermon or something."

"Saturday is not my day off, and anyway you have something important to discuss with me." He could easily have told her that he enjoyed her company but he didn't want to give her the wrong impression.

"I thought we could move our meetings to a day that suited you, but I wasn't sure if you wanted to come to them anyway."

Paul felt uneasy. His day off had been a good and genuine excuse not to go to Rita's meeting but now he had to face the real reason why he avoided them. From what other parishioners had said, Rita's group was charismatic. The members practised the gifts of the Spirit and he wasn't sure how he would fit in or react to the goings on. After all, he was supposed to be the spiritual leader of his flock.

After a moment he said, "I really am keen to have prayer meetings and study groups; they're important to the life of the parish. I'm hoping we can get a few going, perhaps starting them during Lent."

For the next ten minutes Paul went over one or two courses; Diocesan recommended schemes of an evangelical nature. "Perhaps some of your members would like to act as leaders?"

"You have to get people to the meetings to start with. Jim never could. One or two would come at the beginning but they soon lost interest. Our group has gone on for years."

"So I've heard. It's very commendable and shows a lot of commitment," Paul said quickly. He didn't want to alienate her; she was important to his plans, apart from which, he didn't want to hurt her feelings.

"We support one another. Jim would have nothing to do with us. He wasn't exactly anti-charismatic but he might as well have been. Because he didn't support us, folk were suspicious."

"I can understand that, especially after what happened in Peter Millar's day," said Paul, giving her a hint to his own feelings about charismatic groups.

Rita frowned. "You know, Paul, you'll find plenty of parishioners who'll join you if commitment is not involved. You'll get them to do anything if it's social, including money raising. But if it's spiritual, I'm afraid you're on your own except for us. We really do support you."

He knew the arguments; they were only too familiar. In his urban parish, he'd won the people over through the evangelical traditions of the church, encouraging lay participation and bringing in the youngsters. Now, he was in a rural parish and the traditions were totally different. But he believed in the power of prayer. God had brought him there and God would surely show him the way. Was Rita there to open his eyes?

"I have to be honest with you, Rita. Past charismatic renewal movements have done a lot to reawaken the Church to the third person of the Trinity, but they also caused divisions. It's not long since the Toronto Blessing caused upsets. It did in one of my neighbouring churches. They had people laughing and barking during the services."

"I am aware of the problems; they are constantly thrown at us," she answered a little touchily. "But you can't toss aside the work of the Spirit because of mistakes and excesses. Even the first disciples were not perfect. We have to admit our blunders and move on, not deny the gifts God has given to his Church. It's like denying the joy of nuptial union because the couple might enjoy the sex."

"That's perhaps an unfortunate metaphor considering what happened here all those years ago."

"Love affairs happen in the Church all the time, why should charismatics be different?" Rita asked him. "Of course, people expect us to be pure and holy and are ready to condemn us when they act like other Christian sinners. Surely you must know clergy who have fallen from grace? There are some in this diocese who are divorced; you're not telling me it's always the fault of their wives? And what about gay priests?"

Paul was not going to be drawn into that argument. He changed tack. "The Holy Spirit works in many ways and endows the Church with many gifts, not just the spectacular ones. I just want us to keep some sort of perspective when we talk of God's gifts."

"I haven't come to ask you, or anyone else, to join us. Our group is praying for revival, and has been doing so for years now. You arriving at St Michael's has given us hope. Just let us know of anything specific that you want us to pray for. And remember, we are prepared to put prayer into action, and that means using all of God's gifts."

Paul felt ashamed. There was a lot of quiet ministry going on in the parish and Rita's group did much of it. Names were sometimes mentioned, and occasionally the speaker had the person tagged with Rita's prayer group as though that devalued the charitable action. In his mind, he could hear Doreen the verger's voice, "Oh, Betty's being visited. Joan Simmons goes to see her — she's one of Rita Lee's lot. Though what a lot of mumbo-jumbo does for her, God only knows!"

"I'm sorry, Rita. I'm not trying to dismiss the blessing God has given you and others. I guess it's outside of my own experience. When I was converted, I know I received the Holy Spirit; call it a baptism of the Spirit if you will. I felt a strong call to the priesthood and that's never wavered."

Paul suddenly realised that statement wasn't exactly true. When he'd accepted he was gay, he had indeed questioned his vocation. It was in St Michael's church that certainty had returned. Was it for more than ministry that God had brought him there? Did God intend to illuminate him further? Was he missing out on Spiritual gifts that would aid him in his ministry?

Rita was speaking to him. "I wanted to ask you if you would be interested in going to a conference with me on the Spirit's work. It's called, 'Cool to be a Charismatic?' There's a particular emphasis on youth and evangelism. Maggie's had to drop out and her place is paid for. It's just before I'm back at school. Wednesday to Friday of next week at the Riggington Conference Centre. It's only thirty miles up the M6."

Paul was taken aback. Was this from God or a mere diversion

from the way he intended going? But he couldn't dismiss it out of hand. "Can I let you know tomorrow? I must admit I have no meetings next week but I need to pray about it."

Her whole face lit up. "That would be fine. Let me know after the service in the morning." A contented smile curled the corners of her lips. "Perhaps we'd better go over the hymns now; I've kept you from your work long enough."

After Rita left, his mind was in turmoil. There was something about Rita that excited him. Nothing sexual but an indefinable magnetism, which he could only put down to her relationship with God. But to go on a conference with her, was it wise? Perhaps not.

He went back to his study with its bookshelves full of books and heavy theological tomes he seldom, if ever, used. He picked out a huge concordance and looked up references to the Holy Spirit. Sitting at his cluttered desk, he added a few notes to the sermon that he had been preparing before Rita arrived. Turning to his computer, he began to type. He felt very much inspired and now knew what he had to say.

Only a minute or two had gone by when the doorbell rang again. This time it was Angela.

"Has Miss Lee gone?" she asked. "I saw her come here. I don't want to interrupt you."

"Rita came to talk about the hymns for tomorrow. She's gone now." He opened the door wider for the girl to step inside. "Can I help you, Angela?"

"Actually, I wondered if I could help you," she told him with a nervous smile. "I'm getting on well with my secretarial course and I would like the practice of doing some proper stuff. I've got my own computer and printer. Well, it's my dad's really but he lets me use it. I do his typing for him."

He led her into the kitchen. She sat herself down by the stove and spent some time reeling off her achievements. He didn't want to cool her enthusiasm but neither did he want her to be continually around him; dangerous situations could arise. She had already taken over as crucifer most Sundays and filled in for others when they couldn't get there. But she had brought a couple of eager beaver lasses with her and they wanted to get confirmed and help out too. A few lads hung around outside the church waiting for them and before long he would get them inside. Angela was good for business!

"It's very generous of you to offer. I'll have to think about it," he told her.

Angela was not going to be put off. She removed her damp jacket and made herself more comfortable. "I could easily have done those carol and hymn sheets for you, and those special service booklets you did for the Christingle — anything. It would be such a help to me and it would save you time."

"Paul smiled at her eagerness. "I already have a lot of stuff on my computer, so it hasn't been such a hardship to do it myself. But it really is kind of you to want to help. I'm sure I'll find something."

"I know how to use photocopiers too. I can do all sorts of things," she said enthusiastically. "Wouldn't that save you even more time?"

It was true; if he had help with his admin he would be able to do more visiting. He'd heard a few grumbles that the Bradmire folk received less attention than the others did. He had to admit that he couldn't even remember the names of most of their PPC members. There was plenty to do but was Angela the right person? If he found someone else though, the girl would be dreadfully hurt. There was no question of getting paid help; two of the churches couldn't even pay their way. He decided to chance it.

"Tell you what, I'll show you how to use my computer. Everything I need has been put into it. Next week, I'll show you how to do the baptism sheets, complete with hymns and baby's name. Then you can print and fold them ready for the service. We'll see how you get on and take it from there."

Angela was overwhelmed with joy. "Thank you, Mr Stringer. I won't let you down. You'll see, I'm good at that sort of thing; I've been using my dad's computer for yonks! When do you want me to come? It'll have to be evenings or weekends."

"Ah, yes." Paul didn't want her in the evenings if he could avoid it. "How about Saturday mornings? We'll have to change the time when we have weddings but come at nine if you can manage it."

"I'll be here. Oh, I'm so excited! Thanks ever so, it's the best Christmas present ever!"

"No, Angela, I should be thanking you for offering to help. I really appreciate it. Just make sure your mum and dad approve."

"Why shouldn't they? They both do things for the church."

"Quite right, but ask just the same. I have to go out now; a bereavement visit to make in Bradmire."

He ushered her to the door and was about to help her on with her jacket, when he looked outside. The sky was dark with rain clouds and it was bitter cold. Her denim clothes were quite unsuitable for the weather.

"Your jacket is still damp. Your jeans must be too. You can't go home like this, Angela. I'll drop you off on my way to Bradmire."

She made no objection. He slipped her jacket over a radiator and went to his study to get his funeral notebook. He picked up his keys and returned to the hall. Angela was looking at herself in the big mirror. She was pursing her lips as she tidied her hair, and pushing forward her comely breasts in a very alluring manner. He smiled at her teenage vanity.

"Put your jacket on, Angela. Time to be off."

Within a few minutes she was going up the drive to her house. It was now pouring with rain but she wasn't hurrying. Once again, someone was looking out of the window. He didn't hang around. In his mirror he could see Angela standing waving him off, the front door opening and her being pulled inside. He could imagine the scene taking place inside her house. He'd often seen her with a red mark on her cheek and bruising on her arms. But, although Kevin shouted at his daughter in the church, he hadn't witnessed her being physically abused by him.

Within five minutes, Paul was knocking on the cottage door of the Cranford family's home. Old Mrs Cranford opened the door. Sitting cramped together in front of a television were her immediate family of son, daughter-in-law, four grandchildren and two great-grandchildren. He recognised them from the recent Christingle service. They were watching football oblivious to anything else going on around them. Mrs Cranford shooed a cat off a dining chair at the back of the room and indicated for him to sit on it. She sat down beside him. The others in the room ignored his presence.

It was hard work getting anything out of Mrs Cranford about her late husband. Even then, the television and whoops of excitement were drowning out anything she did say. Eventually, Paul asked if they could talk elsewhere or turn down the telly. She took him into the untidy kitchen. She offered Paul the only chair, but he insisted on her doing the sitting. Before she sat down, she picked up a dirty mug, swished it round with water from the washing up bowl and poured him tea from a chipped pot. She handed it to him and then looked at him through red-rimmed eyes.

"I'm sorry, Vicar, it's not fresh, we're out of tea bags. They all landed on me yesterday and there's nothing left in the house. They're drinking pop and beer. They're off early evening until the funeral on Wednesday morning."

Paul sympathised with her on her loss. She nodded in response but said nothing. Holding the cup of vile tea, he asked her specific questions about her husband. Before long she was talking freely, memories of times good and bad causing her to smile or frown. He sat on the edge of the table empathising with her: smiling during happy moments and holding her hand when tears rolled down her cheeks. Eventually, he wrote down the hymns she requested.

"My lot can't sing, they just mumble. Will you sing the hymns too, Vicar? I heard you singing at that Christingle service — you've a lovely voice. My Fred was there too. He enjoyed that hymn about walking in the light. Would you sing that for him at the funeral?"

"Certainly, I'd be pleased to, Mrs Cranford."

"I'm glad you've come here," she told him with a quivering smile. "They're a lot of old miseries at our church; they need a bit of livening up. I'm going to come every week now. Couldn't get before. It took Fred till dinner time to get up in the morning, what with his heart and crippling arthritis. Had a bad time of it — poor lad. But he's at peace now."

After a little while, the kitchen door opened and youngsters came in searching for goodies. Mrs Cranford gave them a tin of biscuits, still wrapped in Christmas paper. Paul took his leave, saying that she and her family would be remembered in the parish prayers.

Back at the vicarage, he put some tea, milk, sugar and biscuits in a bag for Mrs Cranford. On a little card, he wrote a note saying he hoped they would come in handy, and that he looked forward to having a cuppa with her during his visits in the weeks to come.

Sighing at the thought of someone losing a loved one, especially at a time when festivities were going on, he sat down and said a prayer for Mrs Cranford. How sad that her family had cut themselves off from the feelings of grief, making them unable to share in the old lady's loss. Perhaps he was judging them too harshly. Everyone reacted differently. Of one thing he was certain, he must get a better pastoral system going in the parishes; he didn't even know Mr Cranford was ill. Both Mr and Mrs Cranford should have been receiving Communion at home. Why hadn't anyone told him about them?

How many more of his parishioners were in need of spiritual and emotional support? He needed a pastoral team to cover the three parishes and someone to coordinate it, making sure no one was missed. He couldn't do everything himself. Rita came instantly to mind; she was already involved in visiting within her own area. She only need organise a rota system; he would recruit and train. Apart from being the St Michael's church organist, she knew many people within the three parishes through her school connection. Rita could be given an official title, and the whole team be commissioned by the bishop during a Confirmation service. At the same time, members could receive an official badge. It wasn't new, something similar had happened in his last parish. But would his PCC's accept the proposal?

He was asking a lot of Rita; was it time to give something in return? She'd asked him to go to the charismatic conference with her. It could be a good opportunity to get to know each other better and discuss pastoral and spiritual matters, and youth work. But it would also be an acceptance of her and her spirituality. It meant losing his day off with Nick too, that was the hardest thing. He would have to make up for it; Nick would understand. Since the conference was unlikely to start until the afternoon, he could go straight after Mr Cranford's funeral. Right — he would do it.

He made himself a sandwich and a cup of tea. It was with a feeling of elation that he went to say Evening Prayer in the church. When he returned home, he rang Nick and asked if it was all right to come over. Nick was delighted and asked him to stay the night. It was what Paul wanted. He put on his answerphone, intending to ring through from Nick's to check on any emergency calls that might come in. With a clear conscience he set off to visit his lover.

# Chapter five

Paul's journey to Riggington with Rita by his side was quite stimulating. While she was driving up the motorway, she talked to him about the time when St Michael's had been aglow with life and creative activity during Peter Millar's incumbency. Talking about the work of the Holy Spirit both excited and scared him. He wanted his parish to come to life but he didn't want bitter divisions.

She told him, "When I gave my heart to Jesus, I gave him my whole self to do with me as he willed. I started playing the organ after my conversion but it really took off after I was baptised in the Spirit."

Paul felt a little uncomfortable at Rita's reference to baptism in the Spirit. He believed it happened at conversion but he had to admit that although his ministry had been greatly blessed, he felt a certain something missing from his life. Falling in love had largely filled the gap; being with Nick was like being in paradise. In his mind he went over the previous evening, his body reacting to the pleasurable memories.

But Nick had not been enthusiastic when told about the conference. "Don't be brainwashed, Paul. I'm not saying it's all rubbish; it most certainly is not. I speak in tongues myself — have done for many years. Unfortunately, a lot of it is now going way out, especially when anything not understood is attributed to demons. And in certain circles when this is combined with pressure to dig up memories, which are sometimes false, I think it can be very dangerous. But then, that is my opinion; you must judge for yourself."

That Nick could speak in tongues had come as a great surprise and Paul had asked him about it. Listening to Nick's story of how the gift had come to him during a time of prayer was a very moving experience. Could he too receive this gift? Nick said it had been a great help to him, especially in times of difficulty and uncertainty. Now he was on his way to a conference where most people would have that gift, and more besides. The hairs on his neck were creeping up again. Rita's voice broke through his thoughts.

"Nearly there; we turn off at the next junction."

A thrill of excitement and expectation ran through Paul's body.

He was absolutely certain something was going to happen within the next couple of days. The feeling grew even stronger when, just as they were coming off the motorway, the dark heavy clouds parted and a brilliant sunbeam shone down over the conference centre a mile in front of them.

His heart was racing and his breathing became heavy.

Rita pulled her Ford KA into a lay-by. "Are you all right, Paul?"

Her voice seemed far away. He murmured, "I feel odd. Something's happening to me."

"I'm going to pray for you," she told him softly. Putting a hand on his head, she began praying in a language unknown to Paul, and yet it seemed right and the proper thing to do.

Warm feelings flowed over his head and spread over his body like soothing oil. He cried out in ecstatic delight, which was even greater than his rapturous moments with Nick. His tongue formed words he had never learned and he found himself to be praying in the Spirit. His joy was boundless.

Gradually, he started coming back to earth. He turned to Rita with tears flowing down his cheeks. "I think I've been baptised in the Spirit."

"I'm certain you have," she said, elated and laughing joyfully.

He put his head in his hands and cried like a baby. For in truth, he felt his experience to be a sacred consummation of his love for God; similar in emotional feelings to that which he shared with Nick in their most precious of times together, but many times so, and there had to be a spilling out.

Rita rested her hand on his shoulder. "Paul, let it out, let it out," she said tenderly, like a mother soothing a sorrowing child.

He turned his head to her chest. She put an arm around him and pressed a cheek his hair. Taking hold of his hand, she said, "I knew you were the one, Paul. I knew it from when I first heard you."

He pulled away from her. "The one?"

"The one we've prayed for. Ever since I first saw you and heard you praise God in the church, I knew He had sent you to us. 'Your word is a lamp unto my feet', is what you shouted."

"You heard me?"

"I'd locked myself in the church while I had a quiet prayer about the man I knew had been interviewed that morning. I was in the organ loft to practice a few hymns when you came into the church. I didn't want to disturb you so I went on praying."

Paul sat back in his seat and looked at her in surprise. "I had no idea someone else was in the church, that is, until Angela came in."

"I heard you, Paul. I heard you praise and sing. I nearly joined in on the organ. It was beautiful — so very genuine. I knew for certain that God had sent you to us. Then I heard you talking to Angela. You have a way with young people."

"She's a good kid. Did you see her dance then?" Paul asked her, his mind still unable to take in all that he was hearing and feeling.

"I've often seen her dance in church," Rita answered, her eyes far away. "One day, I hope we'll have a young people's dance group. Just imagine in our church — in all three churches — young people filled with the Spirit and praising God with their souls and bodies. Music and movement, singing and extolling God's might and glory. Hands raised to God in thanks and praise. The church full, and love overflowing. Alleluia!"

Paul had followed her every step of the way. Her desires for the church were no less than those he owned himself. The sun was now shining and somehow it symbolised how he was feeling. He was in the light — the light of the Lord. Alleluia indeed!

Fifteen minutes later, they were registering in the conference hall. Still in a delightful daze, Paul went to his room, unpacked and met up with Rita in the hall for tea and biscuits. Within the milling crowd, Rita introduced him to people she knew. He felt nothing but pleasure as they shook his hand or embraced him in Christian love.

"You're the new man in Rita's parish," said a voice from behind him.

Paul turned to see a trendy-looking cleric in dog collar, denim-blue shirt and denim jacket with jeans to match. His trainers looked as it they had just come out of a washing machine — they were white and crisp but not new. His long dark hair was tied back neatly in a ponytail. He had a brilliant toothpaste smile and his eyes twinkled merrily. Paul thought he had seen him before, perhaps recently.

"Yes, quite right. I'm Paul Stringer — Longdale, Penningly and Bradmire. It's my first time at one of these conferences but I've been to others. I think I might know you actually."

"I'm Jason Browning: just one lively parish with a growing church — nothing to do with me though. Tough job ahead of you from what Rita told me. Three churches, large area and the impossible expected."

"Certainly a challenge. Twenty square miles laced with meandering lanes, and each church determined to cling to its old traditions. But I believe God is already at work, and we can expect great things in the future. I guess we all believe that about our parishes though."

"I've met you before," said Jason, ignoring Paul's last comment. "I remember now; your hair was longer and you wore jeans then — more my sort of gear. It was the conference about gay ordinands. You gave an excellent exposition of relevant Biblical texts; I used them in my sermon that week. Canon Palmer's far too tolerant to be a Director of Ordinands. You'd think he was gay himself. Just as well he's married."

Paul was shocked to hear such blatant criticism of such a fair-minded man. "Nick Palmer, is one of the wisest men I know; deeply spiritual and greatly loved by his congregation."

"You sound as if he's changed your mind. Have you altered your anti-gay position?"

"I guess so. Nick put forward a very appealing argument. He convinced me of the rightness of his particular stance."

"Really? Odd, you convinced me of just the opposite!" Jason replied grinning. "We'll be hearing more about it at this conference. Tom Higgins ministers to young people. He's one of the speakers tomorrow. He thinks gay tendencies are the result of environment and upbringing, which can be cured through confession and healing of the memories. Lindsey Patch will be here to cast out lying demons. Should be interesting."

Paul's heart sank. He recalled Nick's warning. Well, he could choose which speakers to go and hear. But perhaps he should at least listen to what was being taught.

Rita came up to him. "The introductory session is about to start. Are you coming?"

In her presence, he could put aside his discomfort. "Sure, lets go," he said, taking her by the arm and steering her through the chatting groups.

Since nothing was said to alarm him, Paul followed the talk with interest. He joined in the hymns and choruses with gusto. It was with a light heart that he returned to his room to freshen up for dinner, and it was with eagerness that he rang Nick on his mobile. He had much to tell him but more than ever he longed for his presence, and to share with him his newfound love of God.

Paul spoke of the joy he'd shared with Rita, his enthusiasm bubbling up like a spring bursting from a rock. "Why didn't you tell me, Nick? Why didn't you talk to me about living water? Because that's what it is — living water! You've had it for ages and kept its secret to yourself."

There was a brief silence before Nick answered him. "I knew you would receive it in God's good time, just as I did. I didn't want to influence you through your love for me; neither did I want you to feel in any way inferior and so put a barrier between us. I'm very happy for you. But remember what I told you; you are going into a highly charged atmosphere. Listen to your inner voice."

They talked for a while with Paul bursting to tell Nick of his love for him. "It's strange, Nick, I feel such a yearning for you; greater than it's ever been. Is this God's doing?"

"I believe so. It's been that way with me ever since we met. You surely must realise that. Only my deep belief that God has brought us together could make me break my vow of celibacy. Take care, my very dear friend, to let nothing come between us."

"Nothing ever will," said Paul. He had a pricking of his conscience. He had to tell Nick about his meeting with Jason Browning.

Nick listened without comment. "You did right. But be careful when you listen to the teaching there. Don't get upset."

Paul felt suddenly fearful. "Perhaps I should come home."

"Run away? Not like you, Paul," Nick told him seriously. "You must listen to the argument. No need to confess your own status — that's between you and God. Don't let anyone use emotional blackmail to sway you. People like Rita can be very powerful. But I have to tell you; if you ever have an honest revelation that God is calling you to give me up, then you must follow your conviction. I will understand."

"We love each other — how can you say such things?"

"Simply because I do love you and want you to go on loving me, even if it means we could never be in each other's arms again. We are both servants of the Lord — our Master is our first love." He was silent a moment. "You believe that as much as I do."

It tore at Paul's heartstrings to hear him say such words but he knew they were true. Even so, from the experience he'd had that afternoon, he also knew that God had brought them together for a purpose, and it wasn't to make them suffer. "Yes, I do." He sighed heavily. "I have to go now."

"We'll meet again soon."

"I'd like to see you when I get back on Friday. Is it possible?"

"Certainly. I have a meeting with the bishop in the afternoon. How about you eat with us? Join us for prayer. Just give me an hour or so to sort out some business and then stay the night. Can you do that?"

"Yes, that's fine. I'll bring some work with me."

"Ring me again tomorrow, I'll be in about this time. God bless you, Paul."

"And you. I'll let you know how things go. Until tomorrow then — God bless you."

Paul switched off his phone with a sigh.

Rita's voice sounded outside his door. He smiled at the way his mother was always trying to get him interested in her. He found her a very attractive person and now he felt drawn to her for other reasons, but there was nothing sexual about the relationship. He hoped she felt that way too.

He slipped on a jumper and went outside to join her. They made their way to the dining room, talking light-heartedly about the afternoon session.

The evening programme consisted of a praise and prayer celebration with a Bible exposition. The hall was almost full by the time they arrived. A band was playing and people were joining in the singing as they entered the room. They found seats near the back and Paul joined in robustly. It was an atmosphere not unlike the evangelical conventions he was used to, but with hands raised and faces aglow with joy.

There was nothing in the Bible teaching that Paul disagreed with. With his new enlightenment, all of it thrilled him. Buoyed up with euphoria, he was riding on the crest of a wave. His singing of hymns and choruses reflected his emotional state; his voice was high, rich and his words full of meaning. Then the singing suddenly stopped and silence fell like a blanket putting out a blazing fire. Even so, the atmosphere was charged as though a tiny spark would set everything in motion again. Gradually peace descended and Paul's tensed emotions relaxed.

It was in this time of quiet that people from the floor participated; prophecies were spoken and tongues were heard with interpretation. One of the messages concerned a brewing evil about to be unleashed on the world and the need for vigilance and earnest prayer. Others told of signs of the Lord's coming and the need to prepare for harvest.

A powerful voice came from the platform. "Souls to be saved. Souls to be saved. Stand like rocks amid the storms, so that struggling souls may cling to God's word and be saved. And let the light of God's love beam out over the raging torrents of disbelief."

A few people muttered, "Amen."

A woman's voice sounded close to Paul. "You must purify yourselves ready for the battle. You must be clean and holy."

A man to the side of him stood up. "Be strong in the Lord. Come to him and he will wash away your sins and will heal you. There are some here tonight who are sick, some who are sorrowing. There is a man who has a stain on his soul. The Lord will wash it away."

Another man called out, "I feel the pain of someone with a serious illness." The man groaned and put a hand to his stomach. "The Lord wants to heal you." He clutched at his head. "There are many needs — take them to the Lord."

The room fell silent again. The band started playing gentle music; a delicious medley of sounds sweet to the ear. Before long, a few people started singing in tongues and gradually the whole room was alive with exquisite music, the like of which Paul had never before heard. Paul opened his mouth and entered into the rapture of it all.

Gradually people started drifting to the front for the laying on of hands. Rita turned to Paul. "Come with me. We need God's blessing for the work we have to do. And we need to be cleansed and healed."

Paul hesitated, but she stood up and reached out her hand to him;

he felt drawn to go with her to the platform. As hands were about to be placed on his head, a feeling of force drove him backwards. He landed in the arms of two men just behind him. He opened his eyes to find they had moved him out of the way and were praying over him. Rita was there too, smiling with happiness.

"You've had a powerful experience, Paul. The Spirit has anointed you. Praise God! I knew you were the one sent to us. Now you will have the strength to do his work."

Paul felt quite strange. He was exceedingly happy and yet overawed with a feeling that was akin to dread. Nick's warnings came into his mind — had he allowed himself to be swept along on a tide of emotion?

The man who'd sat next to him came up and asked if he was all right.

"I'm fine. I feel as though I'm bursting with energy. Quite odd really."

"Great!" said the man. "I'm Steve. Come and help me lay hands on a lady over here, she's in a lot of pain."

Paul hesitated; the significance of what he was about to do was overpowering; he just knew something was going to happen. Rita, having asked the woman what her problem was, had put her hands over her pelvic area. Steve put his hands on her shoulders and nodded at Paul to lay hands on her head. As Paul did so, he felt an urge to pray softly in tongues. Before long, heat began flowing down his arms. A tremendous sense of calm followed and with it the knowledge that all would be well.

Eventually, the woman looked up at him. "Thank God you were here tonight; he's used you to heal me. The pain has gone. I know it won't come back. I saw you when you arrived. You seemed somehow lit up. Sounds odd I know but that's the only way I can describe it — lit up."

After the service, one or two people chatted to Paul but Rita was urging him away. She suggested they go to her room for a coffee. He thought it a good idea; he needed to talk so as to consolidate in his mind what had been happening.

Rita talked quietly to him while he drank his coffee and he began to unwind. As he did so, he realised how tired he was. He needed to get some rest; tiredness made him vulnerable. He rose from his chair and made his excuses.

Rita stood in front of the door. "Before you go, can I ask you something personal?"

"Of course," he answered, a little concerned at what it might be.

"I heard you telling Angela that you're married to your vocation. Did you mean it — really mean it? Or were you just putting the silly girl off?"

Paul turned his eyes away from Rita's penetrating gaze. What could he say to her? The truth? In a way it was the truth. "I have no intention of getting married, if that answers your question."

"Does that mean you intend to stay celibate? Somehow I can't see you as the promiscuous sort."

Paul looked into her eyes and saw the longing she was feeling for him. "I'm so sorry, Rita. If I could love any woman — sexually I mean — it surely would be you. But since I won't marry, there can't be anything other than Christian love between us."

She slipped off her glasses and came up close to him; her eyes sparkling and her lips poised ready to kiss him. "Then let me give you a sisterly kiss before you go."

She put her arms around him and kissed him tenderly on the lips. He hadn't the heart to push her away. In his mind, he let himself feel Nick's lips on his own. How he longed to be with him, enclosed in their love for each other.

He very tenderly moved her away from him. "Thank you, Rita. That was quite lovely. And thanks for everything today. I have to admit it's all been rather overwhelming. I really must go now and get some rest."

"Goodnight, Paul. I'll see you tomorrow," she said smiling. All at once her face was twisted by pain. "It's okay," she said, when Paul showed his concern. "Just a stab of neuralgia. I get it from time to time."

Paul instinctively put his hand to her face. He felt a sudden rush of energy run through his arm. An inner voice was saying, "Be healed." But he pulled his hand away quickly — awed and afraid of what he was doing.

Rita took his hand in hers. "You have lovely hands, Paul — healing hands."

Paul felt embarrassed. "Goodnight, Rita," he said, slipping his hand away from hers. "Sleep well." He quickly left her room.

Returning to his own bedroom, he sat on his bed, took out his mobile and rang Nick again.

"Paul? What's the matter? Got a problem?" Nick sounded anxious.

"Not really, just wanted to hear your voice. You don't mind do you? It's just that so much has happened and I wanted to share it with you. I know it's getting late but—"

"Get on with it," said Nick pleasantly. "I was about to go to bed; you'll give me something to dream about."

Paul told him what had happened that evening. As he did so, strong feelings that he could only describe as 'rising energy' seemed to gather in his body. He told Nick about it.

"You seem to be having some powerful experiences," Nick told him. "You really must get some rest. I'll go to bed myself now. I'll pray for you until I drop off to sleep."

"Nick, I'd rather be with you. I could easily drive over and be back here in the morning. Perhaps not come back — I'm afraid."

There was a moment's silence. "But you will stay there and see it through. Don't worry, you're not alone. Believe me, things will settle down."

"Yes. You're right of course. Goodnight. See you, Nick."

"Stay cool and ring me tomorrow. Goodnight, Paul. God grant you his peace."

Even as the words were spoken, all fear was lifted and a feeling of tranquillity swept over him.

For the first time in many years, Paul overslept the next morning. He missed the early Morning Prayer session and he would have gone without breakfast had it not been for Rita knocking at his door.

Paul was hungry but he only ate a light meal. He didn't want to doze off during the discussion sessions. Rita asked him which one he was going to: the one on teenage drug abuse and related problems, sexual promiscuity, or homosexuality.

"Doesn't really matter which we go to," she told him. "There will be a plenary session this afternoon with a question and answer seminar after tea. Since we've had a lot of discussion at school about our drug problem and promiscuity, I thought the homosexuality discourse might be the most enlightening. The other two problems are straight forward — matters of sin, excess or addiction." She shook her head thoughtfully. "Gay men are a complete enigma to me. I hope Tom Higgins and Lindsey Patch will enlighten me."

"You think they will? Perhaps so," he said in a non-committal way. "I'll go to the promiscuity one."

Paul wanted to get away from Rita for a while. He needed a bit of breathing space from the hype she seemed to generate. They met up again for lunch but Paul encouraged Rita to talk about her teaching career. He didn't want to hear her views about homosexuality, before long she would have him confessing.

Homosexuality was the last of the items at the plenary session. Jason Browning was given the task of presenting the main points and the conclusions drawn. He summed up the problems facing individuals, the church and society, concluding with, "As Christians, we are not here to condemn, but to heal. We are all urged to pray about it. Tom and Lindsey will be ministering to anyone with a problem this evening."

Paul went up to his room during the tea break. He wanted to avoid Rita. She was too intuitive for comfort, and he refused to explain himself to her or anyone else. And he certainly didn't need healing — he wasn't ill!

He joined Rita for the late afternoon seminar just as it was about to start.

"You certainly made an impression on Jason Browning," she told him. "He talked about you quite a lot. He said you had changed your stance recently. How very interesting. It must have been a very powerful revelation for you to do that. You must tell me about it over dinner."

Paul wondered if he was right in keeping his thoughts private, after all, he'd been very willing and eager to put forward his previous views. When the opportunity came to go against the mounting tide of speakers who voiced the opinion that gay Christians were sick, misled by demons, or downright sinners, he decided to make public his convictions. He raised his hand, which brought forth an invitation to use the microphone on the podium.

Taking up the flow of argument he'd heard from Nick, Paul shocked his audience by putting forward his new and honest beliefs.

He didn't find it easy, especially when seeing the astounded looks on the faces of his hearers. Just as Nick had done, he used what lay at the heart of the Christian message to get across his points. Finally, he said, "We should not allow our disgust of those who indulge in flagrant promiscuity, to cloud our vision of what is right and just for those who are in committed relationships. Men can and do, love each other."

"And would you say the same about women?" Jason Browning shouted from his chair.

"Why not?" Paul answered, as he was leaving the podium.

Mutterings sounded around the room, and many eyes followed him as he made his way back to his chair.

"Well, you certainly made everyone look up and take notice," said Rita. "I'm surprised you hold such liberal views."

He was thinking up an answer when an announcement said they were running late and the session was now over.

Rita stood up. "Perhaps we can talk later?"

"I think I've said it all," said Paul, but she didn't look convinced.

He was thankful she didn't bring the subject up during dinner. He was prepared to face her questions but not with other folk around; a few people were already looking at him as though he were about to expose himself in public.

The evening session began with music and singing. Before long the atmosphere became electric. Paul was completely taken over; his heart and mind at one with those around him.

Tom Higgins and Lindsey Patch mounted the platform and each gave a brief reiteration of their previous teaching. Paul was most unhappy about it; they made him feel unclean. Two men each gave prolonged testimonies of why they became homosexuals, and of how they were eventually forgiven and healed of their sinful practices. Then ministry was offered in a side room for anyone who had leanings or problems in that direction. Meanwhile, the band played soft music and those not otherwise engaged sang.

Rita asked Paul to assist in praying for the woman beside her. He refused but she persuaded him to change his mind. "Paul, God has given you gifts to use, not to hide them away and keep them for yourself."

Then others asked them both to lay hands on them. The room had nearly cleared before they were sitting down again.

"It's been a great night. Can I get you a drink at the bar?" Rita asked him.

"Wouldn't mind a long cool drink," he replied, getting up from his seat. "But mustn't stay too long. I have a call to make."

"Perhaps you would like to do that now while I get the drinks?" Rita suggested, smiling at him most engagingly. "I'll bring them into the lounge."

Paul made his way upstairs. Relaxing on the pink-striped duvet of his bed, staring at the featureless ceiling above him, he reported to Nick all that had happened that day. "Couldn't ring you earlier. Guess I made everyone late by my little speech!"

"I'm proud of you, Paul." Nick said with deep emotion. "It took guts to stand up and contradict your previous views. You may well come under suspicion though. Remember you have nothing to confess; what we have is between God and us."

"At least I can be honest about my beliefs now. I've got a great deal out of this conference one way or another. It's going to make a lot of difference to my ministry, no doubt about that."

Rolling over, staring unseeingly at the few framed posters on the pale pink walls, Paul talked enthusiastically to Nick about some of the things he wanted to do during the coming months.

"Well, I'll support you as much as I can, but don't go overboard. I wouldn't want anyone going over my head and making things difficult for you. Anyway, time to talk when you get back. Must go now, Paul. Someone is ringing the doorbell and Lucy isn't back from an emergency call. God bless."

Paul found Rita in the lounge with two empty glasses and two bottles of fruit juice, a bottle of lemonade and one of ginger beer. She also had a few miniatures of spirits.

"Mix your own, Paul. I'll take upstairs what's left."

"Thanks. You must let me pay for this."

"Certainly not. I'm so very grateful that you came here with me. It's been such a joy ministering and praying with you. And to see you come alive in the Spirit — oh, so very wonderful!"

Tears of joy were sparkling in her eyes. She took off her glasses, put them in her pocket, and dabbed her eyes with a handkerchief.

"Silly of me I know, but you have no idea how much we've prayed for this to happen."

"'We', being your group?"

"Not only our group but others we're linked to — right across the country."

Paul looked up from pouring himself a drink and smiled at his thoughts. "Gosh," he said. "Well, I've always believed in the power of prayer. I suppose it's standard practice for these groups to pray for each other's clergy. Knowing what a stubborn lot we are, I guess the prayers can go on a long time."

"Yes, a very long time, but we don't give up. I don't need to lecture you about free will. We were praying for Canon Palmer for ages, and then something seemed to happen to him. At least, that's what I was told. Of course he did get married, but he's changed in a way hard to explain. When he was filling in for Jim Smithson, I thought I heard him praying in tongues. I dare say it could have been Latin or something else. He thought he was on his own, but I was in the organ loft sorting out music."

"Oh, really? I guess I'd better be careful if I have a spy in the camp!"

Paul grinned at his thoughts. Rita had caught out both he and Nick. They were going to have to be more careful.

Rita was silent a moment. Looking at him very carefully, she said, "I know you said you could never love a women because you're married to your vocation, but you didn't actually say you were celibate. Do you ever go out with women, Paul?"

"For sexual gratification?"

Rita frowned. "That's putting it rather bluntly."

"What other way is there to put it? I have friends who happen to be women but that isn't what you're asking."

"I guess not." Her eyes dropped to rest on her glass of bubbling ginger beer.

She picked up a miniature of brandy, removed the top and poured the liquid into her glass. Paul guessed she was in need of comfort.

He took hold of her hand. "The answer is no," he said gently. "Please don't take it personally. I think a lot of you, but I could never take advantage of your fondness for me, and I will never marry."

Rita clasped the hand that was holding hers and gazed into

Paul's eyes. "Have you never been with a woman — not even to do a bit of petting?"

"No."

She looked puzzled. Then her face clouded over. "Have you made a vow of celibacy?"

"No."

"Are you gay?"

Paul turned his face away and let go of her hand. "Don't ask that question, Rita."

"I'm sorry. Of course it's your own affair — sorry that's not a pun. You know, you're in the right place if you want to change and be normal."

"I am normal," he told her pointedly.

"But" she began. "Sorry again. I guess you know I've fallen for you. Well, if you change your mind, I'll be around."

"You are a very beautiful woman. I couldn't think of anyone better to change my mind over, but I never will. Please accept that."

She nodded. "Okay. Thanks for the compliment. At least, I know the handsomest guy in the area thinks I'm lovely; that's a real morale booster,'" She laughed, but her eyes told a different story.

He took hold of her hand again. "Please say we can stay friends; I really need you working with me. You are a very gifted woman. We can be partners in ministry if in nothing else."

She smiled. "Partners in ministry? That's the loveliest proposal I've ever had." She looked into his eyes, "I accept with all my heart."

She bit her lip, and poured herself another drink.

# Chapter six

Paul was on his way to see Nick. It was springtime — the season that held the promise of Resurrection and glory to come. The countryside was teeming with new life and resounding with birdsong. As he drove along the lanes, passing bright green hedgerows and cottage gardens aglow with yellow forsythia, golden daffodils, pink cherry blossom and the jewel-like colours of primulas, his voice sang out with praises.

He had much to be thankful for. Quite a few people had attended the Lent meetings and most of them decided to go on at least to Pentecost. The Easter services had gone well with more lay people taking part. Mary Jones, headmistress of Longdale Primary School and a churchwarden at the Penningly church, had decided to train as a Church of England reader. She had set the ball rolling, and now two members of Rita's group and a member of the Bradmire congregation were considering some kind of training.

Rita had been working with him to get a pastoral team together, and the PCC of each church had given consent in spite of some opposition. One or two committee meetings had been a bit acrimonious as Nick had predicted, but things were gradually moving in the right direction.

Kevin Raymond had complained that the vicar's sermons were getting too long and too personal. He said there was too much talk about the Holy Spirit. If they weren't careful they would be back to where they were when Peter Millar was there: "Clapping, dancing, hugging and all that bloody rubbish. Services should be quiet and holy!"

"Did you never read of King David rejoicing and dancing before the Lord?" Paul had asked him.

He smiled at the memory of Kevin's reply: "He wasn't in the Church of England!"

Paul was not concerned by the grumbles of the few, even if they did have a lot of power — he was happy within himself. Little people like the widow Mrs Cranford, were delighted by the gradual changes and were bringing other people into the services with them. And the monthly Family Services were very popular with newcomers.

Turning a corner, he passed Angela on her bicycle. She gave him a smile and a wave. She was turning out to be a real asset to him. She had matured a lot since starting her college course and now had a very responsible attitude. She prepared all of his service sheets for him and did lots more besides. But Kevin didn't trust him or his daughter; he continually made excuses to visit the vicarage when Angela was there working.

He passed the school in Nick's parish and he thought of Rita. They had bonded at the conference and she seemed to accept they would never be a couple. In some ways it suited him to be linked to a woman, but as time went by without an engagement, speculation could only increase; both their reputations might take a hammering.

Rita had asked Angela if she would be interested in the dance group she was hoping to get started. She was really keen and wanted to know who else was involved. Since then, he'd found her several times in the church with her disc player dancing around in the chancel. It was hard to think that she would be eighteen in six months.

As Paul pulled into Nick's drive, Lucy was coming through the front door. She gave him a cheery wave as she went off to her car. She was looking very beautiful and incredibly happy. Her lovely heart-shaped face was delicately made-up, her grey eyes were bright and her dark glossy hair was bouncing around her shoulders. She was wearing a flowing mid-calf pink skirt to match an attractive pink blouse. Her dog collar was just noticeable at her throat. She had a black jacket over her arm, which she jauntily threw into the back of the car along with her black handbag. She could just as easily have been going out to meet a lover as visiting her parishioners.

Nick met him at the door. They went inside and embraced each other. Today they intended going for a long drive, stop for a light lunch at a pub and walk a few miles. What could be more normal than two friends, dressed in walking gear, to be out walking together? Afterwards, they would spend some time at an indoor swimming pool and then relax in the pool's café. Home to pick up Lucy, dinner out, then back to the rectory for a romantic night in bed. The routine of the day varied but the ending was always the same — it was the climax of their time together.

They tried to avoid 'shop' but sometimes it was the only chance for Paul to have a consultation with his rural dean without having to make an appointment. The PCC annual general meetings were about to take place and Paul wanted to ask Nick's advice. There was so much he wanted to get done and it was difficult to be patient. What's more, with three PCCs, too much time was taken up with meetings.

As usual, Nick was quick in summing up the situation and brief in his advice. "Personally, I wouldn't push for more change. By all means halve the PCC meetings — that will please most of the members and would be just as efficient. You could try for a combined AGM. As long as it was disciplined and the reports kept brief, it might bring the congregations together more."

Paul clenched his fists in excitement. "I see these pictures in my mind of things to do. I have this tremendous urge to bring in the young, and to see the Church as a healing centre — mending hearts, broken relationships, and sick minds and bodies. Oh, Nick, I feel so full of love, I can hardly contain it!"

"But you will, my friend," Nick said calmly. "I know how you feel, but don't burn yourself out. Go steady and take the people with you. You already have lay people doing a lot of work, so don't overburden them. God will bring in the ones to help you in your vision when the time is right, just as he brought you here." Looking at Paul with love in his eyes, he added, "And just as he brought us together."

A surge of desire welled up within Paul; his heart was beating fast as his body prepared for action. "Must we wait until later?"

Nick stretched out a hand and took hold of Paul's. "You know it's impossible, don't make it hard for me."

Paul clasped Nick's hand and held it against his face, brushing it with his cheek.

Nick groaned. "Do you think I don't feel as you do?" He sighed heavily. "Anyone could come to the door, it's obvious someone is home. This house is a public place in the daytime, just as yours is. A few people have keys — you know all the reasons, Paul. We must keep control of our emotions."

"Of course, you're right. It's odd though, Nick. Since this baptism in the Spirit thing, I've been drawn so much closer to you."

"Yes, an upsurge of love doesn't by-pass our sexual desires."

"Perhaps that's what made Rita bold at Riggington. I'm absolutely sure she would have gone to bed with me — wanted to, in fact. I could see it in her eyes and feel it pulsating in her body."

Nick smiled. "Like I can yours?" He became more serious. "I hope you let the poor girl down gently."

"I must admit, I didn't stop her giving me a sisterly kiss, or hugging me at appropriate times, but I've left her in no doubt that our relationship can never go further than what it is now."

"I hope so. You never know what goes on in a woman's mind. Be careful, Paul, that lass Angela hangs around you a lot, and I've noticed other women look at you in a very sexy way."

"Jealous?" Paul asked, shaking his head and laughing.

"No joke. There's nothing like a thwarted female for causing trouble. You're too good-looking for your own good!"

Nick stood up and pulled Paul out of his chair. As if on cue, the doorbell rang. They both laughed. Nick threw up his hands, as if in defeat, and walked to the front door. Paul heard a woman's voice getting louder as she came inside. He heard Nick go to his study and come out again. The woman was thanking him and the door then closed.

"Baptism form. Sorry about that. Let's go, before the word gets around that I'm working on my day off!"

By the time they returned that evening, they were both more relaxed. Lucy was waiting for them. She was dressed ready for their dinner date, although she said she had a bereavement visit to make at nine. Paul was again taken by how lovely she looked. No dog collar this time. Her dress was full and long but the neck was cut low, revealing the tops of her sweetly rounded breasts. She saw Paul raise his eyebrows. "Don't worry, I'm doing a quick change again before I make my visit. I have to let my hair down sometime!"

Nick went up to her and kissed her on the cheek. "Darling, you look wonderful. We'd better get going or you'll be too late to change. No one will take a priest seriously if she looks more like a temptress."

Lucy laughed. "I wonder what they would say about you and Paul!" She suddenly looked embarrassed. "Sorry, I shouldn't have said that. Let's go."

When Nick was alone with Paul that evening, he told him that he was a little concerned about Lucy. "Ever since we've got together, she seems to have become a bit restless. I think she realises she's missing out on life. I guess she sees we have something she hasn't. She obviously hears us in the bedroom. Sometimes I hear her crying but she won't talk about it. I asked her if it was because of me, but she said not."

Paul felt deeply concerned. "Would it be better if I didn't come here?"

"I asked her that, but she said it wasn't a problem."

"Have you no idea what's the matter? She looked so happy when I saw her this morning."

"She's very good at putting on a mask," Nick said, shaking his head. "But we both know what can make a person deliriously happy as well as desperately sad."

"You think she's fallen in love?"

"I'm sure of it. But she's married to me."

Paul asked no more questions. They prayed for Lucy and left her in the hands of God.

The following evening, just after ten, Paul had an unexpected visitor. Angela was on the doorstep and it had nothing to do with the work she did for him. He was somewhat apprehensive about her calling at such a late hour.

"What's the matter, Angela? It's very late. Does your father know where you are?"

"I'm a big girl now, my father doesn't need to know where I am all the time. I saw your light was on and I noticed Miss Lee leave here just ten minutes ago, so I thought you wouldn't mind if I had a word with you."

"Can't it wait?"

"Well, I'll be seeing him shortly. Please — just a few minutes."

"Is it your father?"

"Of course not." She sounded disgusted. "I'm seeing Mark — meeting him at the church."

"At this hour?"

"He's been working late and I promised I'd meet him."

"Well, you'd better tell me quickly what you want." He led her into the kitchen and offered her a chair by the warm stove.

"Mark wants to have sex with me. Should I let him?"

"Why ask me? Do you want to have sex with him?" He could have added that it didn't sound like it when he'd heard them in the porch.

"I don't know. I'm still a virgin," she said coyly.

"If you don't know, then don't. And don't give him expectations that you will."

She looked at him with big innocent eyes. "Is it sinful if you're not married?"

"I think it's better if you are married," he told her, trying to dodge the issue. "But if you don't want to, that's not a problem."

"I might want to sometime — is it sinful?"

"I think promiscuity is. Joining yourself to someone is an emotional as well as a physical act. I believe it can be a spiritual joining too — the blending of two souls in a unity of love. The sexual act can be an expression of deep love and commitment to one another; it cannot be repeated ad infinitum with every boy you meet."

"I've told you, I'm still a virgin. I'll be eighteen this year. I must be the oldest virgin in Longdale." She was pouting again like a young schoolgirl.

"I doubt it. But stay that way until you're sure." He was thinking that her mother should be telling her this.

"How can I be sure if I never let a boy do it? How will I know if we're right for each other?"

"That's just the point. Falling in love leads to sex, not the other way around. Haven't you listened to what I've been telling you?"

She shuffled around in her chair and looked at him sheepishly. "Suppose you fall in love with someone — hopelessly in love?"

"Are you in love with Mark?"

"I don't know. I like him. He's been around a bit. The girls say he's good. If you can't have who you want you might as well have someone who wants you — especially if he's good at it." She gave him another big innocent look. "Don't you think so?"

Paul sighed. He could see the point of her argument. In today's sexual climate she was doing remarkably well at preserving her virginal status.

"There's a lot to think about," he replied eventually. "It's not just important that you have the right person, there could be consequences — pregnancy, diseases, off-putting experiences and disappointments. Don't throw your gift away just to know what it's like. You'll know when the right person comes along."

"I've told you. You can't always have the person you love."

She was looking at him with tears in her eyes. He was moved to pity. He took hold of her hand and tried to find the right words to comfort her.

"You're still young, Angela. You have plenty of time to find someone else. Someone who will love you, with the same love you want to give to him."

She shook her head. Tears were now rolling down her cheeks.

"I can understand that you want to feel loved and wanted," he said tenderly. "Mark does this for you, and you don't want to lose him. But if he truly loved you, he would wait until you're certain."

"I think he does love me; he said that's why he wants us to do it. He said he can have any girl he wants, but he just wants me, no one else."

"Perhaps he's just putting pressure on you to get what he wants. Give yourself time to get over this other man and perhaps you'll see things more clearly," he told her gently.

She had her hanky out and was dabbing at her face. She looked up at him with sorrowful red-rimmed eyes. "Do you believe God sends people for you to love?"

"I guess I do," he said with a wry smile. How could he say otherwise? And yet Angela was pining for someone who didn't love her. "But perhaps we are mistaken and our real partner hasn't arrived on the scene yet. I think both parties would feel an equal attraction for one another. If we are concentrating all our attention on someone who has shown no signs of wanting us or who is married, we could miss out on the real thing."

Angela perked up. "That could apply to the one you love who hasn't noticed you yet, couldn't it? They may be distracted by a she-devil in disguise."

Paul had to laugh. "Oh, Angela, that's putting it a bit strong." He squeezed her hand. "I'm sorry, I shouldn't laugh. Can't say I've ever met she-devils in my ministry."

"But it's right isn't it? It doesn't have to be a she-devil; anyone or any thing could distract a man or woman. God has to open their eyes to what is in front of them."

"Maybe, but don't put your hopes up too high." He was now worried he'd done more harm than good. "I'll just pray with you before you go."

He put his hand on her head and prayed that she would be able to discern God's will for her, and that she would find happiness and fulfilment.

She looked up at him, her face glowing with joy. "Thank you, Paul. I feel so much better."

The doorbell rang. Paul frowned, wondering who could possibly be calling so late in the evening. Surely not Angela's father? He went to the front door, thinking what excuse he could give for the girl being in his kitchen with smudged make-up and puffy eyes.

It was Mark.

"She's here isn't she?" he demanded to know. "Her bike's here. She's supposed to be meeting me at the church. What's she doing here?"

"I take it you mean Angela. She's in the kitchen. I'll tell her you're here."

Angela was already on her way to the hall. "You didn't need to come looking for me. Anyway, I'm going home now. I'm tired."

Mark looked at Angela and then at Paul, fury burning in his eyes. "You're supposed to be meeting me. I got us some chips, they're cold now."

"You should have eaten them. I'm going home," Angela said haughtily.

"No you're not, you promised you'd meet me," Mark bellowed.

"It is rather late," Paul butted in. "Suppose you come into the kitchen and I'll make you both a coffee. I'll heat your chips up in the microwave. You two can talk while I'm in my study."

"Piss off!" Mark yelled. He ran out, jumped on his bike and pedalled furiously.

Paul watched him go. Sadness filled his heart. Once again the young man had had his sexual urges frustrated by a girl who appeared to be teasing him. Angela was smiling.

"I'd better take you home," he said, feeling a little cross with her. "Mark might be waiting down the lane for you. You can iron out your problems tomorrow when he's in a better mood."

"If I decide to see him," she said primly.

"Be honest with him, Angela, it isn't fair to keep a boy on a string." Paul was now wondering if he was wrong about she-devils. Was Angela as innocent as she claimed to be?

She jumped happily into his Discovery while he put her bike in the back. She was looking at herself in the mirror, tidying her face, when he pulled himself up beside her. He was thankful that she was making herself presentable — the last thing he wanted was his churchwarden thinking he'd made his daughter cry.

They passed Mark standing under a tree at the side of the road. He was eating chips out of an insulated container.

"You see for yourself — he tells lies. His chips aren't cold, he was hoping I'd join him on my way home."

"Would you have done, Angela?"

"Maybe. I don't know. Poor Mark."

Was she genuinely sorry for him? She obviously liked him or she wouldn't go on seeing him. He was certainly a good-looking young man. Plenty of girls hung around him on Sunday mornings, so he must have something going for him. How old was he? Eighteen? More likely nineteen, or even twenty. He could probably give Angela the benefit of his experience; she could do worse — if she intended doing it at all. He meant every word he'd said to her, but who was he to sit in judgement?

Angela broke into Paul's thoughts.

"You didn't answer my question," she said, as he was about to stop the vehicle near her house.

Paul was too weary to guess what she was talking about. "What was it?"

"If sex before marriage is sinful."

He pulled on the brake as the Discovery came to a halt. "Oh, I thought we'd finished with that one. We humans are very fallible creatures — we all sin. I guess there are worse things than sharing your body with someone you genuinely love — in a lifetime commitment, that is."

He knew he was fudging it again, but he also knew there were no easy answers if the Church was not to go back to hypocritical condemnation of 'fallen' women. But neither could he give the green light to avid promiscuity.

"What about priests who never marry — don't they ever do it?" she persisted.

He jumped out of the Discovery and hurried to the rear door to retrieve her bike. "Possibly," he said, now opening the passenger door to get her moving.

She jumped out. "Well, that's all right then. Priests are supposed to be holy, so it must be okay."

She pedalled the few yards to her home, turning at the gate to give him a wave and call out, "Goodnight, Paul."

He only hoped Angela didn't tell her parents that sex outside of marriage was okay; must be — priests did it. Mr Stringer said so!

# Chapter seven

So far, the Longdale St Michael's AGM had gone very well. The officers had produced excellent reports, and Paul had given a brief summery of his ministry up to date and his hopes for the future, thanking all those who laboured hard and without whom he could do very little. All the members and officers had been re-elected without opposition and some people were looking at their watches, wondering if they would be in time to see the news on television.

The date of the first meeting of the new sessions was about to be announced when Kevin Raymond stood up and said that he would like to add a small item of business to the meeting that couldn't wait. There were mutters that he was out of order but no one dare challenge him. Paul, who was chairing the meeting, preferred to let him have his say.

"Two years ago it was put to us that we should join with Glenton under a Team Ministry. We turned it down. We didn't know if Canon Palmer would be staying at Glenton — we might have been bloody jumping into bed with anyone. Some of us were worried that when Jim Smithson retired, we might get swallowed up by the bigger parish and be served by a progression of curates in training. Maybe have a woman put in charge — that was one of our biggest fears."

This last remark received a mixed reception; some heads nodding in agreement but most nodding in disgust. Paul was trying not to grin. Kevin continued, oblivious to what people were thinking.

"I think the time is ripe to go ahead and set the process in motion as soon as possible. Unofficially, I've sounded out the other churchwardens and they all agree."

"And what made you change your mind?" asked Rita Lee.

Paul was puzzled too. It was what he wanted, but something he didn't want to push for. He had so many changes in mind. He'd already been flying kites about moving the altar forward to the chancel step so that Communion could be received in the round. He had visions of the choir moving to seats in the side chapel, leaving room for music groups or dancing in the chancel. But joining with Nick's parish was at the top of his prayer list.

Kevin, looking mildly embarrassed, answered Rita's question.

"We have our own vicar now. I should say priest-in-charge, but he's our vicar just the same. We're lucky to have a young eager beaver, but I reckon it would be good for the parish if we had an older man in overall charge — someone to give Paul support and help him adjust to our ways."

Everyone looked at Paul to see his reaction. He was both amused and excited but kept his emotions hidden under an innocuous mask.

"Of course, that's just a minor thing," Kevin continued. "There would be a sharing of ministry and that would be good for all parishes. Canon Palmer was very popular during the interregnum and filling in for Jim Smithson. It would be good to have him as Team Rector and Paul as Team Vicar. Mrs Palmer could help out with the visiting. It would save us having to have these bloody lay workers nosing around the parish."

Paul wondered what Lucy would think about Kevin's plan, but his immediate concern was the hurt feelings of his lay workers. He jumped up to speak before Rita, who was looking ready for a fight, could object to the last remark.

"Well, Kevin has given us something to think about," he said benignly. "I'm sure our Secretary will put it down on the first meeting's agenda. I for one will be very happy to work with Nick Palmer; he's a wise and spiritual man. But I have to say I'm also glad we have splendid dedicated lay people to visit our parishioners. The Reverend Lucy Palmer would need more than twenty-four hours a day to see everyone who's presently visited; she's a very busy priest — like the rest of us."

Kevin Raymond gave a little snort but said nothing. Paul wondered if he was going to change his mind again, but it was too late for doing that now — the Council liked the idea.

The following morning, a Saturday, Paul rang Nick to see if he had an hour to spare between weddings and other jobs. "I'd like to have a word about the Team Ministry proposal," he told him.

Nick was his usual affable self. "Lucy's taking two weddings this morning and I have to visit a prospective ordinand. Not sure when I'll be back, but probably about twelve-thirty. Tell you what; come early if you can. I'll leave a report on the parish merger proposals on my desk. You can to read it while you're waiting. Stay for lunch and we can bring Lucy into the conversation."

"That suits me fine. I have an early wedding this morning and someone's coming late afternoon."

"I have some admin to get through, but Lucy's preaching tomorrow so I've no sermon to prepare." His voice changed to a more intimate tone. "You can stay for a couple of hours or so after lunch. I'll be glad of your company."

It was what Paul wanted to hear. He collected his notes and walked to the church, singing as he went. He loved weddings and baptisms. In a strange kind of way, he enjoyed funeral services too — they were celebrations of life and an anticipation of the joys to come.

As he entered the church, he sang out, "God will show us the path of life; in his presence is the fullness of joy."

As far as Paul was concerned, that short passage from Psalm 16, recited by him at every funeral, would be just as appropriate at any celebration. His heart was on fire with love; God was lighting up his path and his lungs were bursting with joy. Suddenly the whole church was filled with triumphal music — Rita was seated at the organ and picking up his mood in a magnificent display of her musical talent. Paul danced around the church, laughing and singing. When the music came to an end, he ran up to the organ loft. Rita stood up and fell into his waiting arms.

"Wonderful!" he said, kissing her on the cheek. "You are a genius."

A querulous voice sounded from down below. "That wedding's in less than half an hour, don't you think you should be getting bloody ready?"

When Paul entered the vestry a few minutes later, Kevin Raymond was waiting for him.

"It's bloody indecent and disgusting — messing around with women in church. I saw you fooling around too. I suppose you think you're King bloody David? It's got to stop, Mr Stringer. The sooner Canon Palmer's in charge the better. All this Spirit business is going too bloody far. I heard you babbling funny words — or do you call it bloody singing?"

"I'll be pleased to explain it sometime, but not now. You have to realise, Kevin, God is doing a new thing in this place. The Holy Spirit—"

Kevin didn't let him finish, he was too angry. "Don't bloody lecture me about the Holy Spirit, I was churchwarden here when you were in bloody nappies! You talk about a new thing? I've seen it all before. If we'd known you were going to push this bloody rubbish down our throats, you'd never have come here. Bloody fit in — or bugger off somewhere else!"

While Paul was recovering from the tirade, Kevin headed for the door, calling after him, "And don't you dare touch my bloody daughter."

The verger, Doreen Briggs, came close to being bowled over as she came through the vestry door. She was looking at Paul as though expecting an explanation. She didn't get one.

"Thanks for pressing my alb, Doreen; you really do keep me looking neat and tidy. Anyone here for the wedding yet?" he asked her.

"Not when I came in. Just as well; they might have thought they'd come to a pub not a church." She turned her head towards the door to emphasise her point.

"It's a nice day — probably waiting outside for the groom's party to arrive," he said, trying to shift Doreen's thoughts away from what she'd heard.

Doreen prepared Paul's white and gold chasuble. "I'm not the only one looking after your robes, Mr Stringer," she said, running her fingers over the fine gold embroidery. "The Sewing Guild takes care of the fancy stuff, and members of the Mothers' Union help me with the albs and altar linen. Angela's been taking your surplices home to launder — she's a good kid."

"Hardly a kid, Doreen, she's eighteen this year," Paul corrected her. "But you're right, she's an angel. She's helping every Eucharist, assists the sacristan, and does a lot of admin for me."

Doreen nodded. "She'll be helping me with the books too," Her voice hardened. "And staying to sweep up the confetti."

Paul knew her feelings about litter and ignored the severe look she was giving him.

Doreen let out a deep sigh. "Her father doesn't appreciate her — always bawling her out."

Angela came dashing into the vestry. "They're coming inside now; thought you should know." She smiled at Paul. "I'll be at the vicarage after I've helped Mrs Briggs."

"I'll be going out later, will you be okay on your own?"

She looked disappointed. "Of course, I know what to do."

"I'll go over the services with you and leave you everything you need. Don't print anything until I've checked it. But I'll be seeing you in an hour or so, we can talk then."

Angela nodded. "I'll help you on with your things." She gave him a winsome smile. "Doreen will be okay for a few minutes."

While straightening his chasuble, she remarked casually, "Miss Lee's a terrific organist. I like that music she was playing when you came in."

"You saw me come in?" He wondered how many more folk were around to witness his leaping and dancing.

"I was in the corner getting out the books. But when I heard my dad I ducked behind a pew. I thought you were great. I nearly joined in."

"I wish you had, we would have made a good dance duo!" he said, laughing with pleasure at the thought of it.

"My dad would have killed me. I heard him shouting at you, what do you think he'd have done to me?"

Paul felt the pain in Angela's voice. "Does he hit you, Angela?"

She looked away. "I'd better go and give Mrs Briggs a hand. Dad will be in the churchyard somewhere. He's looking for someone's grave for burying ashes this afternoon. See you."

She dashed away. Paul picked up his service book and notes and went out to greet the wedding party. It was proving to be a very emotional morning. He hadn't realised how much Kevin resented him. The last thing he wanted was to inspire hatred in his flock. But then, Jesus did the same amongst his own people. He breathed in deeply, said a prayer for wisdom and understanding and, smiling, went forward to greet the groom.

Before long, Paul was once again in an ebullient mood. The bride arrived on time, the service went well and everyone seemed happy. It was a simple wedding, not one of the expensive affairs that most couples had. No choir, no extra flowers, no bridesmaids and only about twenty guests. The bride was heavily pregnant. It hadn't been so obvious when he'd seen them before, but in her white dress her bump swelled out like a ski slope. At the end of the service, the groom kissed the bride and then fell on his knees and kissed her satin-covered belly. Paul was greatly touched. For the first time, he was gripped with a desire for a child within his relationship to Nick. It was ridiculous — a sentimental aberration. He tossed the feeling aside and concentrated on his duties.

Back in his vicarage, Paul prepared the notices, readings and details of everything needed for the service sheets the following day. He already knew the content of the sermon he would preach but he would make notes that evening; right now, he was eager to be off.

Angela arrived and he went over the details with her. Before leaving, he told her to make sure the house was locked up if she had to go out and when she left. He went to a small cupboard in the corner of his study and took out a spare key. "When you go, put the key through the letterbox."

"I'll still be here when you get back. I've got that other typing to do, and those sheets you wanted for your school visit."

Paul had forgotten the work in the pipeline. "Gosh, I do give you a lot of work. I hope I'm not imposing on your good nature. You will tell me, won't you?"

"I enjoy helping and it's good practice. I'm doing really well in my college work. My mum's ever so pleased."

"What about your dad?"

Angela ignored the question. "I loved the way you were dancing and singing in the church. Will it be long before you get that dance group going?"

"Hope not. Perhaps when the school exams have finished we can see who's interested, and get things going after the summer holidays. But I must go now. Make yourself drinks and help yourself to anything in the tins or the fridge. I wouldn't want my angel to starve!"

"Thanks, Paul. I'll print the sheets after you've checked them. I can pop in tonight if you come back after I've gone."

Paul put an arm around her shoulders and gave her a hug. "You're a good lass, Angela. Take care. Don't open the door unless you know who it is. If the phone rings, the answerphone will take the message. Pick it up if you hear my voice. I'll be off then."

He was a little uncertain at leaving Angela alone in the vicarage, but he saw no reason not to trust her. He realised it was her father looming in the background that really concerned him. The man was turning into his adversary. On his way back from the wedding, Kevin had warned him that if he tried to get the church furniture moved he was in for a fight. Neither was he going to have all that hugging in church — he'd got rid of the last bloody menace and he'd get rid of him too!

It wasn't long before he pulled into a lane close to the Glenton rectory; Nick's drive having been blocked by a thoughtless driver — the man had clambered out of his car and dashed off before Paul could stop him.

Paul walked up the drive and rang the bell. As he expected, no one came to the door. He used the key Nick had given him and entered the house. He quickly tapped in the number to cancel the security device and then casually walked to Nick's tidy book-lined study. He took off his jacket and sat in Nick's comfortably padded armchair, picked up the report left for him on the highly polished mahogany desk, and began to read.

Five minutes later, he heard someone come in through the back door. Lucy's voice could be heard and it seemed someone was with her. Paul was about to call out when he heard Lucy say, "It's okay, Tony, we're alone. Nick won't be back for half an hour or more. We'll go to my study; if he gets back early, he'll think we're discussing tomorrow's services."

"I can't wait to get upstairs — lets do it now; I've always fancied it on the kitchen table," said the man with her.

Lucy laughed. "And what would our flock say if they looked in the window and saw a randy ram in the rectory kitchen? You watch too much television."

There was the sound of feet on the stairs and then Paul heard the pair go into the room overhead — Lucy's study.

Paul recognised the voice of Lucy's lover; it was Tony Mayhew, St John's lay reader. He felt like a spy but he could hardly show himself now. Before long the talking upstairs ended and the sounds of a copulating couple reached his ears. The groaning went on for some time. Paul tried to read but it was quite impossible. Soon he heard bumping just above his head and he knew they would be on the old studio couch sometimes used for guests. Did Nick know about Tony? Surely not, he would have told him. How long had it been going on? Paul knew that he was in no position to sit in judgement, but what implications did Lucy's adultery have to his relationship with Nick? He put his hands over his ears and tried to read.

Ten minutes later, he heard the Mondeo on the drive. He looked through the window blinds and saw Nick getting out of the driver's seat. He was carrying a document case and a large bunch of flowers, plus other items, which he was trying to balance while reaching for his keys. Paul hurried open the front door for him. As he did so, Lucy came running down the stairs. She stared at Paul in shocked surprise.

"Say nothing, Paul. Please," she begged, flashing a quick glance upstairs. "I'll tell Nick myself when the time is right — I promise."

Paul nodded and turned to open the door. Lucy ran back upstairs again.

Nick's face broadened into a smile. "Hi! I'm surprised to see you. I thought you hadn't arrived yet. Where's your car?"

"Parked around the corner; your drive was blocked when I arrived." He smiled at Nick's juggling act. "Let me take those flowers off you. Would you like them in the kitchen?"

"Thanks," Nick said, offloading the huge floral spray. "They're for Lucy. I think she needs a bit of TLC. Has she come home yet?"

"She's in her study."

Lucy called to Nick, saying that she would be down shortly. "I'm discussing tomorrow's service with Tony Mayhew. We won't be long."

"Don't rush, Lucy. I'll make us all a coffee," Nick called back. "Paul will help me get the lunch ready." He turned to Paul. "All right with you?"

A few minutes later, Paul was preparing meat for grilling while Nick took coffee to the pair upstairs. The flowers had been placed in a jug of water on the worktop, waiting for Lucy to see them. Paul could have wept at the poignant irony of Nick's tender concern for his wife and his gracious hospitality towards her secret lover.

"Tony can't stay for lunch, so there's just the three of us," Nick said when he returned to the kitchen.

Paul washed the meat juices from his hands and sat down to drink his coffee with Nick. He looked across at the pink carnations and roses, remembering when he saw Lucy dressed in pink and looking so beautiful and happy. Had she been going to see her lover that day? "Pretty flowers. Lucy will be pleased. You know, you make a lovely couple; you really do care for her."

"I'm rather concerned for her, she works so hard." He grinned. "I hope you're not jealous. I'll show you later where my affections lie."

Paul felt a thrill running through his body. He held out his hands for Nick to take hold of. The warmth of their love for each other passed between them. "I've a lot to tell you," he said, trying to pull himself away from Nick's tender but lustful gaze. "But I'd better get on with the lunch."

During the food preparation and while sitting down to lunch, Paul talked about the AGM and the problems he was having with Kevin. Nick listened with interest, but Lucy seemed far away. As soon as the meal ended, Lucy said she would clear away before she went off to town to do a bit of shopping.

"She wants to give us some time together," Nick confided. "But while we're on the subject of your ministry, there's something I have to say to you as your rural dean."

Paul was puzzled. "Sounds heavy stuff." He frowned at the possibilities.

"I've received a complaint and I have to take it seriously."

"Don't tell me, it's my friendly churchwarden, Kevin Raymond. He wants you to give me a good dressing down for seducing the women of Longdale!"

"He rang me this morning just as I was going out — insisted it couldn't wait. He said you were profaning the church with lewd dancing, babblings and sexual activities. He said you were in league with Rita Lee, and dubious practices went on at her house. He complained that his daughter Angela had been sexually assaulted by you at one of Rita's sessions."

Paul didn't know whether to laugh or to cry. "You are joking aren't you?"

"No, Paul, I'm not. Raymond will go to the bishop if I don't deal with the matter. Then it could turn nasty. However groundless the complaints, they have to be looked into."

"Of course. This morning he caught me coming into church in a joyful mood. Rita started up a triumphal piece on the organ and I danced and sang praises to the Lord — probably in tongues for part of it. I joined Rita in the organ loft, kissed her on the cheek and we hugged each other. It was an exuberant, happy celebration of life. I had no idea that we were being watched but I can assure you that it was all very innocent. He's probably seen me at other times doing the same thing."

"What about Angela? Have you touched her?"

Paul was hurt. "That you can ask me that?"

"Think, Paul; there must be something you've done that's been exaggerated beyond recognition," Nick was clearly agitated. "Angela is above the age of consent but this isn't a straightforward accusation of sexual assault, it's something quite sinister. From his statement of what Angela had told them, you performed something lewd with her in the presence of others."

Paul couldn't believe what he was hearing. "Angela has told her parents what? I'm supposed to have done something indecent to the girl in public? Her father's made it up; his daughter's an angel, she wouldn't lie. Oh, maybe over her age, but with nothing serious like this!"

"You know, Paul, when angels lie, all hell is let loose and demons fly. Perhaps she isn't as innocent as she would have you believe."

Paul vehemently shook his head. "No, I can't believe it. It must be Kevin trying to cause mischief."

Nick was now looking quite worried. "Do you think Rita Lee could throw some light on what he's talking about? The incident is supposed to have happened at her house."

"Ah, just a minute, I think I have it," Paul said with relief. "Just after I got back from Riggington, I went to one of Rita's meetings. Someone had brought Angela along — she had been having problems with her periods. Rita asked her to lie down on the couch. Rita and someone else put their hands over her pelvic region. I put my hands on their shoulders and we all prayed. Someone said something in tongues and Rita interpreted it. I can't remember what it was. I know it wasn't exactly that she had been healed; I think it was a promise that she will find wholeness."

Nick nodded. "Nothing different from what all Christians hope to find in Christ. You know the girl; what do you think she could have told her parents — Kevin in particular?"

"When I dropped her off, she was in a happy mood. I expect someone was looking out of the window, as usual, and saw us laughing. She was probably interrogated; I know Kevin shouts at her a lot. I suspect he physically abuses her too. Angela may well have told them the truth, but in Kevin's warped mind he saw me as the one touching her in sensitive areas."

Nick sat thinking for a few moments. "Paul, you must be extra careful where women are involved. Kevin Raymond has good reason not to trust young charismatic priests. Hardly surprising that he's completely paranoid where his womenfolk are concerned."

"Yes, I know, but I can't do anything about that. If I refused to let Angela help in the church, he'd take that as a personal vendetta — he's very proud that all of his family are committed workers. He comes from a long line of Raymond churchwardens and it gives him a lot of influence. He'd probably get it around that I'd dismissed her because she wouldn't let me have a bit. Apart from which, it would hurt the girl terribly — it would be rejection and she gets enough of that from her father."

Nick nodded. "There's more. He seems to think Rita Lee is a witch in church robes — she gets even more stick than you do. Kevin seems to think she's got you bewitched since your arrival in the parish. According to him, you were all right when you came for your interview. He said he would never have accepted you in your present state; you're useless in rural parishes and should go back among the druggies in the urban jungle."

Paul looked at Nick and saw humour sparkling in his eyes. He burst out laughing and Nick, unable to keep his face straight any longer, had to join in.

"It isn't funny, Paul," Nick said when he stopped laughing. "I'll tell Kevin that I've discussed the matter with you and find you have nothing to answer for; there's been a lot of misunderstanding. I can hardly criticise you for praising God, as long as the manner in which you do so doesn't bring the Church into ill repute. That is only likely to happen if biased or unfounded rumours circulate. Affectionately kissing one's organist on the cheek after she's played splendid music hardly merits a rebuke.

"As for his daughter," Nick continued. "I would need to hear from her own lips any accusations of improper conduct. As far as I can ascertain, the ladies touched a fully dressed woman on the site of her problem and you prayed, which, of course, is your priestly function."

"Thanks, Nick, it can't be easy for you."

"All part of the job. But can I give you a bit of advice?"

"Of course, with a troublemaker like Raymond on my back, I'll welcome it."

"Go easy. If you want to dance in the church, try to do it when he's not there. You'll be getting your dance group together soon. When people are familiar with it, it won't come as such a surprise when their vicar does it too. But don't be surprised if you're accused of being a puff. I expect Rita will be blamed for that too!"

Paul did an imitation of how a gay man is supposed to act. He strutted across the kitchen with little steps, swinging his hips, bending his elbows and flapping his hands. He concluded the act by striding over the vacuum cleaner and racing across the floor as though flying on a broomstick. "Bye darlings!" he said in a high-pitched voice. They both roared with laughter. Paul fell off his make-believe broom and rolled on to the floor. Still laughing, Nick helped him to his feet and put the cleaner back in its cupboard. They both sat down again.

"As for Angela," Nick said, returning to his official position. "It seems to me it's her father she needs protection from. Even so, take warning from what's been said and avoid all compromising circumstances."

"What's going on here," Lucy asked as she walked into the kitchen. "Can't leave you two alone five minutes before you're up to mischief. I'm off shortly, do you want me to get the lunch?"

"Has Tony gone?" asked Nick.

"Yes. Did you want to see him? I might just catch him."

"Don't bother, Lucy. I'll see him in the morning. His wife seems to think he spends too much time on church business. I'll have a word with him. I don't want to break up a happy marriage."

"What makes you think his marriage is happy?" Lucy asked him, and then the flowers caught her eye. "Are those for me? They're beautiful! Whom do I have to thank for them?"

Nick gave her a broad smile. "Just to let you know I appreciate the hard work you do." He kissed her on the cheek. "Now, for a real treat, the master chef will prepare your lunch." He moved over to the hob.

"My pinny first," Lucy said, placing an almost naked woman over his head to hang over his blue clerical shirt and the front of his trousers. "Now, that's what I like to see — a woman in the kitchen." Laughing, Lucy picked up her flowers. "I'll do them in the utility room. You two fill this kitchen."

"Is Tony having trouble with his marriage?" Paul asked Nick when Lucy had gone.

"His wife Jane came to see me the other day. She says Tony's always at church doing something or other. Actually, I think the marriage is on the rocks. I've heard the way she constantly nags and embarrasses him in front of people. She's a good-looking woman but a bit of a shrew. Not much love lost between them I should think. At least, I get that impression from the way she talks about Tony. But that's between us; I don't know if Lucy knows about their problems — she hasn't mentioned them, and I don't want either of the Mayhews to think they are the subject of our dinner conversations."

Paul felt like a traitor. Lucy should have told Nick about her affair; he would understand. If it all came out at a divorce hearing, Nick would get unwelcome attention; possibly more than Lucy would. He tried to put the matter from his mind. "Want me to prepare the salad?" Playing at happy partners was his favourite pastime.

If Paul was fearful for Nick before the meal, he was even more concerned for him during it. The conversation had turned to baptisms. Lucy said that she had never expected to miss having children but holding babies during baptisms had moved her maternal instincts.

"I don't expect you men to understand that," she said, as she forked a piece of steak cooked to perfection. "I suppose a woman is born with an urge to nourish a child in her womb, just as a man has a subconscious urge to plant his seed there. You don't realise it until these feelings well up inside of you." She turned to Paul. "Don't get me wrong, I'm not saying that I regret marrying Nick, I'm just stating that we are subject to our biological urges."

"I can understand that," said Paul, thinking that it also helped to explain Lucy's orgasmic encounter with Tony Mayhew. "Only this morning when witnessing the groom kiss the belly of his pregnant wife, I got this crazy desire for Nick and me to have a child. I can understand gay couples wishing to adopt, so why shouldn't I understand your innate urge to bear a child?"

"Why didn't you tell me, Lucy?" said Nick, who'd been sitting listening in silence. "These are things we should discuss — the three of us. Is that why you've been unhappy at times? I can understand it now. I feel I've let you down. We must think of the implications of course. What it would do to our interrelationships is very important."

"Forget it, Nick. I was only making conversation, not asking you to sleep with me. Would you have me sharing a bed with you and Paul? I'd get a baby with two dads. But who'd look after the poor thing? Since Paul's getting daddyhood urges, perhaps he could come over to change the nappies. That would make for lively gossip in all of our parishes; might actually fill up the pews for a while."

She turned to Paul, "How do you fancy that? Your instincts still urging you to procreate? Would you really like to have a child to rear and bring up in your own likeness? Personally, I've chosen to follow my vocation. Children don't come into the equation."

Lucy started giggling. "You should see your faces. I'm not sure whether the both of you are relieved or disappointed. But I must be off now. At least, I've given you something to chew on besides tough steak!" Still laughing, she left the room.

"The steak is great, Nick. I'll finish Lucy's if you don't want it."

"Help yourself. I don't know what's happened to Lucy lately. She certainly gave me a shock just then. We talked about the implications of no children before we married. I said at the time, I'd never deny her motherhood if she changed her mind. But how would you feel about it, Paul?"

Knowing what he did, Paul couldn't see Lucy desiring Nick to father any child of hers; surely that would only complicate her relationship to Tony Mayhew. "I need time to answer that question. But it doesn't arise so why anticipate it? More important, what are we going to do for the next hour before I go back?"

"I'll put the answerphone on, but I'm going to have to be prepared to answer the doorbell," said Nick, stuffing his last piece of meat into his mouth and smiling impishly.

"Well, that limits the options but I'm sure we'll think of something," said Paul grinning. "Unless someone is spying on the place, no one knows I'm here."

# Chapter eight

Paul had been eagerly looking forward to Pentecost. At least, Kevin Raymond and his buddies could not possibly complain about a sermon centring on the work of the Holy Spirit on this special Sunday. In no way did he want to give the impression that being baptised in the Spirit was some kind of magic, but neither did he want to dismiss the gifts of the Spirit as being unimportant in today's Church. As far as Paul was concerned, they were important signs of Christ working within his followers.

From the pulpit, Paul interacted with his congregation in the retelling of the Pentecost story, bringing life and credibility into a remarkable event. "Imagine it — feel it — see it for yourselves," he told them. He then gave his personal witness, concluding, "Seek what Christ has to offer you — not just for yourselves, but for the coming of his Kingdom in this place."

Throughout his preaching, Paul's eyes had never left his congregation. He had spoken from the heart, trying to put over his message in simple terms rather than by deep theological argument. He wanted to share with them what he himself had received, and he felt certain that people had been truly listening — it was written on their faces.

As usual, after the service, Kevin Raymond grumbled that the sermon had gone two minutes over the twenty minute preaching slot. "You've got a captive audience; you should have more consideration. It wasn't even a proper bloody sermon!"

Later that day, Rita told him that it was his manner, his personal conviction and passion, rather than the words he'd used that had moved many of his hearers that morning. "It was wonderful; I felt the power of the Spirit present among us. Don't worry about the opposition. It shows the Spirit is working in men's hearts, even our disgruntled churchwarden's."

Paul's heart was gladdened when a few people turned up at the vicarage wanting to know more, and those in the study groups said they were going on and asked him for a course with plenty of 'meat' in it.

He'd always tried to get to the prayer and study meetings from time to time, but now he decided to have a large fortnightly meeting at the vicarage to get the groups together. It was to be a time of prayer and praise as well as teaching — something suitable for interested casual enquirers. The first one was a bit of a squash. He played his guitar and they sang choruses. Rita played the piano and they sang modern hymns.

Rita reported that her own meeting had grown by six new members and the other groups likewise reported growth. Paul was not entirely happy when Rita confided in him, "This vicarage meeting is just like it was when I was a girl and Peter was here. As big as this room is with the folding doors drawn back, the piano had to be moved into the hall, and even then youngsters were sitting on the stairs."

Paul found it hard to share Rita's bubbling enthusiasm. He didn't want things to go too fast; he wanted the growth to be genuine and not fizzle out if for some reason he was moved on. For a moment, he felt as though they were in a time warp, and he understood the fears of some of his congregation. At least, he could never be removed for the same reason as Peter Millar had. But he did hope that none of the worshippers, especially the women who visited the vicarage, would get mysteriously pregnant.

He received a large number of requests for Confirmation, and some adults had asked if they could have an exploration group with an option to be confirmed. He was pleased that people were relating their inner experiences to the normal workings of the Church of England, and did not want to separate themselves from the local congregation.

Four teenage boys he often casually chatted to in the churchyard, asked him about "this weird Spirit stuff" Angela had told them about. He invited them to eat their takeaways in his vicarage while he talked to them and played lively music on his guitar. It was the beginning of a youth group.

It was all heady stuff. Nick told him to be careful and not rush into things. But by July, a lot was going on — not just the usual fetes and outings but activities involving young people. He soon had some of the youngsters gathering around him. One wanted to play Paul's drums while he strummed on his guitar. Another lad went home to get his guitar and brought his flute-playing sister, who was one of Paul's servers, back with him.

The vicarage soon became a gathering place for youngsters from the local villages and housing estates with time on their hands. Before long a lively music group was getting into shape. Others came along just to listen, chat, drink Paul's coffee and play football on the large vicarage lawn. Fortunately, a keen married couple, both of them teachers who were part of Rita's group, volunteered to help organise the youth in meaningful activities with a view to getting them evangelised.

A few girls, who were known to Rita, wanted to be in the dance group they'd heard about. Rita and Angela between them worked out a few routines and, after one or two workouts, decided, with Paul's approval, to produce something suitable for the Harvest Festival on the last Sunday of September.

Paul did not anticipate problems about that but he had no intention of introducing a music group into the church until they'd had considerable practice and most of the PCC members were with him. He could see the possibility for youth services on Sunday evenings, but he knew Kevin Raymond was going to be his biggest stumbling block to any progress on that front.

On the last Saturday evening in July, he was preparing his sermon for the following morning when Kevin started banging at his door while ringing the bell at the same time. As soon as Paul, deeply concerned, opened the door to him, Kevin came storming in accusing him of desecrating the church, ruining the vicarage grounds, encouraging louts into the area and now abetting theft from the church safe.

"I knew we'd have problems when you started practising your bloody mumbo-jumbo! You're supposed to be a priest of God not the Devil's disciple! You should be doing your duty visiting our parishioners, not spending your time with bloody delinquents." Paul was about to protest, when Kevin, after giving himself time to breathe, continued, "We, and especially the other churches, rely on legacies and contributions. We won't get them now — not with that bloody lot you call a Pastoral Team knocking on their doors."

Before Paul could defend his pastoral strategy, Kevin was back on tack.

"The bloody louts will drain our resources — not add to them. We don't want them in the church. They can't even talk bloody English. Always swearing with the f word — bloody disgusting. Sex, sex, sex! That's all they bloody think about. Now, see what you've bloody done. One of your bloody ne'er-do-wells has got into the safe and taken the money collected at yesterday's funeral, and this morning's wedding. Huh! For his bloody drug habit no doubt!"

Paul ignored the tirade and calmly walked back into his study, indicating to Kevin that he should follow him. Paul sat down and waited for Kevin to do the same. When he could get a word in, he addressed the problem of theft.

"Perhaps you'll tell me exactly what's happened? How could anyone get into a safe that's always kept locked in a vestry that's also locked? First, they would have to get inside the church — the outside vestry door is bolted. Are you telling me that both church and safe have been broken into?"

Kevin's face grew red with anger again. His eyes were even beadier than usual and glittering like polished jet between narrowed lids. The veins in his neck were swollen and sweat had broken out on his brow. "What do you think I'm trying to bloody tell you?" he yelled at Paul. "Whoever took the bloody money must have had a bloody key — and it wasn't mine!"

"But only you and I have keys to the safe — not even the treasurer has one. And the sacristan has to have the safe opened for her," Paul said, more by way of clarification for his own sake than for argument.

"Do you think I'm a bloody cretin? I keep telling you — it's those bloody tattooed louts with the red hair and bloody studs. You let them into the bloody vicarage!"

Paul was worried that Kevin was about to blow a blood vessel. "Can I get you a drink, Kevin?"

"I haven't come for a bloody social chat! Get the police in — and do it bloody now!"

Paul may have been keeping calm but he was very worried. As far as he could see, the only person who might have borrowed his safe key was Angela. He had the keys to the vestry and safe in the back of his locked filing cabinet. He'd put the keys back after the wedding, but left the cabinet unlocked while he was clearing up a bit of admin prior to his holiday.

Angela was working on the computer at the time, so he took his work into the dining room for privacy and also to spread out his papers. She stayed for lunch, and after printing the service sheets, took them into St Michael's ready for morning. She then came back to get her things from his study.

But he couldn't believe Angela would do such a thing. She had never given him cause not to trust her. She seemed happy and contented, especially after having had an experience of being filled with the Spirit whilst at Rita's. Sometimes she joined him for Morning Prayer and came to various groups and meetings. No, it couldn't be his little angel; there must be another explanation.

"Well, are you just going to sit there chewing your cud and looking bloody gormless, or are you going to ring the police?"

"Was anything else taken? Is the silver all there?" Paul asked, feeling certain that a thief from outside would have taken the lot. If some of the taggers-on who came with his regular lads had been involved, he couldn't see them just taking money — not after all the bother of getting into the safe, and the silver would be more important to a professional burglar.

"Just the money. Two hundred and fifty-five bloody pounds! They'll get a lot of dope for that!"

"You're assuming they got hold of my keys. Not possible. They're locked in my filing cabinet, and only I know where."

"Since mine never leaves my person—"

"Not even at night?"

"Don't be a bloody fool, man. I put them on the bedside table until morning. We've had enough of this bloody nonsense. I'll ring the police!"

"No! We'll investigate this ourselves. There could be a simple explanation."

Kevin thumped the desk. "You're bloody off tomorrow. I'm not being left to explain to the bloody treasurer where the money's gone."

Paul rose from his chair and reached into his back pocket for his wallet. "I'll give it to you myself. I've got some cash for my holiday. I'll sort it out when I get back."

"No you bloody won't! I want that bloody kid found and bloody punished!"

"Suppose the thief — if there is one—"

"If there bloody is one? Do you think I'm bloody-well making this up? Or maybe you think I'm so bloody hard up I need to rob the bloody collection?"

With difficulty, Paul kept his voice steady. "Nothing of the kind. Maybe there is another key that neither of us knows about. Maybe someone borrowed the money and will be returning it in the morning ready for the banking of the weekly collections."

"And maybe bloody pigs can fly? He rose from his chair. "I'll ring the bloody police myself."

"Well if you do, don't be surprised if you yourself come under suspicion. Everyone knows you want me out."

"That's bloody ridiculous!" Kevin's fists were clenched ready for a fight.

"Just let things rest a bit," Paul said, taking five fifty-pound notes and a fiver from his wallet. "I'll get to the bottom of it."

Kevin snatched up the money. "You're a bloody fool, Stringer. You know who took it and you want to protect him. I'll take your bloody money because the church can't afford the loss. It bloody-well serves you right. But I'm informing the rural dean — you won't get away with it."

"Well, you'd better be quick about it, he's off on holiday in the morning." He led Kevin to the door. "I doubt Canon Palmer will be staying behind to sort out this little problem."

As Kevin went off down the drive, Paul's mind focused once more on the possibility that Angela was involved in the theft. He could hardly face her with his suspicions. Why would she do it anyway? If he found the opportunity, he would ask her if anyone had ever quizzed her where the key was kept. He hated to think what her father might do to her if she came under suspicion by the police. But if they were brought in, he'd have to tell them about her whereabouts that afternoon.

Perhaps it would blow over by the time he arrived back from holiday. Tomorrow he would hand over his church keys to Kevin and clear off for almost three weeks. The church hadn't lost anything and somehow he'd get to the bottom of it.

The thought of the coming holiday revived Paul's good humour. Meeting up with Nick and Lucy for a rented cottage holiday in the north of Scotland was ideal. Lots of healthy walking and maybe a bit of golf — Nick intended teaching him. Lucy would be there for just a week. She wanted to take two weeks off later on to stay with a friend in France. She would be driving Nick's Mondeo home and telling folk that Nick would be getting a lift back, which, of course, was true.

But he still had the next day to get through, with Kevin to glare at him throughout the service at St Michael's. He settled himself down to complete his sermon but it wasn't easy. Restless, he picked up his keys and went to the church. He was surprised to find Rita playing the organ. He sat in a back pew for a while, allowing the music to penetrate his mind and body. Soon his soul felt refreshed and he went to the sanctuary rail to kneel in prayer.

He knew the music had stopped but he didn't hear Rita coming up behind him. As he was in deep meditation, he felt a warm glow over his head and then a feeling of utter tranquillity spread through his entire body. Rita's voice sounded and the tongue with which she was speaking was sweet and melodic. Paul knew Rita was praying for him with her hands over his head.

When they were sitting together on the sanctuary steps after a time of prayer, Rita said, "I'm glad you came in. I won't see much of you tomorrow and then you'll be off for a while. I've decided to go away too. I've managed to get a late booking for a tour of Egypt. I'm really going to miss you."

"I'll miss you too, Rita. I guess we've been drawn together as kind of soul mates."

"Only soul mates? You know I love you, Paul. I'm sure, deep down, you love me too."

He felt sad that she was unable to let him go. "We are all called to love one another," he told her gently. "It can never be more than Christian affection. Please don't hope in vain; you'll only be disappointed and prevented from finding the right guy for you."

"You're wrong, Paul. You only think you're gay. I do believe you've never slept with a woman; you're probably afraid to and can't admit it to yourself. There could be many reasons why you find it difficult to relate sexually to women. We could pray about it and find an answer. God wants you to be whole and live in unity with yourself. You can't do that if you hanker after sexual union with your own gender."

"I know you mean well, but you're wrong. I know who, and what, I am."

"You only think you do. Living a celibate life isn't easy — I know," she said to him with deep meaning.

"I'm sorry, but there's no reason for you to be without a man if that's what you really want. I see the way men look at you. You're a very desirable woman — intelligent, accomplished and beautiful. Give yourself a chance, Rita. Stable loving relationships are very important, and if you were in one, I'm sure you'd find the contentment I have."

She looked at him in utter disbelief. "Are you telling me you're in a relationship? Impossible! I'd know it. If you were a practising homosexual God could not work through you like he's been doing. You're just trying to put me off."

Paul shook his head. "Accept it, Rita. You said you were happy for us to be partners in ministry; to want more will only make you unhappy."

She took hold of his hands and gazed into his eyes. Smiling, she said, "God has brought us together. He's given me a deep and tender love for you. He wants me to help you through into wholeness. I will go on praying for you — I'll never give up."

Paul felt the warmth of her love for him and he was deeply moved. But she was wrong about him. He loved Nick. Had it not been for his lover, he wouldn't even be there listening to Rita. He wanted to press home the fact that he did indeed have a lover, but to do so would only make her be on the lookout for his partner. He couldn't risk it. Judging by her reaction, he'd said too much already.

He held her by her shoulders and said gently, "By all means pray for me. I certainly need wisdom and discernment at this present time. But it has to do with my ministry, not my sexuality."

She moved forward and kissed him on his lips.

He gradually pulled away and told her sadly, "I'm sorry, Rita; women do not move me sexually, even if I truly welcome your affection."

She looked at him puzzled. "But God will heal you, Paul. Then you will want me just as I want you. I know it, I just know it."

A voice from the back of the church rescued Paul from his awkward situation.

"Can I speak to you, Mr Stringer, please? It is rather urgent."

Angela was standing just inside the door and looking a little nervous. "I went to the vicarage first. You didn't answer and so I came here. I'm not spying, truly I'm not."

Paul was greatly concerned at her nervousness; it wasn't like her. He stood up and walked over to her. "Of course you can speak to me. What's the problem?"

Angela looked towards Rita, clearly not wanting to speak in front her.

Rita said she had to go. "I'll leave you both to chat. See you in the morning, Paul; you too, Angela." As she was going out, she turned and said cheerfully, "Thanks for taking the dance group this week, Angela; they're coming along fine."

The door closed and Angela looked up at Paul. "She's real nice. You're an item aren't you? You don't have to answer — everybody knows it anyway." She sighed and looked away.

"Well, everybody's wrong, Paul assured her. "We like each other and we work together but we're not a couple."

She immediately brightened up. "Really?"

"Yes, really. I've told you already; I'm married to my vocation. What did you want to see me about?" Was she going to confess about the money?

"Can we sit down? I won't keep you long but I had to walk here. My bike's had it." She pulled a face. "My dad ran over it on purpose when he came home in a temper."

Paul didn't like the sound of what he was hearing. He signalled for her to sit next to him on a bench near the back of the church. Golden evening sunlight, streaming in through the west window, once more caught her hair like a glowing halo. Her troubled big blue eyes moved him deeply. "What is it, Angel? Trouble at home?"

"You could say that all right. Dad says you're a liar and a thief, or in league with one. He says money's been taken from the safe and you know where it's gone. He says he'll inform the police if Canon Palmer won't do anything about it." Her voice began to quiver and tears formed in her eyes. "He says I'm not to go to the vicarage anymore or to Rita's place."

Paul took out his hanky and dabbed tears from her cheeks. As he moved her hair from her face he saw a red angry mark under her left ear and spreading across her cheek. Even worse, the side of her right cheekbone and her jaw were bruised. He was very angry.

"Has your father done this to you?"

"Yes, but it's nothing. Poor Mother usually gets it. My sister moved out but Mum's nowhere to go. Anyway, she doesn't want to leave him."

It was no more than Paul suspected. No doubt Kevin had threatened his wife with what he'd do if she left him; he'd seen it a number of times in his last parish.

"I know why he's angry but why did he hit you?" Paul was afraid it was because of him; or had Kevin found out she had taken the money?

She hung her head and rubbed at her wet cheeks with her fingers, but she said nothing.

Expecting the worst, he lifted up her chin and looked into her red-rimmed eyes. "Angela, why did your father hit you?"

"Because I told him he was a liar."

"But why, Angela? It was bound to make your dad angry."

"Because of all the things he said about you."

He put an arm around her to comfort her. "Oh, my poor child."

"I'm not a child," she said crossly.

He pulled away from her. "Sorry, of course you're not."

She moved back up to him, her bruised face resting on his chest. "He said horrid things. All lies! Anyway I know you didn't take the money, and you couldn't possibly know who did."

He turned to face her. Grasping her shoulders, he tried to read her eyes. "How can you be so certain, even clergy can be tempted?"

She hung down her head. "My mother took it. She was in the church clearing up after the wedding. Dad came in to check the money and to put the silver candlesticks and vessels back in the safe — the sacristan had just polished them. While he was having a pee in the vestry toilet, she took the money from where it's always kept after it's been counted — under the velvet bag that the chalices are kept in. He didn't even know Mum had been in the vestry; when he locked up, she was helping Doreen to sweep up outside you see."

"But how do you know all this? Why would your mother want to take the money?" Paul found the story hard to believe but it did explain things.

"That's the irony of it," Angela said with a sigh. "She wanted him to be blamed; pay back for the pain he's caused her. Mum was hoping he'd get locked up, or at least get kicked out of the church and leave us in peace. She showed me the money and told me about it just before I came here. She was going to plant it in the house where the police would find it, but you refused to call them in. I've got the money here." She put her hand inside her pocket and took out an envelope filled with banknotes and cash.

There was still something unexplained. "Why did your father go back to the church this evening? Why did he go into the safe?"

"That's the big laugh! He forgets things but won't admit it. He's even left the safe key in the lock before now. He suddenly remembered that he'd left the registers out and came back to put them in the safe."

Paul took the envelope from Angela. "What will happen if your father finds out what really happened?"

"He mustn't — he'll kill her! Me too probably. Her eyes were wild with fear. "Please don't tell him. Make it all right. Oh, please, Paul, never let him know."

"Don't you worry; I have an idea. But you and Diana must keep quiet about the whole affair. Can you do that?"

"Yes. Neither of us will say anything." Her eyes opened wide as she looked around the silent church. She whispered, "What are you going to do?"

He smiled at her caution. "You'll probably find out tomorrow. Don't worry; I'm sure your dad will relent about you working in the vicarage. You'd better go now, Angela. Are you going straight home?"

"I'm meeting Mark. We're going to a disco," she said smiling. "He's got a car now. He's picking me up at the crossroads. He won't come to the house — doesn't like my dad."

"Better be off then, it's getting late."

She went off much happier than she arrived.

Paul walked over to the vicarage and returned with the vestry and safe keys. Making sure he was alone in the church, he locked the door and went to open up the vestry. Unlocking the safe, he took out the velvet bag that contained the heavy silver chalices. He pulled open the drawstrings and dropped the collection money inside. The weight of the coins carried the envelope to the bottom of the bag. He placed the bag back inside the safe, exactly as he'd found it. He locked up the safe and then the vestry door. First making sure the church was completely secure, he went back to the vicarage to finish his sermon.

Paul arrived in St Michael's church vestry just in time to hear Jean the sacristan speaking to Kevin. "I guess you must have slipped it inside absentmindedly. Old Mr Smithson did it several times."

"Are you saying I'm going bloody senile? I put it under the bag. Someone stole it, and came back in last night to put it inside the bloody thing!" Kevin roared. Suddenly realising how stupid he sounded, he started mumbling about a frame-up.

Jean, who refused to let the likes of Kevin Raymond upset her, merely looked at him with raised eyebrows and carried on with her job. She left the vestry murmuring, "Perhaps it was the tooth fairy playing tricks."

Paul greeted Kevin with a cheerful, "Good morning."

Kevin turned at the sound of his voice and looked at him with fury in his eyes. "You must have done it!"

"Ah, you found it then — splendid! I'll have my cash back sometime. Don't bother to apologise, we all make mistakes."

Kevin opened his mouth to speak when members of the choir came in from outside.

"Good morning, Vicar," they said in chorus, as they made their way to the robing room.

Paul patted his churchwarden on the shoulder. "Let it go, Kevin. The money's been found. Where was it anyway? Inside the wedding register?"

"You know bloody-well it wasn't."

"Language, gentlemen," said Jean, who'd just returned to the vestry. "We're in the House of the Lord."

Kevin gave her an angry look but said nothing. Locking the envelope inside the safe, he simmered down and went about his work.

Paul carried on robing, trying to keep up his normal good humour. "Kevin, I'll give you my keys before I leave for Bradmire. Mary Jones and Bill Smith are taking the Family Service at Penningly. The people there are quite happy for their churchwardens to take the service. Mary's getting some of her schoolchildren involved. It's a great blessing to have a church school in the area, especially with such a good Christian in charge don't you think?"

"Our own church school should never have been bloody-well closed," Kevin groused. "The new one's almost in Penningly."

"I seem to remember you complaining about the kids running around the gravestones," said Jean grinning. "My grandchildren are much better off at the new school. They've got a football team now, a choir, and a mass of computers to mess about with."

"Mess about is all they bloody do these days." Kevin muttered. He turned to Paul with narrowed eyes. "Don't think I'm going to let this money business drop. I'll get the police in tomorrow."

Paul shook his head. "Accept the money's here. As safe as it's always been."

Fury was turning Kevin's face from red to purple. "You put it there," he snarled. "I'm not bloody daft!"

Jean looked at him derisively. "You must be mad. What do you think they'll say when I have to tell them that you left a valuable silver paten out last month? Mr Stringer opened the safe for me to put it away. You were lucky it wasn't stolen."

Kevin was utterly deflated. "No one told me," he muttered.

"No one wants to be reminded their memory's going. I know that," said Jean in sympathy. "But it happens and we just have to accept it."

Kevin was looking puzzled. He mumbled something incoherent and left the vestry.

More members of the choir arrived and joined their chatting comrades. Just five minutes before the service was due to start, a group of teenagers rushed into the vestry to get themselves robed and prepared for the service. Paul noticed that both Angela and her mother had not yet arrived. With them in mind, he went to the sanctuary for a moment of prayer.

The procession was lining up when he returned to the vestry. The outside door flung open and Angela entered. Her head was lowered and golden hair was almost hiding her face. Someone helped her on with her robes and another handed her the cross — she was the crucifer that morning.

"Do try to get here on time, Angela," said Jean. "And you should get your hair tied back. I'll do it for you."

"No," said Paul quickly. "She looks the perfect angel as she is." He smiled at Angela as she glanced up at him. Hiding the anguish that was in his heart, he said gently, "Do you need a minute to calm down?"

She shook her head in reply.

"Right, we'll let Rita know we're ready."

With choir and congregation singing, the procession went forward. Paul was thinking how appropriate it was that Angela should be bearing the cross that morning. He had seen the nasty bruises on her arms when the sleeves of her alb had fallen back, and he knew what would be under her unusually heavy make-up.

They passed by Kevin Raymond at the back of the church. His head was lowered and he was looking very sheepish. When he came up for communion later on, his eyes were down and Paul thought that he detected moisture on his cheeks. Had the sight of his abused daughter carrying the cross moved him to tears — tears of shame and sorrow? Or was he merely feeling humiliated and fearful of being ridiculed? Perhaps a mixture of both.

At the end of the service, before moving to the back of the church to speak to his flock, Paul whispered to Angela that he would drop her off at her home on his way to Bradmire. "That is, if you can wait until I've finished here. You don't have other plans for getting home do you?"

Keeping her eyes down, she shook her head. "No. Thank you, I'd like that."

Paul was prepared to be five minutes late at Bradmire rather than leave for his holiday without knowing what had happened to Angela. He stopped his vehicle down a side lane that was little more than a dirt track he sometimes used as a short cut. He turned to Angela and gently lifted her chin, smoothing back her hair to examine her face. The bruises on the side of her cheekbones and jaws were now showing through the make-up. And the eye she'd kept covered with hair was red and the lids swollen.

"Dear God, what has he done to you?" Paul said, tears of anger and sorrow forming in his eyes. He pulled her to him and wrapped his arms around her, as though to protect her from further harm, as much as to give her comfort.

"Oh," she squealed and instinctively drew back.

"I'm so sorry, Angela," he said tenderly. "I didn't mean to hurt you. Tell me what happened."

She gingerly put her head on his shoulder and took hold of his hand. He stroked her hair with his cheek. Fighting back tears, she whispered in a quavering voice, "I was home late and Dad was waiting for me. He said I was a slut like my mother and needed teaching a lesson. Mum woke up and came downstairs to tell him to leave me alone. He thumped her in the stomach and she fell over. He was going to kick her and I tried to stop him, so he started hitting me again." She sniffed back more tears and looked defiant. "But I fought back. I told him he was a dirty liar. My mum isn't a slut and I'm still a virgin. He hit me sideways and I fell on the floor. I thought he was going to kick me, but he suddenly stopped and went upstairs. When I helped Mum back to bed, I heard Dad sobbing in the bathroom." She looked up at Paul. "What's wrong with him?"

"Some would say he has a demon but quite honestly, Angela, I think he's a very unhappy man who needs professional help. You and your mother don't have to put up with it. You both have enough evidence to take legal action."

"Mum would never do it. She's afraid of him but it's more than that. She told me last night that she deserves everything she gets. Not just because of the money business but something that happened long ago. She wouldn't say what it was though. She says what happened over the money only proves how bad she is. She says she married my dad and has to stick by him. For better or for worse, it's God's will."

Paul sighed. What could he say to her if neither of her parents were willing to tell her the truth about her birth? "God is all forgiving. Whatever Diana did, God would not punish her in this way. It isn't good for your father to get away with it either."

"But if God will forgive Mum, then surely he'll forgive Dad and I must forgive him too. He does a lot for the church and I've heard him pray for forgiveness lots of times."

Paul had a vision of Kevin at the Communion rail that morning, looking very much the repentant sinner. But what about next time? It was a very dangerous situation. Whatever the cause, and however contrite he may appear to be afterwards, the man had an uncontrollable temper. "You'll soon be eighteen, do you intend to stay as your mother's support for ever?"

"I just can't leave her," Angela protested.

"Because she won't leave Kevin, you don't have to suffer too you know. Perhaps your dad would cool down a bit if he didn't have what he regards as a problem child around." Paul was actually thinking more in terms of Angela being a reminder of Kevin's own inadequacy and of his wife's adultery, than of the girl being troublesome.

"I'll think about it when I've got a job. If I had a place of my own, Mum would have somewhere to stay occasionally," she said.

"Good. Well, I must go now — they'll think I'm not coming. I'll see you when I return. But promise me, Angela, whatever you do, don't provoke your father."

"I'll try. I'm going to miss you," she said, looking at him woefully.

"You'll survive without me." He opened his door. "I'll come round and help you out."

He jumped out and went to her side of the Discovery, opened the door and carefully helped her down. He kissed her forehead. "Keep smiling, my little angel."

"I'll try."

He watched her walk the few muddy yards to the road. "To please me, see a doctor and get checked over." He called after her, but he knew she wouldn't. She was too loyal for her own good.

He drove off to Bradmire. Assuming no one would hold him up, the service would only be five minutes late starting, but for some of the old biddies it might as well be five hours. But he wasn't concerned. He knew he'd get a welcome from the likes of Mrs Cranford and the rest would mellow by the end of the service.

Not wanting to waste even a few minutes, while carefully watching out for deep ruts in the lane and steering clear of overhanging branches, he prayed for the Raymond family. And for himself, that he would have the discernment to get to the heart of Kevin's problem, wisdom to know what to do, and the love to carry it through. Something was nagging at the back of his mind. Was Angela deliberately trying to get his attention? He refused to even consider the proposition.

# Chapter nine

Paul was reviewing the past year in preparation for a combined meeting of all the PCCs within the new Glenton with Longdale, Penningly and Bradmire Team Ministry. The highlight had been Bishop Lionel's visit to confirm the largest group of candidates for many years and to commission his pastoral team. But it was the young people themselves that gripped his heart and mind the most.

On the whole, the dance group had been well received at St Michael's Harvest Festival, and Penningly PCC had formally invited them to perform at their Christingle service. The enthusiastic music group was now really good. The singers and musicians had got together with the dance group in the Penningly church hall for regular open nights as well as for practising. Mary Jones, Bill Smith and the Petersons added a Christian teaching element, and Rita Lee and Angela a creative one.

With the approval of the Penningly PPC Standing Committee, he had invited a Christian rock group to a special youth night in the Penningly hall. The event had brought in teenagers for miles around and from other churches, including Nick's. Some youngsters had been converted that night and were now regular worshippers; they, and others, were urging for a regular Sunday service catering for youth. Kevin Raymond and the rest of his diehards were determined that it would never happen, at least, at St Michael's.

There was still much to do and most of it centred on the position of the altar. Nick was in complete sympathy with him. The altar at Glenton St John's church had been moved forward some years ago. The whole atmosphere was different — warmer and friendlier without losing any sense of the sacredness of the occasion. It was going to be discussed at a combined PCC meeting at Glenton that evening. As he sat thinking about this, and how he was to get it over to his own flock, the doorbell rang.

Angela was standing outside.

"Can I have a word with you, Paul?" Her voice was urgent and pleading.

"Of course. Come in; I'll get us a drink," he said, feeling a little concerned that Angela might be having trouble with her dad again.

Since the business with the stolen cash, things had improved for Angela. Her dad had softened a bit and he hadn't hit her or her mother again, or at least, so Angela had told him. Kevin clearly wasn't happy at her spending so much time at the vicarage or at Rita Lee's house, but she was now eighteen and he had to accept the fact that she was an adult with a mind and will of her own.

They went into the warm, if untidy, kitchen. Paul put the kettle on while Angela spooned coffee into the mugs.

"I don't have long before I have to go out. What's the problem, Angela? Shouldn't you be in college today?"

"I've got a free period this morning. Exams all next week."

"I see. But, what's so desperate to keep you from your studies?"

She sat in one of the comfy chairs by the stove. "Mark wants us to get engaged. Do you think we should?"

Paul leaned back against the worktop and folded his arms, waiting for the kettle to boil. "Only you can answer that. I suppose you're both a bit young but I take it you're not thinking of getting married yet are you?" He was feeling awkward about giving any kind of advice. "Shouldn't you talk to your mother about it?"

"I can't talk to my parents about men, sex or marriage — it's kind of taboo in our house."

Paul hoped she wasn't going to bring up Mark's heated carnal desires again. "I seem to remember you two having problems. I take it everything's okay now?"

"Since he got his car, we've been going places and he gives me lifts to college; saves me having to get the bus. I never did get my bike replaced."

"That's handy for you. I assume you both love each other — it's not just one-sided on Mark's part?"

Her pretty face wrinkled into a frown. "I don't know whether I love him or not. I expect my parents must have loved each other once. I don't want to end up like them. What turns love into hate, Paul? I'm afraid to love anyone."

The kettle automatically switched off. Paul finished off the drinks and handed a mug to Angela. He sat in the chair next to her, thinking about the girl's background. She should be told about her true parentage, how else could she understand her home situation?

But he was not the one to do it. "Talk to your mother about these things, it's important for your future happiness. There can be very loving relationships within marriage but sometimes things just go wrong for all sorts of reasons."

"Half of my friends have divorced parents. Engagement is one thing, I don't know if I ever want to marry though," she said mournfully.

Paul sighed. "I can't deny the difficulties in human relationships. But when you truly fall in love, you want to spend your life with that person and you look forward with hope. The whole of life is about risk. Perhaps you're not ready to make a commitment to Mark."

"To be honest, I love someone else and I'd marry him tomorrow if I could. Mark is okay — second-best is better than none at all, don't you think?"

She was looking at him with pleading eyes, desiring something from him but he wasn't sure what.

"Angela, if you're in love with a married man, I can't condone any sexual relationship you may have with him," he told her firmly, but feeling a bit of a hypocrite for doing so. "But don't use Mark as a substitute; it won't work and it isn't fair. You're young; someone will come along — someone you can give your whole heart to. If you go on hankering after what you can't have, you'll only be unhappy." He sighed and added, "I seem to remember us having a conversation like this before."

"The man I love isn't married. I'm not that wicked," she said defiantly.

"It wouldn't be wicked if you were in love with a married man, you can't help your feelings. Acting on them and breaking up a marriage is different, although I do realise the difficulties faced by people in love." He was thinking of Lucy and Tony, and thought that perhaps he understood Lucy's moral dilemma. "But this isn't the case with you, so why give Mark hope if your heart is elsewhere?"

"You think we shouldn't get engaged then?" She was looking at him intensely; her wide-open blue eyes making her appear so very sweet and innocent.

"Does he know you love someone else?"

"You don't understand; it isn't as if I'm committed to another man. I'm trying to forget him and love Mark. That's why I think it might be good to get engaged. Why should I upset Mark by telling him there's someone else?"

Paul then had another thought. "Angela, is this other man aware that you love him? I hope you aren't using Mark to make him jealous."

"How can you say that? I wouldn't do such a thing," she said angrily. "Mark wants us to get engaged so I'll have sex with him but neither of us wants to marry yet. But if we're engaged, then it's okay to do it isn't it? If Mark's as good as the girls say he is, then maybe things will be okay for us and I can forget about this other guy."

Paul was amazed she'd held out so long. But clearly, she must have some deep feeling for Mark — giving up her treasured virginity was a significant step to take. There were other considerations though.

"This other man you speak of, does he have a girlfriend?"

"Yes, but I don't know how far they go. All the way I should think. They're not engaged but I know they're very close." She gripped Paul's hand and cried in anguish, "That's why I'm trying to get him out of my heart."

He lifted up her hand and kissed it. "It must be very difficult for you," he said tenderly.

She sighed deeply. "It isn't easy."

"I'm so very sorry."

Paul felt her pain but he had to admit that, for him, there was relief too. At the back of his mind there had been a nagging thought that he was the object of her devotion, even though he'd told her that he was married to his vocation.

She looked at him with tears in her eyes. "So you see why I want to forget him and give myself to Mark. God can't always answer our prayers. Or maybe he sometimes wants us to suffer, so we know what it's like for him to have his love rejected. Perhaps he's given me Mark as a kind of compensation."

Paul wasn't completely happy about her theological surmising, but it seemed to give her comfort. "Perhaps you should give it more time before you get engaged; it's a big step to take."

"And not have sex with him?" she asked, looking him straight in the eye.

"I didn't say that. It has to be your own decision — you're an adult, Angela."

"But you are my father in Christ. Old people call you Father Paul even though you're young."

"Maybe that is so, but being called Father doesn't make us founts of wisdom in matters of the heart. You already know my thoughts about promiscuity but, unlike Mark, you've not had other partners. All I can say is, if you do go all the way with Mark, be careful and make sure he takes precautions. And remember, you can only lose your virginity once."

She was thoughtful for a few moments. "Men like to have virgins for lovers don't they?"

"Quite possibly. Literature is often full of that sort of thing." He was unable to speak from his own point of view. "Just be sure that isn't the only reason Mark is attracted to you. If and when you come together, let it be in love," he advised, giving her hand a squeeze before letting it go.

Paul rose from the table and reached up to a cupboard. He put a plastic container in front of her. "I have to go in a few minutes. Drink up your coffee and try one of these delicious ginger biscuits Mrs Cranford made me. I'll get my things. If you like, I'll drop you at the college." He smiled down at her. "I just know you'll do well with to your studies. The work you do for me is of a very high standard. Even Canon Palmer comments on your secretarial and computer skills."

Angela smiled proudly at the comments, and accepted a biscuit to nibble.

A few minutes later, they were going out of the door when Kevin Raymond turned up. Unusually, he was dressed casually in an open-necked shirt with tweed jacket and cap, instead of the formal white shirt, striped tie and dark suit he usually wore as a kind of churchwarden's uniform. He looked puzzled at seeing his daughter. "I thought you'd gone to college," he said, looking very suspiciously at both of them.

"Mr Stringer is going to give me a reference for when I start looking for jobs," she told him a little nervously. "He's going to drop me off at the college. Did you want to see him?"

"I don't need you as a bloody go-between," he snapped. Looking at Paul, he grumbled, "That Mother and Toddler lot have been in the church again. There's mud on the nave carpet and twigs, flowers, and other bloody rubbish on a table in the chancel. Someone left a wet nappy in the toilet washbasin for God's sake. They shouldn't be in church. It's bad enough bringing kids in for the Family Service." He looked at Paul accusingly. "Who let them in?"

"I did," said Paul, unperturbed by Kevin's attitude but concerned at the way he spoke to Angela. "Joan, who now runs the group, and the mothers themselves, thought it would be good for the kids to have a little service in church to help them understand what's happening on Sundays. We combined it with a Pram Service. It was great — pity you missed it. We did a bit of praise and thanksgiving. The kids brought flowers and little treasures to put on their own little altar."

"I should have been told. Someone has to clean up the bloody mess!" Kevin said resentfully.

"Doreen's coming later — all organised. I have to be off; was there anything else?"

Kevin looked at Paul and then at Angela. He was about to say something but changed his mind. He grunted and started walking back down the drive.

Paul called after him, "By the way, Canon Palmer rang. He thought it a good idea for us to have the PCC meeting preceded by Communion. He would like you to read one of the lessons. Are you happy with that or would you rather I ask one of the other churchwardens?"

"I should think I can manage it," Kevin answered in a condescending manner.

"Good. Well, that's settled then. Can I give you a lift home or do you have your own car?"

"I'm walking," he snapped. Clearing his throat, he added more graciously, "Thanks for the offer."

Paul helped Angela into the front seat of his Discovery. He couldn't help but notice how much she had matured during the last two years. She was now taller, slimmer and quite shapely. Most of the time, she wore tailored clothes — quite different to the midriff revealing, clinging garments she wore not so long ago. Thinking about it, since turning eighteen, she'd changed her image considerably. He suspected she thought her smart jackets and fitted skirts of moderate length were more suitable for the type of job she intended getting. Apart from which, she seemed to want to distance herself from the trendy youngsters in her dance group. He thought her to be quite an elegant young woman, and he told her so.

She smiled at him. "You must have thought me a stupid little girl when you first met me," she said with a laugh.

"Not at all. You know, you might have grown up a lot but you're still my little angel."

They both laughed. Paul's mind went back to that teenage kid with the jewel in her belly. He then remembered picking up that sparkling blue stone after seeing her run from the church crying. What did he do with it? He told her about it.

"I wondered what had happened to it. Actually, it was one of a pair of earrings my mother gave me. I would like it back if you could find it. I wear the other one when I go dancing with Mark. You don't approve do you?" she asked him sheepishly.

"I thought it looked utterly charming. It matched your sparkling blue eyes. I should imagine that's what your mother thought when she gave them to you.

She smiled up at him. "Mum's always talking about my eyes. I don't know where I get them from — certainly not my dad. I don't look a bit like him thank goodness!"

The college came into view and Paul dropped her off. He didn't feel he'd helped her much with her problem but she seemed happy enough. He put his mind to thinking where he'd put the earring Angela had lost from her navel. Could it still be in his pocket? He hadn't worn that jacket since moving out of his last parish; he'd bought himself much-needed new clothes.

When he returned to his vicarage that afternoon, he looked for the treasured earring. When he found it, he put it into his trouser pocket ready for when he saw Angela again.

At the end of the combined PCC meeting held in Glenton, Rita asked Paul if they could meet the following day in the church before 7.45am prayers. "I must see you and I can't be late for school. I'll use my key and I'll be in church praying at seven fifteen. If you can, join me before anyone else arrives. It is very important, Paul. Things are on the move and we must have a sure foundation."

It was typical of Rita; it wasn't the first time she'd asked him to meet her early in the morning. Normally he wouldn't mind — he'd often been there at the crack of dawn to meditate anyway. But he was spending the night with Nick and he didn't want to rush off. So he told her he would be in church but not quite that early. He didn't say why; she was still praying about his sexuality. She brought it up from time to time and he didn't want her, or anyone else, to link him with Nick. It might be natural enough for the clergy to confer together and to socialise, and with Lucy in the rectory staying overnight was no big deal but, even so, he felt he had to be cautious.

Paul was feeling less than alert the following morning. With folk talking excitedly about future possibilities, the meeting went on well past the agreed time. Afterwards, the intensity of making love with Nick into the early hours had left him short of sleep.

Rita was in the side chapel deep in prayer when he arrived at St Michael's. He had showered and shaved at Nick's to wake him up for the drive home, but he should have called in at his vicarage for a hot drink and a bite to eat before joining her — he wasn't at his best. What did she want to talk about anyway? He wasn't in the mood for deep theological discussions. What with all his recent workload, he was ready for his day off; he'd given up his last one because he was moving it to Mondays. As much as he enjoyed talking and praying with Rita, he would prefer to meditate — or go back to bed.

Rita looked up when she heard his footsteps. "Hi, Paul. It went well last night. Nick's a smooth talker; looks as if we'll get the altar moved. It'll cost a bit but there's more money coming in now — shouldn't be a problem."

"Is that what you wanted to discuss, Rita? It can wait you know." His voice revealed his utter weariness.

"No it isn't. But the fact that you're too tired to discuss anything is a symptom of your problem, Paul. You need a woman by your side, just as Nick Palmer has Lucy. Oh, I know you say you're okay, but it's not right for someone in your position to live alone. We're getting to a sensitive stage in the renewal that's happening here; we don't want the Devil to get a foothold and destroy what God is doing, just like happened last time.

"Knowing what you do about that affair, is it really likely to happen?" he asked her, smiling at the thought of him getting a woman pregnant.

"Paul, just listen!" Rita snapped, obviously very angry at his casual attitude. "Women are hankering after you. Did you know you're getting a reputation because of the females who visit the vicarage when you're alone? I'm hearing comments all the time. When I contradict them I get smiled at. The gossips think I'm just another of your secret lovers!"

"That's ridiculous, Rita. Is that all you wanted to tell me, that you're not coming to the vicarage any more? That's okay, I can see you here in the church."

"Oh, I'm not worried what they say about me, it's you I'm concerned about. You need a woman for your ministry to be complete, and for you to be a whole person. Surely you can see that?"

"Frankly, no!"

"Where would Nick Palmer be without Lucy? With his looks and smooth speaking, women used to be queuing at his door. But of course, there were others who said he was gay and were on the lookout for known homosexuals visiting the rectory. Lucy arriving scotched that, but they had a hard time of it until they were married. Now they have a perfect ministry together."

"That may be. But I will never marry."

"But why, you—"

He threw his hands up in protest. "I've already told you why — accept it!"

"But, Paul—"

"No, Rita. I don't want to hear another word," he said tetchily.

She gripped his arms and looked into his eyes. "I've been praying for you. You can change; you can be healed. Let me pray for you now — here."

"No."

"I beg of you, Paul. Get rid of this sickness before you yield to it. It's sapping your spiritual energy."

"Rita, I'm not sick!"

"You're tired; you're not well — anyone can see that."

"Okay. I admit it — I do get tired. But let's face it, I've been working hard and need a rest — not hassle about my sexuality!"

He pulled his arms away from her hands, sat on a chair in the side chapel, and closed his eyes.

"Let me lay hands on you, Paul," she pleaded. "God's power and love will bring you healing."

"I tell you what," he answered wearily, "we'll just sit quiet and meditate until it's time for prayers."

"I'll pray for your strength and health."

"Thanks, but I'll just be quiet for a while.".

The next thing he knew, Rita was behind him with her hands on his head. She was speaking in tongues but he had no feeling for what was being said, and that was unusual. It didn't feel right — he was uncomfortable about it. What was she up to? He moved his head to free it and grasped hold of her hands. "No, Rita, I must know what you're praying for. I feel neither strength nor peace coming into me."

"The peace will come, Paul. Let me rid you of this lying demon. I won't harm you — I love you. God loves you — let him use me to heal you."

"Rita, just leave me alone — please," he said, trying to keep calm. "I can't handle this. We'll talk about it some other time — not now!"

Feeling confused and giddy, he put his elbows on his knees with his head in his hands. He heard himself moan wearily.

Suddenly, he felt Rita pressing her hands down on his head and demanding a lying spirit to come out of him. He wrestled to free himself but she was determined to get her way — gripping his head all the harder. They both fell on the floor but she didn't stop. He knew he was shouting but his voice seemed separated from his body. He gave up the fight, moaning as he went limp. He had a vague impression that he was passing out. Somewhere, far, far away, Rita was praising and giving thanks to God.

He opened his eyes and found Rita sitting on the floor beside him. His head ached and he wondered if he'd bumped it. When he looked at Rita, she was smiling jubilantly. Her hazel eyes were almost glittering in spite of the dim interior of the church.

"You're free, Paul. Free!" she shouted. "Free to love — free to love me."

He looked at her, wondering what on earth she was talking about. Then everything clicked. He was about to struggle up and tell her how wrong she was when she lay over him and kissed him passionately. He didn't want to hurt her but he pushed her away. She had to know the truth.

"I'm sorry, Rita, I can never marry you. I can't give you the kind of love you want from me. You've got it all wrong. I'm so very sorry."

She sat back and looked at him puzzled. Before she could say anything they heard noises at the back of the church. Angela was standing there and Ron and Jill Peterson were coming up behind her, asking her if she had walked down and if she would like a lift back.

As far as Paul was concerned the whole scene was surreal. He picked himself up off the floor, just as the Petersons noticed he was there. Rita stood up and faced the newcomers. "It's okay, folks. Paul had a little accident." She turned to Paul; "Are you all right now?"

"I think we should pray for you," Ron said, looking concerned.

Paul felt hysterical at the suggestion but, in spite of shaking a little, managed to keep calm. "No thanks, I'll be okay. I had no breakfast this morning. I went a little dizzy."

The Petersons nodded. "Fasting? Don't overdo it," Ron advised.

Paul was getting tired of the sheep telling the shepherd how to run his life. But he knew weariness was making him touchy. "Quite right," he agreed. Now he had an excuse to get away and recover his wits. "If you don't mind, I'll go and get a cup of tea, a bit of toast and a lie down."

"I'll come with you," said Rita. "I'll get you a proper breakfast."

"No, please don't. I can do it myself. You have to go to work soon. Have your prayer time — it's important. I'll pray later; we have a lot to be thankful for. If you have time, please tell Angela about last night's meeting."

Angela had been standing there, looking at him in awed silence. She mumbled something as he went past her. He gave her a little kiss on the cheek. "I'm okay — don't worry," he said wearily.

He went home, made himself a cup of tea and sat down, wondering what on earth Angela had seen.

# Chapter ten

Paul felt shattered after the incident in church that Friday morning. He did what he had to do then put on his answerphone and went for a walk to think things through without being interrupted.

It was true that being single had its drawbacks but it would seem that Nick's solution, although fine on the surface, was not entirely sound. He had no idea how things were between Lucy and Tony but Nick had said nothing to indicate he knew what was going on. Maybe nothing was anymore.

He thought it most unlikely that he would find such an accommodating partner as Lucy. Rita, a little older than him, dedicated, gifted and normally sensible, was too much in love with him to consider such a relationship; apart from which, she would be forever working on his demons! Perhaps he should put a notice on his door — 'No suitors. Confirmed bachelor lives here'.

On his way home, he stopped at a quiet pub along the long lane leading to the vicarage, to get an early lunch. It was a place he often used when on his own. He enjoyed the country-pub ambience: no games, music or fancy menus; just simple well-cooked fare served with a cheerful smile and, most importantly, odd corners where he could tuck himself away. His hunger having been satisfied, he found it pleasant to sit at his small window table looking out across the fields, quietly meditating on the good things of life. With glass of shandy in his hand, sipping at the bitter-sweet liquid, he was once more at peace within himself and ready to return to his duties — he had a funeral that afternoon.

"Fancy seeing you here!" It was Bill Smith, Penningly St Mark's churchwarden. "Rita rang this morning to say you needed prayer. She had me ringing around the prayer circle." He sat down beside Paul, whispering quietly, "I hope it's nothing serious."

Paul felt embarrassed. It was typical of Rita. A kind heart maybe, but too overpowering at times. He always made sure he had a sick person's permission before asking others to pray for him or her; too much gossip spread around if you were not discreet. But Rita was a law unto herself.

"She shouldn't have bothered you," he told Bill. "I'm fine. I was up early and went out without eating and drinking. Stupid of me. I fainted in church — that's all."

"Are you sure? It sounded more serious than that. I think you're being too macho about your health. Can't afford for you to be ill, we need you more than ever. Let me get you a tot of something."

Paul protested, but Bill fetched him a glass of brandy just the same.

"Thanks. Just as well I'm walking," he said as Bill returned to the table.

"Well, I think you've walked enough. I'll drive you back," Bill insisted. He was doing a balancing act with the brandy, a glass with ice in it, and two bottles — one of beer and another of lemonade.

Frustrated at being nannied, Paul immediately raised a hand to decline the offer of a lift — just as Bill was bending over with the bottles and glasses. The brandy-glass slipped from his fingers and hit the edge of the table, causing the contents to run down Paul's trousers. Then ice followed the liquid as Bill juggled to save the glass and bottles. It was a bit of a shock to Paul's system but he managed to apologise for his carelessness. Bill insisted on getting him another drink. A double this time since he wasn't driving. Meanwhile, Paul picked up the broken glass and ice and then dabbed at his trousers with his handkerchief, forgetting that he had recently blown his nose on it.

His tranquillity now in tatters, Paul resigned himself to listening to Bill going on about the previous night's meeting and the way ahead for Penningly.

"Our finances have greatly improved since your arrival; we can now manage some alterations," Bill said enthusiastically. "Our congregations have increased and the family services are so popular there's hardly a seat free, especially when they're combined with the Eucharist. Mary Jones has a great ministry, but it's your ability to inspire people that's got us all going these last two years. Who'd have thought we could get young people back in church? You certainly know how to encourage them. It's that baptism in the Spirit that's done it. You've changed: more aggressive, more powerful. It just oozes out of you!"

Paul considered that remark somewhat appropriate since he was wet between his legs! But he couldn't cope with any more. "Sorry, Bill, must go. I need to get back home and change. Funeral in an hour's time."

Bill jumped up, insisting on taking him. Paul gave in; with his pants wet and his breath smelling of alcohol, it would be best to get back as soon as possible before it went around the area that the vicar was drunk and unable to control his flow of urine!

A few minutes later, Bill dropped him at the vicarage. As Paul hurried to his door, Angela came from around the back.

"There you are. I've come straight from college — not in this afternoon. Are you all right? You looked very odd this morning. Rita said that you needed prayer."

"I'm fine, Angela. But I must get in and change my clothes." He didn't want guests but he couldn't turn her away — it was a long walk from the bus stop, apart from which, he hoped to find out how much she'd heard that morning. He gave her a welcoming smile. "Would you like to come in and make us both some coffee?"

Angela walked into the kitchen as Paul picked up letters that had been delivered while he was out. He put them down on the hall table to sort later. Meanwhile, the doorbell rang. It was his churchwarden, Kevin Raymond.

Kevin looked and sounded like a man in a hurry. "There's been a delay with that funeral," he announced brusquely. "They've been trying to reach you but all they could get was your bloody answerphone. Someone's been taken to hospital — it's Mrs Blake's sister. You're wanted there — they think she's dying. They're all in a bit of a state."

Paul indicated to Kevin to step inside. "Are you saying the funeral's been cancelled for today?"

"They're having it an hour later — unless they've gone home. They're all at the hospital. Are you going?" It was more of a demand than a question.

Paul mentally estimated how long it would take. "I'll pop in now and make a proper visit after the funeral. I'd better get ready."

As he was about to disappear upstairs, he caught Kevin glaring at his crotch area. He followed Kevin's eyes. His trousers were still damp from the brandy and ice but worse still, smudged over the dark stain were ominous shiny patches of an off-white colour. Paul suddenly remembered dabbing the stain with his handkerchief.

"Oh, I had a bit of an accident — knocked a glass over and

dabbed it with my hanky," Paul explained casually. "Stupid of me. I'll get changed."

But Kevin barred his way. "A likely bloody story. You've got alcohol on your breath and semen on your bloody trousers. We've a grieving widow by her dying sister's bedside waiting for her priest to comfort her — and where are you? Don't try explaining — your bloody answerphone's been on all morning, your bedroom curtain's still drawn and you answer the bloody door flushed and sweating! God man! You can't even clean yourself up!"

Angela came into the hall and stared at her father. "Dad, what are you saying? Paul's only just got home — he's been out!" she shouted at him.

"Don't call me Dad — you're no bloody daughter of mine. You never have been and you never will be. You're just a bloody slut — same as your bloody mother," Kevin bellowed at her.

"I haven't done anything — it's just your dirty mind!" she screamed at him.

Kevin, speechless with fury, clenched his fists.

Paul jumped in front of the girl. "Angela is right," he said, trying to hold back his anger. "Bill Smith dropped me off just a few minutes ago — he'll confirm that. Angela arrived here just as I got home."

"Oh, yes? So it was just a quickie in the bloody kitchen was it? Or are you telling me you had it off with that Bill Smith — always thought he was a bloody puff!"

Paul was seething inside. He forced himself to stay cool. "I've explained what happened. Everything can be verified. I'll change my trousers and you can have these — check them out yourself. And here's my handkerchief — it's still damp with brandy." Paul pulled his hanky from his pocket and held it out to Kevin.

Kevin pulled a face and waved a hand — as if to ward off obnoxious contamination. "I don't want to touch your filthy bit of rag!" Then something caught his eye. "What's this?" He snatched the handkerchief from Paul's hand.

Angela sprang forward. "It's my earring. I lost it and Paul found it. He's been keeping it for me." She held out her hand to retrieve her sparkling blue jewel.

"You bloody harlot." Kevin took a swipe at her hand and Angela cried out in pain.

Paul pulled her to his side and glared at Kevin. "You're so blinded by your own ignorant assumptions, you can't recognise the truth when it stares you in the face."

"The truth is staring me in the bloody face and I recognise it all right. Look at her! She's the image of that bloody Peter Millar. Everybody knows it — they all titter behind my back. Bloody miracle baby? The only miracle about her birth is that I didn't kill her bloody father!"

Angela stared at him — her mouth open in shock. Kevin suddenly realised what he'd said. A flash of regret crossed his face, but he quickly recovered his blustering stance. He looked at Angela with piercing eyes. "Your bloody mother shamed me — and you go on doing it — fornicating with bloody priests." Tears of anger and pain were now welling up in his eyes. He began to shake.

"Come and sit down, Kevin," Paul said, reaching out to him. "I'll get you a drink."

Kevin pushed him off. "I don't want your bloody drink — I'm going."

"I need to know what's happening about Gerald Blake's funeral, and what's happened to Mrs Blake's sister. Come on, man. You do a fantastic job as churchwarden, don't ruin it over misunderstandings."

Angela was still staring at her father in shocked disbelief. "You've always been my dad. Mum wouldn't go with another man — she's not like that," she told him, as though trying to work out an impossible puzzle. She turned to Paul. "It's not true is it? A priest doesn't do such things — it can't be true."

"Leave it now, Angela," Paul said tenderly. "We'll have a chat in a minute or two. You can talk to your mum and dad later. How about that coffee for the three of us?"

Angela, in a daze, drifted off to the kitchen.

Kevin hadn't budged. He sniffed back his tears. "It's time she knows the truth — everyone else does. Diana refuses to admit it — it makes me so bloody angry!"

He beat his palm with his fist. "Why can't she admit it — it's so bloody obvious. Cock and bull story about miracles. It's bad enough I've never been able to give her a child. Everybody thinks I'm not bloody man enough. Now they see their Sunny Jim vicar in the face of my daughter. I might have got rid of him, but he's returned to bloody haunt me. No one respects me — I'm the bloody laughing stock for miles around. I've tried to bring her up as my own child — teach her right from wrong, but she's as bad as her bloody mother. After all I've done for them, they both bloody hate me."

Paul felt Kevin's pain. The man needed help but a priest would never be acceptable to him. "You need to talk it through, Kevin — you must see someone. The Diocesan Counsellor is very good."

Kevin shook a little, and then pulled himself together. "Forget it. Get on with your bloody job and I'll do mine. Mrs Blake's sister is called Elizabeth Johnson. She's had a stroke. She's in Glenton A and E the last I heard — she might be in a ward by now. The immediate family went with her. Funeral arrangements for Gerald Blake as before but an hour later. Since I couldn't get hold of you, I informed Canon Palmer. He said he'd take it if you couldn't. As you know, the organist from Bradmire church is playing today and I've informed him of the change. The funeral directors have been in touch with the crem. They can fit it in for the last slot but don't be late. If the sister dies, the burying of ashes next week will be put off until later. Mrs Blake says, come what may, her husband's being put to rest today." Having finished his reporting, Kevin turned to leave.

He hesitated by the door. "I'm sorry," he said bluntly. "I said things I shouldn't have." He cleared his throat and muttered, "I must get on. I haven't got hold of Doreen Briggs yet; she was out this morning."

As he went through the door, Paul called after him, "Thanks, Kevin, you've done an excellent job. I'm sorry I was out when you rang."

Kevin snorted and was gone.

Paul rang the hospital. Elizabeth Johnson was now out of immediate danger, although her condition remained serious. Quickly deciding that Angela was in more urgent need of his ministry, he asked the nurse to inform the relatives that he would see Mrs Johnson straight after Mr Blake's funeral.

After changing his trousers upstairs, Paul went to the kitchen to talk to Angela. She was leaning on the sink and looking out of the window with a blank expression on her face. A mug of coffee was in her hand and two more were on the table.

"Take your pick," she said, without looking at him.

Paul looked at her carefully. She was smartly dressed in one of her suits. She could easily be mistaken for a high-salaried working girl. He didn't think that Angela was earning money, so she must be getting a reasonable allowance. Although her father was retired, she never appeared to be short of anything she needed or wanted. Even so, he obviously found it hard to give her his love.

She turned round to face Paul. She was still looking bewildered. "He must be my dad. He's always been my dad. He would have thrown Mum out if she'd been with another man." Her brow wrinkled. "But Mum would never do that. She never looks at other men."

Paul put a hand on her shoulder. "I guess your dad is a jealous man. Diana was obviously attracted to Peter Millar. Whether it was his ministry or Peter himself, I'm not in a position to say."

"Do people around here think the priest is my real father? Dad obviously thinks they do."

"I think perhaps your dad is paranoid. A lot of folk have only recently moved into the new houses. Of the rest, only half would have been around at that time and some of those would have been too young to remember. There's been a lot of coming and going in the last eighteen years or so."

"But it's true — I look nothing like my dad." She gave a deep sigh. "I don't look like my mum either. I used to think I was adopted like my sister."

"I know lots of people who don't look like their parents, but it will be somewhere in the past generations," he tried to reason with her. "But you must talk to your mother about it."

"You heard what Dad said. Mum's denied having an affair with Peter Millar — she's hardly likely to tell me different." She went thoughtful for a few seconds. "There's DNA now, that should prove something one way or another."

The idea had already occurred to Paul some time ago. But it would seem the Raymonds preferred to live a lie rather than face the truth. Were they concerned they would lose Angela? Did Diana want to believe in miracles? Or did she want to hide the truth of her adultery from Kevin and the world? As for Kevin, did he cling to the smallest of possibilities that Angela was his child rather than know for dead certain she couldn't be? To stir it all up again and have people talking behind his back, pointing a finger and questioning his manhood, would be very hard, especially as he was a pillar of the church and local community.

"Do you really want to force this issue?" he asked Angela. "It's something either of your parents could have pursued but haven't. They have their reasons. Suppose it turned out that Kevin can't possibly be your father would you, or they, be any happier? Would you seek out Peter Millar — who may well be married and with a wife and family? And if he denied it, would you force him to be tested? He must have known your mother was pregnant — the church was rejoicing over a miracle. But you know, sometimes the doctors do get it wrong and miracles do happen."

Angela looked up at him with tears in her eyes. "Mum knows I'm the priest's child. That's the truth of it — isn't it Paul?"

"Angela, I have no idea."

"I don't know who I am any more," she said, shaking her head in a gesture of hopelessness. She burst into tears. "How could a priest do such a thing?"

Paul's heart went out to her. Kevin had treated her badly. She was in need of love and to feel secure in her own selfhood. He wrapped his arms around her. Pressing her head to his chest, he stroked her hair. "I honestly don't know what happened between Peter and your mother," he told her gently; "but you have to realise that priests have the same emotions as everyone else. We may try to subjugate our sexual impulses but it isn't easy — especially when we fall in love."

"Are you in love, Paul?"

It was something he had to give serious thought to before answering.

She pulled away from his chest so she could look into his eyes.

"You are — I can see it," she said with certainty.

"Perhaps you see what you want to see. I've told you before — I'm married to my vocation."

"Did Peter Millar say that to my mother?"

"I wouldn't know. But the fathers and husbands in my parish have no need to worry."

She put her head back on his chest. "Rita loves you. I thought you loved her but I saw you push her away. You said you could never marry her — you couldn't give her the love she wanted. Are you impotent?"

Paul laughed nervously — he didn't like the way the conversation was going. He gently pushed her away from him. "Really, Angela, I thought you'd stopped asking me personal questions. Seriously though, about what you heard, please don't repeat it to anyone. It would be very distressing for Rita."

Just then the phone rang. Paul picked it up before the answerphone came on. It was Nick asking him if he was all right. "The Petersons rang to tell me you had fainted in church this morning — asked for my prayers."

"I'm okay. Just a bit under pressure."

"I don't like the sound of it," Nick said, sounding concerned. "Can you manage lunch tomorrow? You can tell me what's happening."

"I'd like that. Can't talk now. See you." Paul put down the phone and went back to the kitchen, picking up his letters from where he'd left them on the hall table.

"Do you want me to help you with anything, Paul," Angela asked him. "I can take some of the pressure off you."

Paul smiled; she'd been listening while he was on the phone. "Well, I made some notes last night, would you like to type them up for me? If you come into the study a moment, I can find you some other things to do. Would you like to do the service sheets today instead of tomorrow?"

"Sure. No problem," she said happily.

He spent a little while sorting things for her. Being quick and intelligent, it didn't take her long to pick it up.

"I'd be pleased if you could get the notes done today — the rest can wait. I must be off shortly. Use the phone and let your parents know you're here; after what's happened, they might worry if you're late home.

He checked the messages left on the answerphone and then left Angela to get on with her work. It would give her something positive to think about. He changed into his cassock, placed his surplice over his arm, put his keys in his pocket, collected his notes and picked up his service book. Telling Angela that he'd be back after visiting the hospital, he left her to it, utterly confident that she would do a good job. As he was about to leave the house, the phone rang again. This time it was Rita.

"I'm fine, Rita," he assured her. "I'll see you in the morning if you want to go over Sunday's hymn list. We'll meet in the church if you prefer."

"No, I'll see you in the vicarage. I'll be bringing two friends — if that's okay with you?"

"Two friends? Do I know them?"

"Jan Norris and Toby Manning. You may have seen them at the Riggington conference but I don't suppose you will remember them. I've met them a few times since — we've worked together. They offer seminars on demonic influences."

"Thanks, Rita, but I have no intention of meeting them — here or in church."

"That's not you speaking, Paul. When have you ever closed your mind to exploring the truth? Are you afraid? Is there something inside you that's telling you to resist? You were so close to healing this morning, but the deceiving spirit is too strong for me on my own. We need help to overcome it. Jan and Toby have had a lot of experience in these matters."

Paul sighed. "I'm sorry, Rita, I have to go now. I have a funeral to conduct and a hospital visit to make. I'll ring you in the morning about the hymns; don't come here until we sort this out. I'm off. I can't approve of what you do with those two, but take care." He put the phone down and left the vicarage.

Tired and exhausted from emotional strain, Paul arrived home at five-thirty and was surprised to find Angela still there. She met him at the door saying that she wasn't sure if he had his spare key with him. "I had visions of you trying to fish this one out of your letterbox after I'd dropped it in." He didn't tell her that Nick also had a key but he was happy to see her.

She told him that after telephoning home, her dad had come down to have a word with her. "He was ever so nice — said he was sorry. He told me that he shouldn't have said such things because he had a grandmother who looked like me. He actually kissed me on the cheek," she added with a radiant smile.

Paul didn't believe a word that Kevin had told her. He was probably worried that the local gossipmongers would have a field day at his expense; and maybe that Angela would leave home. But he said to her, "That's good, Angela. I'm very pleased for you. I expect your dad was tired and hassled by today's funeral. No doubt he was angry with me for being out of reach. He's wanted my mobile number for ages. I'd better give it him, but it won't do him much good — I keep it switched off most of the time."

Angela smiled. "Well, at least, it would be something less for him to complain about."

"Mm — until it proves of little use."

"I'll make you a pot of tea."

Paul put his things away and, after making brief notes in his desk diary, flopped into the old leather armchair in his study. There was something to be said for having someone to welcome you home with a nice cup of tea. Angela brought it to him and asked if she could cook him some eggs and bacon. "I've been looking in the fridge," she said with a sheepish grin.

"How about cooking some for both of us?" Why spoil her happiness by rejecting her kindness?

He was late saying Evening Prayer. It was partly deliberate — just in case Rita turned up. He realised he was dodging the issue but he wasn't in the mood for confrontation. Angela was the only one with him and he asked her to take part. It was all very peaceful and pleasant. Afterwards she went with him to the Penningly church hall for Youth Night.

The Petersons were surprised to see him. "Bill Smith said you were a lot better but he's worried about you. Said you seemed not quite with it — knocked over bottles and glasses or something or other. You were in a heck of a state this morning, are you sure you're all right?" Ron asked him.

Before he could answer, Jill Peterson asked him if they could pray with him. "Rita is quite distressed about you. She phoned me just before we came here."

Paul sighed. Shrugging his shoulders, he held out his hands sideways and declared, "I am as you see me — fit, healthy, sane and perfectly normal. Thanks to Angela, I'm well fed, relaxed and ready to go!"

They both looked at Angela who was smiling happily. She said, "He doesn't realise how bad he looked this morning. But he's okay now."

Rita's voice sounded behind them. "I'm glad to hear it. So Angela's been looking after you? I hope her boyfriend doesn't object."

Paul quickly turned to face Rita. "I didn't know you were here. As you see, Rita, I'm fine. But there are people who really do need your prayers, so you can happily take me off your list. Thanks for your concern though."

Rita looked at him puzzled. "We'll see, Paul. Perhaps our prayers have been answered." She turned to Angela, "I thought the girls needed a bit more practice with that new dance movement. Are you joining us? I see Mark's at the coffee bar. He's looking cross, so perhaps it would be better if you joined him and his friends. We can manage without you."

At that moment the drummer started up with the rest of the group joining in. Angela turned to see Mark getting up and heading her way. Paul saw him too and stepped forward to greet him.

"Hi, Mark. Angela's been doing the angel of mercy bit. You'd better take her off before Rita gets her working again."

Mark nodded to Paul in greeting and then wrapped his arms around Angela and made a demonstration out of kissing her. It was a clear signal to all present, 'she's mine — hands off'. Paul smiled at the young man's jealous lover routine, but he couldn't blame Mark for wanting to hold on to a lovely girl like Angela. He turned to the Petersons and said he'd move around and chat to the youngsters. He found Rita following him. She pulled him over to a corner.

"Paul, what's happening? Is something going on between you and Angela?"

"Rita, really! This morning you were trying to cure me of being possessed by demons and now you're accusing me of having it off with my secretary!"

"Keep your voice down, Paul," she said, looking around to see if they could be overheard. "This is no joke. I haven't said you're possessed as such, it's a deep subject and we must talk about what's involved. But you and Angela. I saw the way she was looking at you — with sexual desire burning within her. Has something happened? Were you cured this morning? Do you need guidance and help in adjusting? Promiscuity is wrong, Paul — especially for a priest."

Paul sighed. How the woman jumped to conclusions.

"Nothing is changed, Rita. I can love my fellow Christians without confusing affection with sex," he told her plainly. "I am what I've always been — it's part of being me. Please accept it. I don't want constant battles with you over my sexuality. We need to work together in ministry. Don't let your love, or your prejudices, get in the way of our working relationship or everything we've achieved together will fall apart."

She looked at him with pain in her eyes. "I know at one time you were totally against gay priests. What happened to change your mind? What got into you, Paul? Ask yourself that question."

"Maybe I had a revelation; perhaps I fell in love. Does that make sense to you?" As soon as he said the words, he regretted having done so. Now she was going to be like a terrier determined not to let go of its quarry.

"You fell in love with a man? That's it, Paul," she said excitedly as though a light had been switched on in her mind. "Your denial of your sexual appetite over so many years, left an opening for demonic influences to enter your soul. Can't you see it's blinding you to your true nature?"

"Oh, Rita, stop it," he begged. He felt like thrusting her aside and escaping from the corner she'd trapped him in.

"Your natural instincts are drawing you to Angela — not out of love but to satisfy carnal desire," she said, her eyes wide and lit up behind her glasses. "You deny such feelings because your mind has been perverted to think of yourself as being gay. But you know that homosexual relationships are abhorrent to God. Unable to resolve the conflict within you, you choose to be celibate."

Paul lowered his head and shook it in frustration. He was beginning to feel the same weariness as he'd suffered that morning. Rita was watching him carefully. He felt her eyes somehow piercing into his soul, searching for what he was hiding.

"Have you been lying to me, Paul? You are celibate aren't you?" she said, with the voice of the Inquisition, as far as Paul was concerned.

The noise from the band was now thundering in his brain. He gripped his temples. "I have never said that. It was something you assumed," he said testily.

She came very close to him and kept her voice low. "Oh, Paul, you poor man, it's worse than I thought. You think you are in love and have linked yourself to a perverted soul. No wonder I could do nothing this morning. You are being controlled. Who is it?"

"You are still making assumptions," he said angrily. "My sexuality is my business." He gripped her by the shoulders and stared into her eyes. "Rita, leave it!" He came close to adding, "Mind your own bloody business," but he controlled himself.

His temples were throbbing and his mind reeling. He could hear Kevin swearing, Angela crying, the Blake family quietly weeping, Mrs Johnson gurgling her last breath, and above it all the voice of Rita from that morning's episode — all drowning out the noise of music, singing and clapping which was getting louder and louder around him. He had to get out — away from Rita, away from the Petersons who were heading his way, away from the noise thundering in his brain. He dived for the door and then headed for the car park.

Rita caught up with him and grabbed his arm. "You must let me help you," she yelled.

"Leave me alone," he told her abruptly. "I've had enough."

"Don't you realise, you don't belong to yourself — you belong to God. Your body is a temple of the Holy Spirit. You are making it unclean!"

He reached his car, dragging Rita with him.

"Paul, how did this man attract you? Did he stare into your eyes? Did you suck in his breath? You've joined yourself to him and allowed the evil to flow into your body — you have haven't you? You can't deny it. You must confess what you've done and be made free."

He put his hands over his ears, but she didn't stop. He could still hear her hammering away.

"Paul, Paul, you must listen," she said, forcefully shaking his arms. "A great work is happening here but we're having to fight evil forces. Can't you see the Devil has a foothold in your ministry here; far greater than all the other devious methods he's been using?"

Paul pushed her away and dived inside his Discovery. He locked the doors and started the engine. Rita was standing staring at him. Framed by dripping wet hair, her face wrinkled with frustration and colourless in the car headlights. She looked old and careworn but he refused to give way to either pity or remorse. As he drove away, in his mirror he saw the hall door open and one or two people coming out and waving to him. No way was he going to return.

He was driving back to the vicarage but then changed his mind. He pulled into a gateway and reached for his mobile phone, intent on ringing Nick to see if he could stay the night. He wanted him — no, needed him — to drag him out of his nightmare.

He composed himself before dialling. What was he going to say? He realised he was panicking; after all, he would be seeing Nick for lunch tomorrow. He knew his lover would be busy that evening with his considerable workload and it wasn't fair to disturb him. But he couldn't go home just yet as he might be pursued to the vicarage; he needed peace not confrontation. He would drive somewhere quiet and recover his equilibrium. Taking deep breaths, and mentally saying a prayer for peace and guidance, he calmed his pounding heart and brain. After a few minutes, he started up the engine.

He began to drive forward when he caught sight of a familiar figure in his headlights. It was Angela. She was walking alone along the path that ran at the side of the road. She was wet through. He stopped his vehicle beside her. She looked up, saw who it was and jumped in beside him.

"How did you get here?" Paul asked her.

"Mark said he had something to show me. He drove to the gateway back there and told me to get in the back. I didn't want to. He said I wouldn't get it if I wouldn't do it."

"Get what, Angela? I can guess the doing bit."

"An engagement ring. He showed it me. It's very pretty," she added wistfully. "But he said that I had to prove I loved him first. I said that was like being paid for sex. I got out of his car and he drove off. He's only just gone."

"Tell you what, suppose we go to a nice little pub the other side of Glenton and have a bottle of ginger beer and a packet of crisps — my treat?"

"Oo, lovely."

While he was driving, Paul steered the conversation towards Angela's hopes for the future now that her college course had finished and she told him about her job applications. She talked about the various firms, what they did, and what the prospects were for advancement. She had certainly done her homework.

When they were in the pub, Angela looked at him and said, "Are you okay? Have I been wearing you out? I'm really sorry. I'd better shut up a bit."

He smiled ironically. If only a certain other lady would have the same consideration. "You're not the problem, Angela. I'm okay. I guess I should have stayed home tonight. After that nice welcome home, the lovely meal and time in church, I was nicely relaxed. I could have done without the hassle and noise later on."

"Is Rita hassling you? Oh, I know it's none of my business, but I know she loves you. Perhaps she's like Mark — can't take no for an answer."

Paul thought that was a very apt description of Rita's problem but he couldn't discuss it with Angela. "Well, things are peaceful at present. Let me get you another drink."

When he came back with the glasses, Angela said, "You work too hard, Paul. You should relax more. What did you do when you were my age? Surely you had a bit of fun sometime. A good-looking guy like you? You must have had lots of girls hanging around."

Paul thought about it. "I suppose I did, but I was always studying and then Theological College. I didn't have time for girls."

"And now you're married to your vocation and Rita can't accept it," she said, nodding wisely. "But you know, I think if you really loved her, you'd get together. It wouldn't be like adultery or promiscuity, so it wouldn't be a sin."

Paul laughed. He liked Angela's simplistic views after the heady stuff Rita constantly presented him with. "I'm not so sure Rita would agree. Not that it matters because the question doesn't arise. You're fishing in the dark, Angela. I'd better take you home. You'll soon have me making love to half my congregation and defining it as feeding the five thousand!"

She laughed with him and stood up to go. "It's been lovely, Paul. Thanks, ever so."

It didn't take long to drive the few miles. She had been pleasant company and his headache was almost gone. The rain had stopped and it was now a perfect evening. He felt good about himself once more.

As she was about to get out, she turned to him and pulled his face down to meet hers — kissing him full on the lips. It wasn't unpleasant and how could he spoil her night, and his, by pushing her away? She wished him goodnight and then quickly jumped out of his Discovery. As he watched her reach her door safely, he noticed someone looking through the window.

"Oh, Angela," he said aloud. "I hope you're not falling for your vicar; it will only cause you more heartache and make trouble for the both of us." He was determined to tell her so — when the time was right.

It was a little after ten when he arrived back at the vicarage. A note had been pushed through his letterbox. Was it from Rita? He picked it up but did not open it. He checked his answerphone for messages. Mary Jones wanted to see him about one of her training assignments. The treasurer of St Mary's Bradmire was worried about their finances. The Funeral Director, Roger Drayton, was asking him to conduct Mrs Johnson's funeral and said that the burial of Mr Blake's ashes had been postponed. Then a nervous voice came on to say she wanted her baby christening but failed to give her name and telephone number. Then Rita came on:

"Paul, if you are there, pick up your phone. We need to talk. I called at the vicarage over an hour ago but you hadn't arrived home. We're all worried about you. If I don't hear from you, I'll be around in the morning. Anyway, I'll see you in church for prayers."

"Oh, no you won't, Rita, my love," Paul said aloud. He went to the kitchen to relax with a cup of chocolate, thinking it not good that he was now talking to himself. He took two painkillers — Rita was now having that effect on him. He sat down to open the envelope he'd picked up on his way in. It was a card from Mrs Blake to thank him for his kindness. There was a twenty-pound note inside for him to buy himself a bottle of whiskey. She said he was looking thin and poorly and needed a good wife to look after him. Paul smiled. Funny, in this day and age, how many women still thought it the job of their own sex to look after the menfolk — well, at least priests.

He remembered that he still hadn't opened all of the morning's mail. Dutifully, he picked up the letters from where he'd left them on the kitchen worktop. He sorted the bills, put aside a document from the diocesan office that required in-depth reading, threw junk into his bin, and left the letters for morning. Worn-out, he went to the bathroom, struggled to bed, read through compline and promptly dropped to sleep.

# Chapter eleven

It was raining heavily when Paul woke up in the morning. He showered and dressed quickly. Instead of going in the church he meditated for twenty minutes and read Morning Prayer in his study, telling himself that he wasn't running away from Rita, he just hadn't time to argue with her.

He cooked himself a breakfast of scrambled eggs and, while he was eating, read the letters he'd left on the table overnight. One was information on a seminar organised by a powerful evangelical group fighting to uphold Biblical teaching on homosexuality. Sighing heavily, he threw it aside. The other letter was from his mother. Since she usually phoned, he was surprised she had written to him.

It was bad news. His father had suffered a heart attack and had been taken to hospital. His dad had refused to allow his mother to phone him because it might have disturbed him when he was very busy — typical of him! His father was in the intensive care unit, but his mother told him not to worry because he was being well looked after. Not worry? He loved his father, and his mother. How could he not be anxious for both of them?

He immediately telephoned his mother but there was no answer. He telephoned his sister, Ann. All he heard was a bland answerphone message. He decided to visit his parents as soon as Angela arrived. As long as everything was prepared for her, he could leave her to get on with all that needed doing. Rita already had the hymns for Sunday, so no need to contact her. Since she was out to 'rescue' him, he expected her to call him anyway. Too bad, he was in no mood for a discussion.

He started up his computer to check his e-mails. He realised he hadn't done so for a day or so. He was getting slack and must pull himself together.

He had seven e-mails to deal with. He instantly binned two of them — they were junk. Two others were information on various diocesan happenings and could be read later. One was from a former colleague, another from his bank, but the last message was from his sister. He clicked to open Ann's message first.

His sister appeared to be angry with him. She had phoned him but had received no answer, and his answerphone had twice run out before she could speak. She'd tried his mobile several times but it was always switched off. "Where the hell are you when you're wanted? Dad's had a serious heart attack — he's in the Royal. Neither of them can face the fact that he could have an even worse one any time. If you come over — you're no brother of mine if you don't — I should warn you that I've left Brian. He's a swine and I'm getting a divorce. It upset Mum and Dad. I feel the heart attack is my fault. Must dash. Ann."

Paul rang the Royal and soon found out that his father's condition was critical but stable. His mother was by his father's bedside. He sent a message giving them his love, and saying he would be there later that morning. He then phoned Nick to tell him that he couldn't manage lunch. There was no reply. He left a message saying that he would ring later.

He put together the information Angela would need for completing the service sheets. In case his parents needed him, he checked his diary for the coming week. It was pretty full. If it became necessary, he would sort things out with Nick and Lucy. He was about to try ringing Nick again when the doorbell rang. It was Rita.

"Good morning, Rita. Come in, but I haven't much time. As soon as Angela arrives I have to be off. My father's in hospital. I must go back home to see him and make sure Mum's okay."

Rita was sympathetic; she asked him what the problem was and then said she would pray for them all. As they walked into Paul's study she started talking about satanic influences. She sat down opposite him and said emphatically, "You must realise, Paul, you're under attack! Whenever there's a work of the Spirit, the Devil comes along to stop it."

Paul said nothing. He knew precisely what was coming and had no intention of arguing with her — how could she possibly understand? She continued her diatribe:

"He'll search out your weak spots and play on them. Holiness and moral purity are not options for Christians — especially priests. Liberalism strikes at the heart of Christianity. You just cannot reinterpret Biblical passages for your own convenience — the Bible warns us about such things. Liberals may scoff at evangelical conservatism but it's a fact that while the rest of the Church is struggling, the evangelical movement has grown tremendously in strength. You must not ignore the facts and go your own way."

"I'll get you a coffee," Paul said, getting up.

Rita followed him into the kitchen. "You — all of us — will be facing many trials. We must be morally strong. Not just for our own growth and salvation but as ambassadors for Christ. How can you spread the word of Salvation if your conduct is contrary to God's laws? If you're not concerned for your own soul, what about your flock? If it came to be known that you are a practising homosexual, how will people react?"

"Do you want to put your own sugar in?" Paul asked her, ignoring her question to him. After all, he knew the arguments; she could have been quoting from his own past speeches!

"Paul, you must listen. A child of God cannot be possessed but you have allowed evil influences to blind you to God's purposes. All that you have achieved — what God has done in this place — will come to nought if you don't repent. You must take the high moral ground and be beyond reproach."

The doorbell rang.

"That must be Angela," Paul said, getting up to open the front door. He turned to Rita. "I'm sorry, Rita, I have to go now. You can stay if you want to. Angela will lock up when she's finished."

"Angela has a key?"

Paul wasn't sure whether she was shocked or jealous.

"I take the spare key, she puts the other back through the letterbox."

"That's another thing, Paul," Rita said, getting up from her chair. "Angela should not be coming-and-going in this vicarage like she does. People talk."

He didn't answer. He was on his way to open the front door.

"Come in, Angela. Nice to see you but I have to go out. Everything's ready for you. Lock up when you go, I've got a key. Not sure when I'll be back." He tried to keep emotion out of his voice. "My father's very ill you see."

"Oh, Paul, I am so sorry. I'll get the sheets finished off and printed ready for morning. Trust me not to make mistakes. Anything else?"

"I'll show you. Come into the study," he told her, ignoring Rita who was hovering around him.

Angela quickly picked up what she was being told. Afterwards, she asked him, "Would you like me to take incoming telephone calls?"

"Just for today — yes. If it's possible, take the message, get name and number and say I'll ring back. If it's an emergency or from my family, ring me on my mobile." He wrote on a piece of paper. "Here's my mobile number. Leave a message if it's switched off while I'm driving. Can you do that?"

"Of course, part of my training."

"Now, keep the number to yourself, I don't want it going off in delicate situations."

"I understand. I won't let you down. I'm very sorry about your dad — hope he'll be okay."

"Thanks. I'll leave you to it then. Help yourself to drinks and food. Leave the answerphone on when you go, and don't forget to lock up."

Picking up his Bible, Paul left his study and went to get his coat and, just in case it was needed, an overnight toilet bag he kept handy. Rita was following him around trying to get his attention.

"Paul, just stand still and listen. You didn't see yourself yesterday. You looked terrible. It could happen again today; you're already stressed and looking very pale. Hospitals are dangerous places when you're vulnerable to demonic attack. Let me pray with you before you go."

Paul stood still and faced her. "Rita, I appreciate your concern but let it go. Much of what you say, I said myself at one time. Please understand — I am what I am, and I don't have a guilty conscience about it. As for needing a wife, it would be good to have a companion in my home, but since I shall never marry, it can't happen. You and the people here will have to accept that." He picked up his things and headed for the door.

Rita went after him and pulled at his arm. "But, Paul," she said desperately, "I love you and want what's best for you, not just for the church here."

Paul put his things down again and took Rita by her shoulders. Her bright hazel eyes, emphasised by her heavy-rimmed glasses, looked lovingly into his. Smoothing her rich dark reddish-brown hair away from her pale anxious face, he said tenderly, "Please, Rita, let go and get back to the way things were. We work well together in ministry. You are destroying that relationship — not me or some vague demon. I realise what's at the heart of all this — you have fallen in love with me. I love you too, but as a dear Christian sister. As lovely and as worthy as you are, I can never ask you to be my wife."

He turned away, picked up his things and headed out, Rita trying to hold on to his arm. "You're wrong," she was telling him. "My love for you has nothing to do with it. You must repent. You are in danger and your flock could be scattered."

"Goodbye, Rita, I'll see you in the morning." As he was getting into his Discovery, he turned to tell her, "I forgot, the Petersons will be here later to talk about that trip we were planning with the lads. Will you ask Angela to ring them and put them off please?"

"I'll do it myself when I get home," she answered. Paul knew why — they would be having a powwow about him.

It was just after eleven when he arrived at the huge NHS hospital. Oblivious to the Royal's attempts to achieve a pleasant environment by displaying pictures painted by local amateur artists, he walked unseeingly along the bright shiny corridors for what seemed like a quarter of a mile. Finally, with anxious heart, he arrived at the intensive care unit with its few beds surrounded by a confusion of tubes, wires, bottles, boxes with bleeps and blinking lights, sterile instruments and all else that made up the latest in cardiac resuscitation technology. His mother and sister were by his father's bedside. They looked up as he entered the room. His mother's eyes were red and swollen but she smiled and said that she was glad he'd come. His sister looked at him reproachfully. "You have time for everyone but your own family."

"That's not fair, Ann," said their mother quickly. "Paul's duty is to the people in his care."

"How's Dad?" Paul asked, feeling the sting of Ann's remark. He may have come as soon as he could, but he knew it was true that he seldom went home and usually left it to his parents to keep in touch.

"He's very poorly," his mother answered, fighting back her tears.

Paul looked around for a chair but Ann stood up and indicated for him to use hers. "I'm going outside for a smoke. I want to talk to you. I'll see you in the coffee shop by the main doors in twenty minutes. I take it, since you've managed to get here, you will be staying an hour or so?"

Paul didn't like her attitude. But he put her aggressiveness down to sorrow over their dad's condition, her concern for their mother and her unhappy marriage. "I'm here until mid-afternoon. Maybe longer," he added, turning to look at their father. He gave her a weak smile. "I'll see you soon then."

Paul bent over his unconscious father and gently kissed his forehead. He put an arm around his mother and kissed her cheek. "I'm sorry Mum. I didn't read your letter until this morning."

"The post can be delayed," she said, nodding her understanding of the situation; "but your dad wouldn't let me ring. He seemed all right two days ago but he's much worse now."

Tears running down her face, she fumbled around inside her bag looking for a hanky. Paul pulled a clean one out of his pocket. "Here, Mum, use mine," he said tenderly.

"Thanks — silly of me to cry," she told him "He'll be all right — I just know he will. I've been praying half the night. Now you're here, you can pray special prayers. You can lay hands on him — anoint with oil — whatever it is that priests do to make people better."

Paul sighed. If only his mother realised her heartfelt uttering reached God far more than any prayers he could say from a book, even though he would say them with the love of a son. And how could he tell her that it would need a miracle to heal the damaged muscles of his father's heart? The nurse had told him on the way in that his dad was unlikely to survive more than a few days. He framed his words carefully.

"Mum, of course I'll pray for Dad. We'll do it together. We'll thank God for his life, and pray for his eternal peace. You must realise, Dad is very, very poorly."

"What are you saying, Paul?" she demanded to know. Her face was strained with fearful apprehension. "I don't want him to leave me, we've been together thirty-five years. He can't die — you mustn't let him. Lay hands on him. Pray for him. You're a priest — God's your boss — he'll listen to you."

Paul moved his chair closer to his mother and wrapped an arm around her. "You're going to have to let him go, Mum. Deep inside you know that. Pray with me."

He took his mother's free hand and placed it on his father's chest. He put a hand over hers, and prayed the simple words of a son for his father, telling God what they earnestly desired but accepting what must be. He thanked God for his father's life and for all that he meant to his mother and to all of his loved ones.

Tears ran down his face but he let them run, preferring to keep faith with his mother and hold her to him — connecting with his father through their common touch.

"Jack, Jack, don't leave me," his mother moaned. "Dear God, don't take him away."

Paul held her tightly as she quietly wept against his shoulder. He didn't say anything; there was no need. Love flowed between them and out to his father, and words would have shattered that intimate unity. He put his mind into a state of meditation — melting out thoughts and purpose. How long it lasted he had no idea — seconds, minutes, hours would have seemed alike. He became aware of what felt like warm oil flowing down his arm. He spoke softly in tongues — it just rippled from his lips — then he was conscious of nothing but tranquillity.

After a little while, his mother said, "I knew you'd know what to say. He'll be all right now." She was calm, assured and smiling.

Paul looked at his father; he seemed to be sleeping peacefully. He withdrew his hand from his mother's and moved his arm away from her. He stood up, bent over his father again and once more kissed him. "God bless you, Dad. I'm sorry I haven't been around much but I'm here now. I love you; I always have and I always will."

His father opened his eyes and the faintest of smiles appeared on his lips; then he fell into a natural sleep. Mrs Stringer's face lit up with hope. "He's with us — he knows we're here. He'll be better when he's had a sleep."

Paul went to speak to the nurse. The doctor was with her and they both went to see what was happening. "He appears to be a little stronger, but don't get your hopes too high," he told them.

Paul went to find Ann. She came back saying that Paul was only making it more difficult for their mother. "Why are you letting her believe he's been healed? You know it won't happen."

"I haven't said he's healed," Paul objected. "But who am I to say what can and cannot happen? We shall have to wait and see."

His father was still sleeping quietly when they returned to his side. Paul told Ann, "I'll leave you with Mum for a few minutes, I've just remembered I'm supposed to be having lunch with a friend — I'll give him a ring."

Nick was as understanding as always. He was very sympathetic and told him that he would gladly get someone to take his Sunday services and, should the need arise, attend to whatever needed doing the following week.

"Thanks, Nick. I'll be getting back to the vicarage late this afternoon if things are okay here. I can come back tomorrow after the morning services if you could get Tony or someone to take Evening Prayer at Bradmire. I'll see how things go. Dad seems to have picked up a bit but you never know."

His father was still asleep when he returned to the intensive care unit. His mother was sitting relaxed. She told Paul and Ann to go and get some lunch but refused to go herself. "I'll go when you come back; I'll be ready for the toilet by then," she said, smiling happily in the belief that all was well.

"So, I suppose you think you're a miracle worker now." Ann said derisively, as they walked the long corridor to the hospital restaurant.

"What's the matter with you, Ann?" he asked, puzzled by her attitude. "I doubt it's me that's made you so angry. Perhaps you'd better tell me what's eating you up."

"Counsellor as well? Gosh, I do have a talented brother!"

Paul didn't answer. He kept quiet, letting his sister go on with her griping — mostly about him. They found the restaurant and chose their meals, Ann insisting on paying for them, and then looked for a table.

"There's one over in that corner," Paul said, moving towards it. "It's quieter there and we'll be out of the way." He wanted her to be free to talk without being overheard.

They sorted out the plates and cutlery, put the empty trays on a trolley and sat down to eat. Paul looked at his sister picking at her food. He always knew when she was unhappy — she would pile her plate with a fattening main course and then choose the biggest sweet with the most cream. But guilt prevented her from enjoying the calories.

Ann was an attractive woman, the same age as Rita and not unlike in looks. Paul had always regarded her as the brainy one. She was a solicitor dealing with corporate finance. Brian was a senior partner of the same firm. Looking at her dressed in her smart expensive city clothes, no one would have guessed that Ann was keener to start a family than reach the top of her chosen profession. His heart went out to her; it couldn't help when their mother was constantly harping on about grandchildren. And now their father, whom Ann had always been so close to, was probably dying.

"I get the impression you've always regarded me as Mummy's Boy. Sorry, Ann, but I can't do anything about that," Paul said, smiling at some of the things she had been saying about him. "Never mind me though, what's happening between you and Brian?"

She looked up at him with pain in her eyes, and then looked down at the greasy, full English, all-day breakfast she had on her plate. She slowly pushed her fork into the egg, watching the golden yolk running out over the fried bread, and then she prodded violently at a plump pink and black sausage. "It's too disgusting to tell you. I couldn't tell Mum, but Dad got it out of me. It's my fault he had that heart attack. He went to see Brian at work, but Brian was with a client and refused to see him. Dad went home angry and frustrated. He collapsed in front of Mum."

"You mustn't blame yourself. No way is Dad's heart attack your fault. It could have happened any time. Have you forgotten how much he used to smoke?"

"But if I hadn't told him about Brian, he wouldn't have been so upset." She was now stabbing at the sausage as if to kill it before it jumped off her plate.

Paul wondered what that sausage represented. He had an idea but thought it politic not to mention it. He reached over the table and took hold of the hand wielding the fork. "Tell me what the problem is."

She looked at him, tears now welling up in her eyes, "You're a priest, holy and all that, so how can I talk to you about such things?" She wiped her wet eyes with a tissue. "Oh, damn! Now my contact lens has shifted."

Paul gave her a hand to retrieve it from the corner of her eye, smiling to himself at his sister's naive view of his ministry.

"Okay, now we've dealt with the contact lens you've damned, perhaps you'll tell me what the problem is with your swine of a husband; that's what you called him, wasn't it?"

"He's gay!"

"What?"

"I knew you'd be shocked," she said, twisting her face into a grimace. "I heard you talk about homosexuals a few years ago. Unnatural and against Biblical law, you said."

"I'm surprised — not shocked. Never mind what I said, that was a few years ago."

"Oh, so now to accommodate Brian, you can change Christian ethics to suit. How very convenient."

"Things aren't as simple as I used to think," he said, wondering how much harm he might have done with his previous hard-line views. "But you and Brian have been trying for a baby — hardly homosexual activity."

"It happened years ago when he was on his way up. Oh, what an apt phrase!" she added cynically. "It was with a senior partner in the firm. Another appropriate statement!"

"Are you sure it happened? How did you find out?"

"A disgruntled secretary told me that's how my husband got on. His rise to partnership had nothing to do with talent."

"What does Brian say about it?"

"He doesn't deny it. Says anything that happened years ago has nothing to do with us. He claims he's faithful. But I told him, once a homo, always a homo."

"You can't say that, Ann. He may have been pressurised into doing what his boss wanted. Or he could have changed when he met you; realised his true nature."

She looked at him with disdain. "You really are in another world aren't you? Always want to think everyone is pure and innocent like you. Well I've got news for you, little brother; the world is full of people who'll never be anything other than depraved. Do you know what Brian was always asking me to do — until he realised he'd always get no for an answer?"

Paul had a good idea but he wasn't saying.

Noting his reticence, she said with a voice meant to convey her utter disgust, "I won't soil your innocence by saying the regular phrase, but let's say — it's an activity that wouldn't get me pregnant."

"He didn't force you to accede to his desires did he? And hasn't he been faithful ever since you came together?"

"How would I know if he's been faithful? But you just don't get it do you? It's what he is — what he really wants — that matters. If he's not getting it from me, he's probably getting it elsewhere. He obviously prefers men anyway; only married me to be seen as the respectable trustworthy business man."

"You don't know that, Ann. It seems to me that he's always loved you. Just because he wanted to vary the sex you were having, doesn't mean that he wanted a man. Perhaps he thought you'd enjoy it once you'd tried it. I understand some couples do."

"So now you're a sex expert! I can't even remember you ever having a girlfriend. What would you know about what couples get up to? Do you secretly watch them at night in the churchyard, or are you into porn videos?"

"I don't live in seclusion, you know — I'm not a monk. I'll talk to Brian. I think you're being very hard on him. He's always seemed a nice guy to me."

"Well there you are! Maybe that tells me something about you I would never have suspected," she said with a little laugh. "That's what happens when you're Mummy's Boy!"

Paul ignored the jibe, turned his face away from her and got on with his meal. Ann continued to pick at her food. After a little while, she said, "Sorry, Paul. I really am sorry. I guess I'm worried about Dad — Mum too."

He took hold of her hand. "It's okay, Ann. I understand."

She looked at him closely. "You really are a lovely person, Paul. Gentle and understanding — no wonder you're a priest. But you know, nice guys can be very vulnerable in a dog eat dog world."

"I'll take my chances," Paul said smiling.

"Will you talk to Brian then?" she asked him, now more at peace with herself. "He'll tell you the truth. I really do love him you know.

It's just that what he's done seems so — not sure what I want to say — unnatural and dirty I suppose. Not knowing if he's still active with men, makes me feel contaminated — I can't bear to let him touch me."

It was with mixed feelings that Paul assured his sister of his help in finding out from Brian what his present sexual preferences were. How would Ann react if she knew a gay priest was holding her hand?

As soon as Paul finished his meal, Ann insisted they return to their father's bedside. She pushed her food aside. "I've lost my appetite."

Their mother said she had to spend a penny. Ann went with her to the visitors' toilets. "But you're going to get a bite to eat afterwards, Mum," she insisted. "We don't want you ill as well as Dad. You must keep your strength up. I'll take you to the restaurant; you can get a proper meal there. We'll have no picking at food; I'll see that you eat a good dinner."

Bossy as ever, thought Paul. Pity his sister didn't follow her own advice.

He sat by his father and, looking at that peaceful familiar face, realised how little he knew about the real Jack Stringer. His dad may have been a churchgoer, but had he put his faith in Jesus Christ? If only he had discussed these things with him while he had the chance. He took hold of his father's hand and spoke the words he knew by heart from St John's Gospel.

"Jesus said to his disciples, 'Do not let your hearts be troubled. Trust in God and trust in me. In my father's house are many rooms; if there were not I should have told you. I am going now to prepare a place for you, so that where I am, you may be also. You know the way to the place where I am going.' Thomas said, 'Lord, we do not know where you are going, so how can we know the way?' Jesus told them, 'I am the Way, the Truth and the Life; no one can come to the Father except through me.'"

Tears ran down Paul's cheeks. "Accept Him, Dad. Let Jesus into your heart. He has a place for you — you'll be free and at peace, accepted and loved. That's what we all want isn't it? I know I do. Don't be afraid, all we have to do is come to Him — just as we are."

Paul detected a movement of his father's fingers grasping his hand. Encouraged, Paul said the Lord's Prayer — slowly and meaningfully. His father's lips were saying the words with him. When Paul reached the words, "but deliver us from evil," he felt a surge of power sweep through him. Triumphantly, he concluded, "For thine is the kingdom, the power and the glory, for ever and ever — Amen!"

Paul's tears of sorrow had turned to showers of joy. His father was gazing up at him, squeezing his hand and smiling. "I'm okay, son," he whispered. "Don't you worry. I'm going to be fine."

"Dad, I love you," Paul whispered between sobs.

"And I love you too," his dad answered quietly. "We'll chat sometime — must sleep now."

Paul wiped his eyes with the back of his hand. Knowing his father was going to be okay whether he lived or died was wonderful enough, but he was utterly convinced that he would be with them for a few years yet.

"You're crying — what's happened?" came his sister's voice from behind him. "Is he worse?"

"I think he's getting better — he spoke to me."

Ann sat down and looked at her sleeping father. "He spoke to you? Have you told the nurse?"

"No. Dad's sleeping. He's okay — I just know it."

"Well, don't tell Mum when she gets back. It would be cruel to get her hopes up for nothing."

"Where's your mum?" came a voice from the bed. "I want to see her."

"Dad, you're awake! How are you feeling? I'll get the doctor," Ann said, getting up.

"Sit yourself down, girl," said her father, his voice getting a little stronger. "You get doctors when you're ill. I'm fine — just tired."

"I'll get Mum, she's in the restaurant — first meal she's had for ages," said Ann, excitement colouring her cheeks.

"Let her eat then. I can wait. I'll have another nap." He closed his eyes and drifted once more into sleep.

Paul called the nurse and she came over.

"Seems to be getting stronger," she said smiling. "Oh, there's a gentleman in the waiting room. He's anxiously waiting to hear how Mr Stringer is. Do you want to have a word with him?" she asked Paul.

"Did he ask to see me?" Paul queried, wondering why the visitor wanted to see him in particular.

"Well, he came to the nurses' station a few minutes ago and saw you were by Mr Stringer's bedside. He said you were his brother-in-law."

Ann was alarmed. "It's Brian. What's he doing here? He'll give Dad another heart attack."

Paul frowned. "I doubt it, but I want to talk to him anyway." He stood up. "You stay with Dad until Mum gets back."

As soon as Paul walked through the door of the waiting room, Brian put down the magazine he was reading and stood up. He looked a very worried man. "How is he, Paul? I feel as though it's my fault he's in here."

Paul went over to him and tapped his arm in a friendly gesture. "Very poorly but it looks as though there might be a slight improvement."

"Thank God!" said Brian. He sat down again, clearly relieved.

"Amen to that," Paul answered with feeling.

He sat by his brother-in-law's side. After a few moments of silence, he asked him what had happened between him and Ann.

"Ann's told you I'm gay, hasn't she? What happened took place a long time ago. I'm not proud of it. I was young at the time and it was what you might call payment for preferment. The best of it is, I would have got where I am today anyway. I should never have prostituted myself."

Paul could believe Brian's confidence in his own abilities. He was the picture of a successful man: black soft leather shoes, tailored grey trousers, soft roll-necked off-white cashmere jumper that matched his well-groomed hair, and manicured nails tipping his long smooth fingers. Tall, good-looking and in love with his wife? Anne must be crazy to cast him aside so easily. He thought a moment about Brian's youthful mistake. Prostituting himself? "Is that how you see it?" he asked him.

"Of course. Unfortunately, we were caught by his secretary, with our trousers down, so to speak," Brian said ruefully.

"Careless wasn't it?"

"She had an adjoining office. It was after hours and we didn't know she was there — the other door was locked. What she heard and surmised, rather than her ability, has yielded good rises in salary over the years. She became my secretary when Phil died and I took over. That was a year ago."

"She's been blackmailing you for years?"

'Blackmailing Phil up to his death, but only for salary increases and status. You know, Paul, what we did only happened a couple of times, but I have no idea how many partners Phil had. He knew I wasn't keen and after being caught out, I refused to cooperate again. He understood."

Paul found Brian's reticence difficult to believe. "Not keen? From what Ann told me you wanted to try anal sex with her."

"What? Never! Look, I fell for Ann the moment I met her. Being a bachelor priest, you probably find that hard to understand," he said, giving Paul a pitying look. "Going with Phil was a mistake — pure and simple. Well, maybe not pure but I sure was simple. I've never tried it with another man and have no desire to. To tell you the truth, the whole thing rather disgusts me. What on earth did Ann say to you?"

"That what you wanted, wouldn't get her pregnant."

"Shit! I only asked her to try a bit of oral sex. It may not get her pregnant, but it would make a nice change from her feverish attempts to get my seed planted in her garden! You may be a priest, but you're not telling me you've never tasted the pleasures of the flesh!"

Paul had no intention of answering that question. "So apart from a couple of sessions with your boss, you've never had another partner?"

"Men, no. Before I met Ann, one or two women — all men like to experiment when they're young and practice when they're older. But I swear to you — on the Bible if you like — I've never touched another woman since I met Ann."

"I believe you," said Paul. But how was he to convince Ann? Another thought occurred to him. "What made your secretary tell Ann about what she knew?"

"She started demanding a ridiculous retirement package to take effect when she's fifty. I refused to be blackmailed. I was going to confess my past indiscretion to Ann, but that bitch got in first."

"I suppose what happened to Dad made things worse. I'll have a word with her but can't promise anything." Paul rose from his chair. "I'll be getting back now. Did you want to see Jack? It might be better if you waited until you get things right with Ann."

"I'd heard he was dying and was unconscious. I rather like the old guy; we've always got on before. I just wanted to say goodbye I suppose. But I'll wait. I'd better see Ann after you've explained things to her."

When Paul returned to the unit, his mother was there holding hands with his father. They were smiling at each other like a couple of newly-weds. Ann came over to Paul and suggested they leave their parents alone for a while.

Sitting in the coffee shop near the hospital entrance, Paul told Ann about his conversation with Brian.

She was somewhat sceptical. "And you believe him?"

"Yes. In fact I think Brian is a very moral person. He refused to give in to blackmail — in his position that took some doing. The whole firm, and probably half his clients, must know about his past by now. Ann, he's been absolutely faithful to you since the day you met. Believe me, that's quite something these days."

"You think I'm a prude. That's it, isn't it? You're a priest, doesn't it bother you that your brother-in-law has done such a beastly thing?"

"Come on, Ann. It was a long time ago. Believe me, I've heard worse things confessed. He's not the only one that's tried to get ahead by giving way to his boss."

"But this is men doing it together — it's disgusting!"

Paul felt uncomfortable with the conversation. Clearly if his sexuality became known, he would have a very unhappy family.

"It was a long time ago," he said, making light of Brian's indiscretion. "Maybe he should have told you before he married you, but it would have been a high risk to take. And let's face it, up till now, you've had a fairly happy marriage — in spite of not getting the children you so much want."

She went quiet a moment. "Where is he now?"

"Still in the waiting room — waiting."

She rose from her chair and left Paul drinking his coffee. When Paul went back to his father, Ann was there with Brian's arm around her. His mother and father were still holding hands and everyone was smiling.

Paul had a word with the doctor. His father was now out of immediate danger. It had been a remarkable recovery but it did sometimes happen. Obviously his father was a good fighter. They would be giving him more tests and looking at the possibility of an operation to correct any permanent damage.

Satisfied that he was no longer needed, Paul decided it was time he left for home. He told his family that he would keep in touch, and return at once if the need arose. He somehow knew it would not be necessary, at least, for a while. He said he would visit again on his day off. Embracing them all, he left the hospital with the warmth of his family's love aglow in his heart.

When he reached outside, five hours from arriving, the sun was shining and everywhere he looked raindrops were sparkling like diamonds. Paul breathed in the fresh air and stretched out his arms in salutation to God's creation. A few people looked his way and smiled but he didn't care. He walked to his vehicle joyfully singing to himself and to God. He was about to open his car door when he noticed a paper stuck to his windscreen. He'd gone over his parking time and had a hefty fine to pay. Still singing happily, he walked over to the kiosk and paid up in full.

# Chapter twelve

Paul was relieved that Rita had stopped pressurising him and they could now work together as previously. He was puzzled at the change in her — until Angela told him what had happened after he had left the vicarage to go to the hospital. She had confessed to telling Rita to leave him alone. "I told her straight. She's making you ill and driving you away from her. I said I could tell you're not in love with her and she had to accept it and take it easy."

Paul was shocked by Angela's audacity but, after a few days, had to admit her intervention seemed to have made Rita aware of what she was doing to him. The girl was proving to be a godsend in many ways, and he was pleased to give her an excellent reference for the job she had applied for. She was now in full time employment but was still assisting him with the admin.

The house now had a very welcoming feel about it. Most of it was due to Angela's cheerful presence. Whenever she was in the vicarage she helped him feel relaxed. If he was busy with a visitor, she would answer the phone and check his e-mails to get rid of the junk. She was a wizard on the computer and could teach him a thing or two. He could rely on her to get messages correct and get on with jobs without supervision. She had turned out to be a perfect assistant. What's more, the fear that she would cause problems by falling in love with him had disappeared — she was now wearing Mark's ring.

Today was Saturday and he was looking forward to the morrow when it was the feast day of St Michael and All Angels. Bishop Lionel was coming to baptise a number of adults and confirm twenty-three candidates, nearly all of them from the new housing estates. He was also confirming the candidates from Glenton. Altogether, the relatives and friends of those being confirmed, plus the normal congregations, were going to pack the building. Chairs would have to be borrowed from Glenton's church hall.

Just as Paul was mulling over details of the service, Angela arrived to do her usual tasks. It was her nineteenth birthday and Paul had something for her — a little appreciation for all she did for him.

"I hope you like it, Angela, it's not much but it's the prayer that goes with it that counts. Happy birthday!"

She took off the shop-wrapped gift and opened up the box. It was a little gold cross on a fine gold chain.

She threw her arms around his neck and kissed him. "It's gorgeous," she cried. "Please help me on with it."

She took off her coat and stood in front of the hall mirror while Paul fastened the little catch at the back of her neck. She was wearing a white open-neck shirt blouse and, with her high breasts, the little cross fell over her lightly tanned skin almost into her cleavage. Paul looked at her in admiration; had he been attracted to women, he would have found her irresistible. Her golden hair fell smoothly to her shoulders and her brilliant blue eyes were sparkling with health and happiness. Her fitted blouse hugged her youthful figure. The cut of her black skirt showed off her neat hips and shapely legs. Although small, the gold of the cross and chain put that finishing touch of colour to a beautiful picture.

"You look lovely, Angela," he said smiling, but worried he might be sending out the wrong signals, he started walking towards his study. "Right, now let's get down to work, it's a big day tomorrow and there's lots to do. I have a wedding in an hour and then I'm back here for a snack. I have folk to visit early afternoon and a rehearsal for the Confirmation at three-thirty — Lucy Palmer will be bringing over their lot too. This evening, chairs are being put in the church and everything arranged. There's labelling of seats to do sometime. It's all go, Angela, so we'd better get started."

"Would you like cheese and scrambled eggs on toast when you get in? Only take me a few minutes."

"That will be great. Make it for the two us. Now we're going to need souvenir pamphlets tomorrow with separate sheets for notices. I've got the details ready."

By the time he went over to the church, Angela was well on the way to getting a proof copy of the service ready for approval. As usual, he left her in charge of the vicarage.

There were comings and goings all day at St Michael's. Paul appreciated the cooperation between his and Nick's parish. Early evening, Glenton ladies were chatting to the local parishioners as they watered the flowers and put finishing touches to the floral displays. While clearing away the mess, merry laughter sounded as they laboured with brooms and dusters. The men from the two parishes joked and chuckled while sorting out the extra chairs. It was if the parishes reflected the congenial unity of their leaders. Surely it augured well for the future.

By eight in the evening, Paul had done all that was needful. In spite of the hard work, he was feeling happy and relaxed. It had been great to return to his vicarage for lunch, followed by tea, to find both meals ready on the table, but he certainly didn't expect to find Angela waiting in the kitchen to make him a coffee.

"Hello, Angela, you should have gone by now, that young man will be waiting for you. Didn't you say he was taking you to a party?" He was a little worried that she was stretching Mark's patience.

She put the coffee mugs on the table and sat down with him. "He came here for me an hour ago. Said he wanted to see his mates before the party. I told him to clear off. Anyway, I had that filing to finish. It's all done now but can't say I'm anxious to get home. Mum and Dad will be watching telly; the usual boring stuff."

"Don't watch it much myself." He picked up his mug of coffee. "Well, thanks for everything — don't know how I'd manage without my angel."

She smiled coyly and sipped her coffee.

He put down his empty mug. "I'll drive you home. It's the least I can do when you've been working here all day. I'm going out anyway — getting some fish and chips. Would you like some? Not much of a birthday feast but tasty."

Angela's eyes lit up. "Lovely. I'll put some plates to warm. Can we have mushy peas too?"

Paul hadn't thought about bringing the fish and chips back to the vicarage to eat them with Angela. He hadn't thought beyond buying them. Sometimes he brought them back to the vicarage, but usually he took them to a local beauty spot and ate them outdoors — going on to a pub afterwards. But why not share the evening with Angela? After all, it was her birthday and she deserved better company than a television screen.

When he returned twenty minutes later, he found Angela had lit a fire in his sitting room. It was the only place that had some semblance of tidiness and comfort about it. The previous Christmas, his mother had insisted on doing it up for him with new deep-pile beige carpet, red rug with matching chair covers, glossy red and beige brocade curtains and cushion covers. She said he ought to have somewhere to entertain his personal friends. If only his mother could see him now, sharing the deep-cushioned sofa with a pretty girl, she would be glowing with pleasure and thinking of her future grandchildren!

The fire was burning brightly and, with the curtains now closed, the room was cosy and warm — a bit too warm. Paul was getting sleepy — very sleepy. While he was eating he managed to keep up a light conversation, but not for long. With bleary eyes, he saw Angela get up and take the tray into the kitchen. She was saying something about making coffee.

Paul watched the flames of the fire licking the crackling wood. A log collapsed, sending bright sparks upwards into the black chimney and outward to glow then die on the red hearthrug. The smell of burning wool brought him to his senses. Small black burns were appearing on the new rug. He struggled up and put a guard in front of the blaze. Satisfied, he fell back on the sofa — his head on a cushion and his hands behind his neck. Utterly relaxed, he watched flickering shadows through half-closed eyelids. Humming softly to himself, his thoughts were of Nick.

How wonderful if he were with him now. He imagined what they would be doing in the firelight — how they would be expressing their love for each other. He could see golden lights tinting the curls of Nick's now greying hair. As he bent over to kiss his soft full lips, little dancing flames appeared in his smiling eyes. He revelled in the magical light of the fire as it heightened the contours of Nick's naked heaving body — his muscular shoulders, broad chest, flat belly, and that delightful member aroused from sleep to play its essential role in expressing their delight in one another. Coming together in a powerful embrace, he could feel their love flowing between them. He sensed his own strong arousal and heard himself moaning with the pleasure of his lover's touch.

Something was wrong — was he dreaming? But there was an air of reality about it — the sensations were powerful and he didn't want them to stop. What was happening? He forced himself out of his stupor. He couldn't believe what his eyes told him. Firelight was glowing on golden hair and almost naked flesh — but it wasn't Nick's. Angela was all over him. She had opened up his trousers and was giving him the benefit of the knowledge she had acquired

Page 158

of how to please men.

Horrified, he pulled away from her. "Stop this at once. Get your clothes on, Angela."

"Why, Paul? You like it." She sounded hurt by the rebuff.

Paul stood up and adjusted his clothes. He tried not to show the anger he was feeling. "I know you think you're pleasing me, but I can't let you do it."

"I don't understand. You were enjoying it — it's obvious. It isn't hurting anyone. It isn't sinful," she argued, standing up and rolling her hips seductively — the blue gem in her belly button sparkling in the firelight.

"You're going to marry Mark; that should be enough reason, Angela."

"But it's you I love, Paul — only you," she murmured, coming up to embrace him.

He held her away. "I've told you, Angela — I'm married to my vocation." He looked at her with compassion and said tenderly, "I'm sorry, so very sorry."

"I'm not asking you to marry me."

"Mark would be very angry. Think of him, my angel."

"I'm not an angel. I want you to make love to me. I've saved myself for you, Paul," she said, putting her arms around his neck. "Only you, my darling."

'Oh, Angela. I really appreciate what you're offering but it isn't possible. Please get dressed. It's time I took you home."

"I don't want you to take me home. I don't want to go home. I want to stay here with you. I'll let you do what you want — anything," she pleaded, trying to wrap her arms around his neck and push her body up to him.

He took hold of her wrists and pushed her away from him. "Now stop it, Angela. I don't want to hurt you. But I can't give you what you want. Please get your clothes on."

He pushed her on to the sofa and quickly left the room. He ran upstairs to the bathroom and locked the door, feeling utterly at a loss. Girls had made passes at him before, but this was something else. Clearly it was his fault. He should have seen it coming. All the little hints and her willingness to please, should have told him that she was in love with him. Now his angel was badly hurt and there was little he could do about it.

The sound of the front door slamming informed him that Angela had left. Should he go after her and take her home? If anything happened to her, he would never forgive himself. He went downstairs, put on his coat and pocketed his keys. The phone rang just as he was about to leave. He quickly picked it up. It was Mark on his mobile asking if Angela was there.

"She left a moment ago; I'm about to pick her up and take her home. Can't stop. Goodnight." He put down the phone and hurried out. If Mark had been drinking, he didn't want him picking Angela up.

She hadn't got far. He stopped his car just ahead of her and jumped out. He went up to her but she turned her head away and went on walking. He barred her path, trying to get her to stop before she reached the houses in the lane. Tears were glistening on her cheeks, causing pity to well up inside of him.

He held out his hands in a pleading gesture. "Angela, please let me take you home," he said with urgency. "Mark rang. He's on his way to pick you up. He sounded half drunk. He shouldn't be driving. Please get in the Discovery."

"No! I hate you!" she said, her voice betraying the humiliation she was feeling.

She tried to dodge around him but he caught her arms. "Okay, you hate me — but let me take you home."

"Let me go or I'll scream!" she yelled.

"Keep your voice down and be reasonable," he pleaded. "You're just tired. Let's forget what's happened. It's my fault — I let things go too far. I didn't realise what was happening."

She didn't want to listen. She tried to pull away. "I'll scream," she yelled, opening her mouth in readiness.

Paul quickly put his hand across the open gap. "Now just stop it. You're being hysterical."

She tried to remove his hand but couldn't.

"Please, Angela, just cool it."

Her eyes went wild. Lifting her free arm, she made a grab for his face. He automatically backed away but she caught him with her fingernails on his jaw. Shocked, he quickly released her. She looked at him, horror distorting her pretty face.

"I'm sorry. I didn't mean to hurt you," she said anxiously. Lifting her tear-soaked hanky to his jaw, she pleaded lovingly, "It's bleeding — let me wipe it for you."

Paul didn't answer. He couldn't handle her mercurial change-about. He pushed her arm away, turned around and walked to his vehicle. Lifting himself in, he said to her, "You're a grown woman, Angela. Choose what you want to do."

She just stood there, looking at him defiantly. He started the engine and drove the short distance back to the vicarage.

He let himself in and wearily threw his keys onto the hall table. Walking towards the kitchen, he caught sight of himself in the hall mirror. What a mess. Blood was on his jaw, collar and shirt. He stripped off the stained clothes and put them to soak in the kitchen sink — watching the blood billow in the cold water. He put the kettle on for a coffee. While he waited for the water to boil, he sat with a cold damp kitchen towel pressed to his face, all the time thinking he should have handled the sad incident better. Being the senior person in the relationship, he was ultimately responsible. He should have seen it coming. Even Rita had warned him about having the girl around him too much.

Poor little angel — falling for a gay priest! It would never have happened if he'd been honest with her about his homosexuality. If he told her now, would it ease the pain of rejection? He couldn't afford to risk it. It wasn't just he and the parish that could suffer — it was Nick too.

He made his drink and went to the sitting room to make sure the fire was okay. The heat in the room met him as he opened the door. He sat meditating for a while, but his mind was restless and thoughts refused to subside. So he let them flow past like autumn leaves drifting on a swollen stream. He couldn't change the past; he could only ask forgiveness and rest in God.

When he opened his eyes, the fire was no more than a few glowing embers. He went wearily to bed. As he was about to close the curtains, he looked out of the window towards the church. There had been a shower and the lamp in the lane was lighting up the raindrops on the dark trees of the churchyard. It was half an hour off midnight and it would not be long before the church became a hive of activity. He knew the bishop would be looking at him favourably — on the surface he was a successful minister. But in his heart he was only too aware of his shortcomings.

He gripped the curtain to pull it across the window but then stopped. Something had caught his eye — light was coming from the windows at the east end of the church. Had a switch been left on or had someone broken in? Thieves and vandals could do serious damage; he couldn't just forget about it and go to bed. Groaning with annoyance, he pulled on a jumper and trousers and ran downstairs.

He picked up a torch and looked for his church key. It wasn't where he kept it. A key that size could not be slipped into a trouser pocket and forgotten. Where was it? The only thing he could think of was that Angela must have it in that big shoulder bag she carried around. She probably thought she might need it when she delivered the pamphlets late afternoon. When she found the church open and occupied, she would have left her father or Doreen Briggs to lock up. He only hoped the key hadn't reached the wrong hands. Apart from the damage that could be done, his churchwarden would make sure he would never hear the last of it!

Locking the vicarage door behind him, he hurried to the church. As he entered the porch, he heard music coming from inside. The key was in the lock. He carefully opened the door and stepped inside. What he saw and heard made him sick to the heart.

Under the spotlights, a couple were copulating on the altar. Clothes and bottles littered the chancel. Music was coming from a disc player. But what horrified Paul most of all, was that above the usual grunts and moans of ecstasy, he heard Angela shouting, "Paul, don't — not that — you're hurting me!"

"Stop this at once!" Paul bellowed.

The male looked up and Paul saw that it was Mark. "Stop this, Mark — stop it now!"

But Mark was already withdrawing from Angela. He leapt for his trousers, leaving Angela moaning, "Paul, come back — don't leave me."

Paul ran forward to get hold of Mark, but he tripped over one of Angela's shoes and fell heavily against a pew. Pain shot through his body. The torch rolled out of his hand and under a seat. Meanwhile, Mark ran in front of the pews and down the south aisle.

"She's all yours!" Mark snapped as he pulled on his trousers before leaving the building.

Angela was still crazily moaning — in rhythm with the love song coming from the disc player. Paul quickly switched off the music, leaving the girl groaning on her own. As he approached her naked body, she vomited and then rolled over towards him. He just managed to break her fall before she hit the hard sanctuary floor — a pain shot up his bruised arm as he did so. As she lay on the floor, she gazed up at him and a little smile appeared on her vomit-smeared lips. "Darling, Paul, I love—" Her glazed eyes went dreamy and her lids closed.

She was in a drunken stupor, but had she also taken drugs?

Paul shoved her belongings into her large shoulder bag — stuffing the overspill into his pockets. Wrapping her coat around her, he threw Angela over his shoulder and carried her out of the church. With difficulty, he pulled the door closed and pulled out the key, intending to return later to clear up the debris and switch off the altar lights. He carried Angela to the vicarage and put her on the sitting room sofa, propping her on her side in case she threw up.

He sat looking at her. What had she and Mark been up to — beside the obvious? It grieved him to think that Angela might have become involved with drink and drugs. Had he driven her to it? He was sure she didn't make a habit of drinking and it was hard to believe she would take drugs. There was an answer to that and only Mark would know about it. Get the girl drinking, slip a tablet into the liquid when she wasn't looking, and Angela would be his for the night with no recollection of what had happened.

Now what? She was old enough to stay out all night but her parents would worry. If he took her home in that state, there was no telling what her father might do. Should he ring them up — and say what? Had she consented to intercourse when she was in her right mind? The fact that it was his name she was calling and not Mark's, suggested to him that she was not entirely aware of what was going on. Poor girl, what a way to lose her virginity — desecrating the church altar. Mark had a lot to answer for.

He couldn't ring Nick and Lucy — they had the bishop staying with them overnight. He rang Rita, apologising for the late hour. Quickly explaining the situation, he begged her to come over and help him with Angela. She didn't argue or fuss, just said she would get there as soon as possible. He breathed a sigh of relief and went to the kitchen to prepare coffee for them both.

The front doorbell rang — too soon for Rita. Puzzled, Paul opened the door to be confronted by an angry Kevin Raymond.

"Where's Angela?" he demanded to know as he rushed inside the vicarage. "She's been out since early this morning. I saw her in church this afternoon with the pamphlets and sheets. She showed me that cross you gave her. We expected her to be home when we got back — Mark was picking her up. But he bloody didn't. I was on my way out when he drove past me like a bloody madman. So where's my bloody daughter?"

"Angela fell asleep on the sitting room couch; she's still there. She's been working very hard — best not to wake her," Paul told him calmly.

"Not wake her? What's she doing bloody asleep?" Kevin yelled. Then he caught sight of Paul's jaw. He looked at him suspiciously. "What's happened to your bloody face?"

Paul had forgotten the scratches on his left jaw. He put his hand over the wound and said the first excuse that came to mind. "Stray cat objected to being picked up," he lied. "Your daughter is quite safe. She'll be home in the morning."

"You could have bloody rung. Don't think I don't know what you've been up to. Fell asleep? Not bloody likely! Well you can wake her up — she's coming home."

"She's nineteen, not a kid; let her sleep, she's quite safe."

"And you're supposed to be a man of God! You're a bloody disgrace to the cloth. You so called charismatics are all the same — always bloody hugging and touching. If you do that in public, God knows what you do in private!"

Paul struggled with his growing anger. "I think you'd better leave."

Knowing he had no legal right to drag his daughter home, Kevin looked at him wildly — eye's bulging, veins raised, fists clenched. Muttering incoherently, he turned to go. Suddenly, he changed his mind and headed towards the sitting room. Paul jumped in front of him and barred the way.

"Let her sleep. I'll bring her home myself. In the morning when she's awake." His apparent composure belied the fear that was gripping his guts.

"You filthy swine," Kevin snorted, his knuckles growing white with anger. "You're up to something, and we both know it." With that he left the vicarage.

As Paul watched him disappear into the night, he had a dreadful thought — would Kevin see the light on in the church? Would he go and investigate? Well, if he did, he'd be back for sure. He went to sit with Angela. After wiping her face with a damp cloth, he watched her heavy breathing. What could he possibly say to Kevin, that is, without letting him know what he'd witnessed in the church? He didn't want to tell lies but he wasn't averse to being foxy and not telling the full story if it would protect the girl.

The doorbell rang. Kevin was back.

"Ring the police at once. The church has been desecrated. My god, I've never seen anything like it — vodka and beer bottles all over the bloody place. Much worse, there's blood and filth all over the altar. Bloody disgusting! There's been a black mass or something. Ring the police I tell you!"

"I don't think that's a very good idea, Kevin. Come into my study and we'll talk about it."

'If you won't call in the police, then I bloody will!" Kevin went over to the phone and picked up the receiver.

"Put it down and listen," Paul said sharply. "There's something you don't know."

The doorbell sounded. Paul thought it would be Rita. "Hold on, Kevin. It's important we talk about this first and discuss the implications." He left the man sitting thumping his fists on his knees.

Paul let Rita in, whispering, "Kevin's here; he wants to send for the police. I'm trying to put him off. Please look after Angela." He led her to the sitting room.

He hurried back to Kevin. "Look, Kevin, whatever happened in the church, we don't want publicity. Tomorrow's a big day; we don't want folk turning up for all the wrong reasons. Before long it would be on the radio and in the papers — the place would be full of sightseers. We'd get kids from miles around having parties in the churchyard. I'll go over and see what needs to be done. I'll have a word with Nick Palmer — we'll do something about the altar before the service tomorrow. I don't suppose any real damage has been done has there?"

Kevin sat with wrinkled brow mulling over the argument. "You might have a point. The bloody rubbish can soon be cleared, but what's been happening? It must be something bloody evil."

"We'll go over now. I'll get my key."

"How did they get in? That's what I want to know. Too many keys to that bloody door. I'll find out where they got one," Kevin said, looking at Paul in a threatening manner. "I'm convinced it's one of those bloody tattooed shaven-heads that hover around your club. I knew something like this would happen — they've probably sacrificed that bloody cat that scratched you!"

They were on the way out with a full set of keys and a bin bag for rubbish, when Kevin saw Rita's car in the drive.

"Rita Lee here?" he asked abruptly.

"Yes. She's concerned for someone in desperate need. We're going to pray when I get back. Do you want to join us?" Paul was absolutely certain what the answer would be.

"Bloody odd hours some people keep," Kevin muttered.

On the way to the church, Paul was considering that it might be best to keep all the evidence, including the messy altar cloth, in case Angela wanted to make charges against Mark.

It didn't take long to clear up. Kevin retrieved a fresh altar cloth from the linen drawer ready for the sacristan to set out in the morning. Paul told him about keeping the evidence in case they changed their minds about calling in the police. Kevin grunted his approval but he wasn't a happy man; he stayed behind looking around for evidence.

Paul went back to the vicarage and told Rita what had been happening. They both agreed they needed to get in touch with Mark and hear his side of the story.

"I don't expect he gets in until the early hours; perhaps I could get him on his mobile — if we could find his number. I don't like the idea of ringing his home; do you think Angela would have it on her?" Paul said, looking at Angela's bag.

"I don't expect you want to rummage inside a woman's bag. I'll do it. She might have a mobile with Mark's number programmed in."

She pulled out the clothes that Paul had stuffed in, shaking her head at the state of the skirt and blouse. She laid them carefully over a chair. Paul rescued Angela's underwear from one of his pockets.

Rita smiled at the bra and briefs. "With those sticking out of your pocket ready to greet Kevin, just as well you were wearing that long jumper. If I didn't know certain facts, even I would find your story hard to believe."

She found a mobile at the bottom of the bag but it was switched off. She tried pressing the power button and the phone came to life without a PIN number. Within seconds Rita had Mark's number ready to ring. She handed the phone to Paul. "Over to you."

"Right, let's see if he's answering." Paul pressed the send key.

An angry Mark came on at the other end. "Angela? Is that you? What do you want? You've already got me into a mess."

The noise in the background was overpowering. It would be impossible to have a sensible conversation with that racket going on.

"It's Paul Stringer. If you don't want the police picking you up, you'd better get somewhere quiet so we can talk," Paul barked down the phone.

"Who? What the devil has she got me into?"

"I'm not shouting down a phone. Get somewhere quiet."

"Hang on."

The noise of music, laughter, and shouting grew louder and then went quieter until it became imperceptible.

"Police? What are you on about?" Mark sounded very angry. "It was her idea. I thought she was mad. It didn't seem right to me but she wanted to do it."

"It's no use blaming Angela because she's not in a position to defend herself. I need to know what you've given her."

"What she asked for. What's all this about the police?"

"Kevin Raymond came looking for Angela and found the church in that awful mess. He thinks there's been a black mass or some kind of ritual going on. He wanted to call the police but I've managed to hold him back. He doesn't know you and Angela are involved. Now tell me what happened and what you gave her. She was obviously out of it — still is!"

"Shit! It was her fault, man. I picked her up in a bit of a state. She said she wanted it bad — wanted to do it in church. Said she wanted to sacrifice her virginity on the altar. I thought she was barmy. I could hardly say no — I've been waiting for years."

"Oh, yes? Then why is she stoned out of her mind? Why was she calling you Paul? What have you given her?"

"Look, Mr Stringer. She saw I'd got some bottles in the back. They were for this party see? But she wanted to get boozed up. The way she was swallowing the vodka down, she didn't need any boosters. She had the church key in her bag. We went inside and she put on those spotlights over the altar. She got out that player, took her clothes off and started dancing around. She started drinking again. I wasn't happy about it; I wanted her sober. She climbed on the altar and started singing the Magnificat. Then a song came on the player and she sang 'I'll always love you, Paul'. Shit! What a turn off."

"But it didn't turn you off did it? Not the way you were going at it," said Paul angrily.

"It's what she wanted — begged me. Three years she's been having me on. We're supposed to be engaged. I've kept off other women because of her. Shit! You can't blame me for what's happened."

"Okay, we'll talk some more when you come and see me — make it soon!"

Paul switched off the mobile.

"What now?" asked Rita, after Paul told her what Mark had said.

"This must never get as far as the police, Rita," said Paul seriously, putting his head in his hands and sighing deeply. "Poor kid, I feel it's all my fault."

"Angela is not a kid — she's an intelligent female. She knows you don't want to marry, but she's been worming her way into your heart — hoping to make you love her. Surely you must see that?" When Rita didn't get an immediate response, she added testily, "She has only herself to blame — the little hussy catching you out when you were asleep."

Paul had only told Rita that Angela had kissed him; he was now glad he hadn't said where and how. He was feeling that he had betrayed the girl and was now sorry for getting Rita involved.

"I'll have a talk with Nick Palmer about what's happened and what to do about the altar. He'll be sympathetic and give advice," said Paul, trying to think clearly. "But whatever happens we try and play it down — door left open and drunken kids got in. No real harm's been done. They used the altar as their bar and cut themselves on a glass bottle — nothing sinister. Kevin must never know what happened to Angela, even if he does think I've got her for a mistress."

"Well, we'd better get her cleaned up a bit. I'll take her home with me," said Rita adamantly.

Paul couldn't see how she could do it on her own. He looked at Angela — sound asleep and snoring. "I'll have to come with you; she'll need carrying."

"Perhaps we can sober her up a bit. Anyway, get me water, towel and a clean cloth. I'll give her a wipe over — that might help. I'll get her undies on and you can help with the rest."

"Maybe she'd better stay here until she wakes up. She can have a shower and then be taken home. Yes, that's what I'll do. Kevin knows she's here anyway."

"She can't stay here, you know that. What will the girl think when she wakes up? She might believe you've done this to her. She'll be all over you. Bad enough you brought her here. You should have called her parents, she's old enough to take the consequences of her actions."

"But her father—"

"If she's having problems at home, then she should leave. She's not a kid — she's got a good job with responsibility. You've got your reputation to think of. You don't belong to yourself, Paul — you're the Lord's servant. You can't afford to compromise your position here."

"Compassion is more important. Jesus had compassion on all the sick," Paul said reproachfully.

"And how are you going to heal sick souls if people turn against you?" Rita demanded to know. She stood up and paced the floor. "We'll clean her up and take her home. You'll tell Kevin that she went off to see Mark and came back drunk. You wanted me to clean her up before she went home. I'll be with you to verify your story."

"I can't do that. Please, Rita, help me clean her up. Put her into her undies and one of my tee shirts, and then help me get her into bed."

Rita stood over Paul, looking at him accusingly. "You're a fool, Paul Stringer; can't you see what's happening? You're living a lie and it's become infectious — affecting your thinking. How can you minister to others when you need to be whole yourself?"

He jumped out of his chair and walked away from her, putting up a hand as if to ward her off. "Don't start again — I can't argue with you — I am what I am."

"You've given the Devil a foothold in your ministry," she shouted.

Angela stirred and mumbled, "Don't hurt me, Paul darling; I don't want you to hurt me." She moaned a little but was soon snoring again.

Rita frowned and looked at him closely. "Is there something you're not telling me, Paul?"

Paul groaned in frustration. He was about to explain when the doorbell rang followed by an urgent pounding of someone's fist. He hurried to the hall and opened the door. Kevin Raymond burst in cursing and swearing. Paul tried to hold him back but Kevin thumped him on the jaw, knocking him sideways.

Fury flashing in his narrow beady eyes, the churchwarden held up a little gold cross hanging from a fragile chain. "I found this on the chancel steps. The last time I saw it was round Angela's neck. I'll bloody kill her!"

He barged into the sitting room, pushing aside Rita who was trying to stop him. "Get out of the way — you're nothing but a bloody witch."

When he saw his daughter lying prostrate on the couch, he stopped as if unsure what to do next.

Angela began moaning again, "Paul, don't hurt me." Suddenly, she rolled from under her coat and off the sofa. Still muttering his name, she lay on the floor completely naked — trickles of blood staining her thighs and a little blue gem twinkling in her belly button.

"What the hell?" bellowed Kevin, rounding on Paul.

Paul, still shaken by the earlier assault, felt a painful blow to his stomach and then to his chin. The room swam around him....

# Chapter thirteen

Out of a painful haze, Paul heard Nick's voice. "Take it easy, Paul, you've had a bit of a rough time."

Paul tried to focus his mind on what had happened to him. Nothing made sense. "Nick?"

"Yes. You've been unconscious. You'll be all right now."

A warm glow of assurance swept over him — Nick was with him. His eyes began to focus. He was in a side room of a hospital ward; the door was open and he could make out the nurses' station. "How long have I been here?" he asked, wincing with pain.

"You were brought in during the night. Rita Lee rang me at seven this morning to say you were here. I came over straight away. You won't remember — you were drifting in and out of consciousness. You've been asleep for the last six hours."

Paul tried to take in what Nick was telling him. "What time is it?"

"Half past three."

"Afternoon? Of course — stupid question. The Confirmations?" He wanted to say more but it was a painful effort.

"Everything went on fine. It was a beautiful holy occasion. No problems. People were concerned that you had been taken into hospital, and no doubt rumours abound, but the service went as planned."

Paul sighed with relief, "Thank God."

"Indeed, it was a greatly blessed occasion in every respect. Bishop Lionel prayed for your healing and also mentioned you, with considerable warmth, in his sermon. He popped in to see you but you were asleep and he had to get away — another service elsewhere." Nick's voice was soft and gentle — soothing to Paul's ears.

"Something terrible happened yesterday, Nick. I wanted to ring you but I knew Bishop Lionel was with you."

Nick patted his hand. "You can tell me later. They've done some tests and you're fine — very badly bruised and shaken, but nothing serious. I'm collecting you tomorrow and you're staying with us for the week. You need a bit of TLC."

Images were floating in Paul's mind. "Is Angela all right? Poor kid, it's my fault." His voice was wavering, and he felt almost detached from his body.

"Much better than you. They brought her in too. She was checked over and then Rita Lee took her home. Kevin Raymond spent the rest of the night in detention."

"What? But why?" It didn't cross Paul's mind that Kevin was the reason for him being in hospital.

"The police will be here soon to see if you want to charge him with assault. They also want a statement from you as to what happened to Angela. Kevin Raymond is claiming you raped her, but Rita Lee gives a totally different story. She understands the girl came back to the vicarage drunk and confused with most of her clothes stuffed into her bag. But Angela says she can't remember anything."

"That isn't the full story, Nick. I must tell you what happened. Poor kid, in a way, I'm to blame."

"I can't believe that," replied Nick with conviction. "For a start, she's not a child. Leave it for now, you can't think clearly. I'll tell the police sergeant that your mind is fuzzy at present and he can see you at my place tomorrow. You can't make statements that afterwards you might regret."

Paul sighed deeply. "Well, I'm certainly not going to charge Kevin with anything. In a way, I'm pleased he cares that much for Angela."

"Maybe, but I think there's more to it than that. Anyway, I'll tell the sergeant of your decision. For what it's worth, I think you have decided wisely."

Paul tried to ease himself up in the bed but a sudden pain shot up his body causing him to gasp. "I take it I was hit more than on my jaw and in my stomach. I'm glad I passed out before I received the blow down under."

Nick tried to help Paul into a more comfortable position. "You'll find bruises in other places too. It was damage to your head that kept you in here."

While Nick had his arm around him, Paul squeezed his hand. "Thanks for being here."

For the briefest of moments their eyes met and Paul felt that joy of an inner communion of love.

Nick sat back and looked at him with both concern and affection. "The service went very well this morning, so don't worry about that. I've brought you reserve bread and wine for us to take together. Would you like it now?"

Paul was about to reply when a nurse came in. "Nice to see you awake. I just want to check your pulse and blood pressure," she said in her cheerful friendly manner. "Do try to take plenty of liquids, Mr Stringer," she added, pouring him out a glass of water.

As she was on her way out, Nick asked her in his courteous pleasant way, "I would be most grateful if we could have a little privacy — say for fifteen minutes? We're about to have a short service of Communion."

The nurse beamed at him, "Certainly, Vicar. I'll close the door and stick a notice on to keep out intruders."

There was a small viewing window on the door; she closed the blind on her way out. Nick took out his Home Communion box and placed the contents on the bedside table. He took Paul's hand in his own. "The peace of the Lord be always with you," he said quietly.

Paul felt the warmth of Nick's love for him adding to the intimacy of the formal greeting. "And also with you," he answered softly.

Nick left him after the Communion; he had to get hold of Paul's diary and start sorting things out for the following two weeks.

Rita called to see Paul in the evening. She told him what had happened after Kevin Raymond attacked him.

"The thug started kicking you when you were down. So I gave him a touch of his own medicine with the toe of my shoe." She swung her crossed leg up so that Paul could get a glimpse of the deadly pointed weapon.

He groaned in painful empathy, "Ouch!"

"It stunned him enough for me to ring for an ambulance — they sent a police car too. Kevin had calmed down before they arrived. I think he was really scared at the way he'd lost his temper. He sat weeping while I took care of you."

Paul listened, amazed at what he was hearing. "What can I say, Rita? I might have been seriously injured if you hadn't intervened. I'm very grateful."

She leaned over in her chair and took his hand in hers. "Paul, can't you see that God prompted you to call me last night. I think you regretted having done so, but an unseen power guided you — you must believe that. And believe what I tell you about other things too," she added pointedly.

Paul sighed. He was too tired to argue. "I'll give it some thought."

"I'll just tell you what I said to the police and then I'll go — you need to rest."

When she reached the end of the tale, she said, "The young policewoman checked over the house to make sure it was locked securely before they left. She saw your things soaking in the sink and asked me if I knew how blood got on your shirt. They had already noted the blood on your trousers and the scratch on your jaw."

"Angela will soon put them right," Paul said confidently. "I take it she's okay now?"

"She says she doesn't remember what happened," Rita said frowning. "She's probably too ashamed to tell the truth. But we know she was blotto during later events. At least, she isn't making any allegations."

"That's okay then. I can sleep easy knowing I'm not a rapist." He gave Rita a weak smile.

"No joke, Paul. They haven't discounted the allegation Kevin was making — that you'd raped Angela in the church. He pointed them to the bag with the bloodied altar cloth and bottles, which you'd left in your hall, and to the cross he'd found which placed Angela at the scene. But of course, clearing up the mess fits with the story I gave them anyway; only the scratch on your face is causing them to take Kevin's allegations seriously."

Paul gave a deep sigh. "Oh, dear. Well I can't say what led up to that sorry incident. And I'd rather not have to bring Mark into it. If he tells the story he told me, it would ruin Angela. As long as she isn't making allegations, I don't see a problem."

"She was bloody, and she's quite bruised in a number of places," Rita told him. "They also noticed her torn fingernail with what might have been skin underneath. But I guess it's up to her whether anything goes further. That is, unless Kevin wants to try getting you into trouble with the Church."

Paul smiled wryly. "Kevin's out to get me one way or another.

But since I am innocent of what happened to Angela in the church, I can't be charged with anything. I think my reputation is strong enough to take any flack. Let's hope so."

Rita kissed his cheek. "You have the truth and God on your side, Paul. I'll leave you now. Canon Palmer said you're staying at Glenton rectory for a week. Nice of them to take in a wounded soldier."

She put her hand on his head, closed her eyes and said a prayer for his healing of body, mind and spirit. Afterwards, she looked at him with love unashamedly beaming from her eyes. "See you when you get back then."

He watched her leave, giving her a smile and a wave as she turned to say a farewell. He breathed a sigh of relief; she hadn't brought up his so-called 'deceiving spirit' — thank goodness! The only thing holding him back from discussing the Christian Healing Ministry with the Parochial Church Councils was Rita's attitude to the dark forces of evil. He didn't want Rita spreading her ideas of demonic influences — the whole area would be awash with hysterical sightings!

Gingerly walking around Nick's garden a few days later, Paul revelled in the autumnal golden sunshine; it somehow took the sting out of his painful predicament. There was something very peaceful about a wall-enclosed old rectory garden. Death and decay somehow had meaning as the whole cycle of life followed its natural course. In a corner, nature's gardeners were transforming rotting apples and pears, dead plants, grass cuttings and leaves into food for Lucy's lovingly tended borders. The ancient deciduous trees, and the high stone walls supporting a variety of espalier fruit trees, roses, clematis, jasmine, honeysuckle, pyracantha, and a magnificent ancient wisteria that arched over the high garden gate, provided a haven for the many birds that nested, fed and sang in happy harmony with man.

"Hi, Paul," Lucy shouted from the kitchen door. "You have a visitor."

Paul waved and said he'd come inside. But his visitor came outside to meet him. It was Rita, looking attractive as ever, in an outfit of rich golds and browns. A multicoloured skirt reached down to her fitted tawny high-heeled boots, and the billowing sleeves of her matching blouse were drawn into neatly buttoned deep cuffs. A suede jerkin hugged her full breasts and slender waist. She looked truly elegant. Her rich brown hair lifted and bounced as she walked towards him. Her sparkling hazel eyes smiled in harmony with her lips. She looked incredibly young for her age. She kissed him on his cheek.

"How are you, Paul? You're certainly looking very much better."

"You're looking pretty good yourself. I like the colours. You blend in with the garden — watch out for birds!" Paul smiled at his little joke.

She smiled with him. "Thanks; I'll do my best. Shall we go inside or would you rather go on with the exercise?"

"I've had enough. Anyway, Lucy will be making coffee. We'll go in to save her bringing it out." He was more concerned that she would want to deliver him again.

"It is important I have a word in private, Paul. I don't expect Canon Palmer and Lucy know about — you know." She refrained from saying what, but Paul was in no doubt that it was his sexuality.

"There's nothing to discuss on that subject, Rita. Sorry, but I'm not in the mood for it."

She sighed. "Don't you think this awful mess should be convincing you of something?"

They were almost at the back door. "Yes — not to trust women!"

Lucy was at the door. "That's nice to know," she said, feigning offence. "Well, at least you can trust the coffee will be good — Nick's made it!"

A few minutes later the four of them were discussing Angela and her convenient loss of memory.

Rita told them, "She's not making any charges, but not admitting the truth is harmful enough. The whole parish is gossiping about what happened at the vicarage, and speculating on the cause. Angela is not saying why she was taken to hospital. I've had a word with her but she sticks to the amnesia story."

"Perhaps the best thing to do in the circumstances," said Nick, sitting back and looking relaxed about it all. "Everyone knows what a temper Kevin Raymond has. It wouldn't take much for him to KO the vicar. He may not have done it to the last one, but his constant bickering was a factor in Jim Smithson's breakdown. If Paul is stalwart about what happened, it will all blow over and Angela won't get hurt."

Lucy rose from her chair. "Sorry, but I must leave you. I have to be at the nursing home in ten minutes. Nice to have seen you, Rita. I'll phone you later. I'm taking the service at St Michael's and we need to discuss hymns."

Rita gave Lucy a broad smile. "Right. Look forward to having you with us."

"Lucy must be quite an asset to you, Canon Palmer," said Rita, as the front door was heard closing. "Wife and curate — quite a combination. Personally, I think all vicars should be married. Handsome single men cause a lot of speculation."

"I dare say, ugly elderly ones do too," laughed Nick. "I suppose you have in mind this business with Angela. But you know, Miss Lee, married clergy can still be the object of gossip. There are plenty of bawdy jokes about vicars and bishops. Of course we're expected to live virtuous lives — that's why clergy satire can be so funny. But we are all human and have our temptations and failings. It's illogical to expect perfection, even supposing there could ever be a consensus of what constituted the ideal vicar."

"But what do you think about practising homosexual priests?" Rita asked casually.

Paul felt distinctly uncomfortable. Had Rita guessed Nick was his partner?

"Ah, now there is an opener for a good joke I heard," said Nick, smiling at his thoughts. "But to give you a serious answer: a man's sexuality is his own affair, as long he doesn't bring the Church into disrepute by licentious living. That surely applies to all relationships."

"Maybe, but I think Scripture has something more to say on the subject," she persisted.

Nick said affably, "If you want to argue Biblical interpretation to prove a point, I can give you a small book I wrote on the subject. I haven't time to discuss it now — I'm due to preside at Communion in fifteen minutes and must be off." He rose to go. "I have a bereavement visit afterwards so I won't be back for a while. But do stay and talk to Paul — he knows my views."

When he had left the room, Rita said, "What a lovely man. You know I overheard at the last Diocesan Synod that he's in line for suffragan bishop — but you must know that yourself."

Paul had heard rumours but that was nothing new; Nick had said nothing to him about preferment and that's what mattered. "It's always a possibility," he told her casually. "Nick has considerable experience; he's academically brilliant and a good pastor. He has a doctorate; he's been a college lecturer and chaplain, and found time to write a couple of books. For a man in his early forties, he has a lot of responsibility in this diocese. What's more, he holds similar views to the incoming Archbishop."

"Mm — not everyone's happy about that appointment, and I'm not sure a pro-gay bishop is Biblically sound," Rita said frowning. "But the Palmers would be greatly missed if they left here."

Paul wanted to get off the subject. He asked her something that was puzzling him. "Shouldn't you be at school?"

"I have a free period — I can make up the time later. I'll let you know what's been happening and then get back." She looked at him with great concern. "Do pray about your healing, Paul. I'm not sure it's good for you to be close friends of Nick and Lucy with their liberal views on such an important matter. Do they know you're gay?"

"You heard what Nick said. He's hardly likely to ask me if I'm gay. What people may suspect I can do nothing about. But understand, Rita, if I ever marry, it won't be to a woman."

"Gay marriages may go on over the Atlantic but they'll never happen here," she said adamantly. "You have to face it, Paul, your relationship to this man will never be sanctified by the Church, or recognised in law in the same way as marriage is. You are living a promiscuous lie, and we've seen what it leads to."

"Please stop this, Rita. You simply don't understand how I feel. You say you love me — can't you accept that I love someone too?"

She looked at him, hazel eyes shining with tears she was trying to hold back. "It's because I love you that I can't give you over to self destruction. I don't know who your partner is, but I pray for him just as much as I do you. I only hope he isn't a priest or some other servant of the Church."

Paul was determined to give nothing away. "If you're fishing, you'll go home without a catch."

Rita stood up and walked over to him, a mixture of love and frustration showing on her face. She went down on her knees and touched his arm. "I'd do anything to stop this folly — I can't give up. God loves you, Paul and he's given me this overwhelming love for you too. There must be a purpose behind it." She bent forward and lightly kissed his bruised face.

Feeling pity, he turned to look into her eyes — now freely shedding tears. He whispered, "Give me up, Rita. You're fighting a losing battle. Don't destroy the affection I have for you; it's bound to happen if you keep going on."

She moved forward and kissed him on the lips. Paul did nothing to stop her but neither did he give anything in return. She rose from her knees and took off her glasses, drying them on a hanky.

"I'll go now. I'm pleased to see you looking better." She picked up her bag and hurried out of the room, leaving Paul to breathe a sigh of relief.

Tired from his morning's efforts, Paul closed his eyes and rested. He came out of a light slumber to hear Lucy's voice in the hall.

"It's okay, Paul's having a sleep. We'll go up to my study. Nick won't be back for a while, but I don't want you late for work."

"I won't be missed — flexi hours remember? So let's get flexing!" It was Tony Mayhew with Lucy.

So they were still in a relationship. Paul supposed Lucy wasn't terribly concerned at his presence in the house since he already knew about them. But was Nick still in ignorance? He felt very uncomfortable about the situation. He was colluding with the lovers in keeping Nick in the dark. He determined not to let it go on.

Nick came home at one. "Did I see Tony's car leaving the drive," he called to Lucy who was busy in the kitchen. "Is he all right for the service at Bradmire on Sunday?"

"Yes," said Lucy, meeting Nick in the hall to greet him with a hug. "We've been talking about it. Since he's at St Matthew's in the morning, he's going to use the same readings so he can preach the same sermon."

"Fine by me," Nick told her. He came through the open doorway to see Paul. Their eyes met in warm greeting. "How's the invalid?"

"All the better for seeing you."

Nick sat down next to Paul. "Mmm. Can't say the bruises do

much to improve your appearance but I can live with it for a while. But how's your bruised ego after Rita's visit?"

"It's something I have to live with. You know, Nick, I never realised the emotional battles gay clergy face when I was busy telling them to live a monk's life. I guess you can't get into other people's shoes when your egoistic foot's too big!"

Nick laughed. "How true. But it applies to many things in life."

"You had a number of phone calls. Most of them are on the answerphone but since I was passing by the phone when it rang, I took one message. Roger Drayton wants you to ring him. Sam Curry's funeral's next Monday. I'd be happy to take it, Nick."

"No, definitely not. I want you to keep your head down for a while. Apart from my concern about you, we have to think of those you minister to. They don't want speculations going on about their minister at such sensitive moments in their own lives. We can wait until most of the bruising has gone and everything is back to normal. That is, if anything can ever be considered normal in Church ministry."

Paul could see his point. "Of course, you're quite right," he said humbly.

Lucy called from the kitchen. "Come and get it."

Nick gave Paul a hand out of his chair. "I feel for you. Must still be very painful."

"I deliberately provoked him just to get a holiday here!" Paul laughed — then winced as a sudden pain shot through his body.

They all sat down at the kitchen table with its pretty blue-flowered cloth.

"Just a quick meal today — cheese on toast. Been too busy to cook. We'll dine tonight after prayers," Lucy told them.

Nick said grace, and then spoke to his wife. "You have extra work with Paul being here; I'll cook tonight. Paul will be glad to do the preparations while we two are busy. I'll finish off when we get back." He smiled at their guest. "All right with you?"

Paul nodded; he loved being part of Nick's household. Even so, he felt entwined in Lucy's deception and it was hard to live with.

"How's Tony getting on since his wife left him?" Paul asked, looking directly at Lucy.

"Actually, it was the other way around — Jane threw him out.

She's claiming the house, furniture — the lot. He's living in a caravan at present until everything's been settled."

"Of course, Jane did put a lot into their home. It was originally her father's wasn't it?" Nick said.

"Maybe, but he's had to cough up for all the changes she's made. She's treated him terrible — kept him at arm's length for ages."

"You seem to be on very personal terms with Tony," Nick remarked.

"Oh, I guess people talk to me. It must be my pretty face and big ears," she laughed, throwing a quick glance at Paul.

Nick smiled. "Pretty face maybe, but no one could call you Big Ears, my love."

Lucy rose from the table. "Coffee and fruit cake?"

The phone rang. Lucy went to answer it. As soon as she returned it rang again. "This one's for you, Nick," she called from the hall.

While Nick was out of the kitchen, she whispered to Paul, "Please say nothing to Nick. He's enough to worry about. Don't you think our lives are complicated enough? Nick needs a wife. I have no intention of leaving him. I love him too, you know."

Nick was soon back. "Another meeting to go to. Certain members of the Board are not happy with my views on selection and want further discussions. I think some folk have got the wind up over the choice for our next Archbishop."

The following Tuesday, Paul returned to his vicarage to begin a gradual take-up of his duties. Ladies called with cakes and goodies and Mrs Cranford had left him a bottle of home-made wine. Messages, mostly of sympathy and concern, were waiting for him. But there were others not so nice. One told him that brawling with a churchwarden was not consistent with a minister of religion and he should resign. Another told him that he should marry the girl whose reputation he'd ruined. Others informed him that promiscuous behaviour was unacceptable and that he should either get married or leave the priesthood. He had no doubt similar things were being said behind his back.

On Wednesday evening, Angela came to see him. He wasn't surprised and he'd already been going over in his mind what he should say to her. Wanting to steer clear of the sitting room, kitchen or anywhere remotely intimate, he took her into his study and offered her the chair opposite his.

"I'm sorry for being a pain," she said with tears in her eyes. "I didn't mean for you to get hurt, and my dad to get into trouble."

"Just tell me one thing, Angela — why did you desecrate the altar?" Paul asked her gently. "Everything else is easily forgiven but that is something I just cannot understand. Apart from the sacrilege, if what happened ever got out, there would be a dreadful stink and your reputation would be in tatters. Bad enough that some folk, especially your father, think I've raped you, and that orgies have been going on in the vicarage."

She broke into tears. Paul offered her some tissues from a box he now kept on his desk. As much as he would like to put an arm around her, he intended keeping the desk between them. He waited for her to compose herself.

"I don't know what you're talking about," she said. "I can only remember having fish and chips and waking up in hospital. Soon after I got home, Dad came back from the police station demanding to know what had happened in the church. I told him I didn't know what he was talking about — and I still don't know."

Paul sighed deeply. Had she got drunk while in a state of denial over her attempt to seduce him? There were several options over what could have happened and he was no psychiatrist. Of course, Angela could be a fine actress playing the part of the innocent raped virgin. He would have to see Mark and get him to repeat his story. Perhaps if he did so in front of Angela, they could get at the truth. But then, if Angela genuinely couldn't remember what had happened, Mark could say anything. The only thing Paul knew for certain was that the couple were having sex on the altar.

"Angela, we must try to get things straight. Apart from Rita, I haven't told anyone about seeing you and Mark in the church. I brought you here that night because you were in no fit state to go home. Your father seems to think I seduced you." Paul saw no reason to give the full story until Angela came clean about it.

"I don't know anything about the church. Miss Lee's told everyone that I turned up at your door — drunk and incapable."

He handed her more tissues. "I think that's a story worth sticking to, at least, until you get your memory back."

Angela didn't say anything; she was too busy mopping up her

tears.

"How are you, Angela? You were in a sorry state the last time I saw you."

"I was found here with nothing on. You must know everything that happened to me," she muttered dolefully.

Acting or not, he felt nothing but deep compassion for her. Had it not been for his rejection of her, she wouldn't be sitting there feeling utter humiliation.

"Yes. I went to the church because the light was on. I saw you there. I could hardly leave you alone in that state. I brought you here and sent for Miss Lee to look after you."

"Thank you," she whispered. "The bruises have gone now."

He passed her the box of tissues so she could help herself. "But you are still hurting inside — I can see that for myself."

After a few moments she said, "Can I still work for you? It's very important to me."

"I really don't think I can let you do that, Angela. Your father would be angry, and after what happened that night — you know — after the fish and chips, you may not feel comfortable."

She looked up at him with red-rimmed eyes, her brow puckered with puzzlement. "I don't understand. What happened after the fish and chips? Was I sick? I don't understand anything. Dad says I'd been in the church because he found my cross there. But I was in the vicarage when he knocked you out. You say you found me in the church, but Miss Lee says I turned up on your doorstep. Is Miss Lee lying?"

Paul thought hard before answering. "We want to protect you, Angela. Getting drunk is common enough these days, but even your father wouldn't want it getting around that it happened in the church. Questions about why you were taken to hospital don't necessarily have to be answered, after all, the ambulance was here already."

"Dad says I've been raped."

"Yes, I know — all too well actually. Certainly you were bruised and bleeding — so Miss Lee told me," he quickly added to spare her blushes. "Your father doesn't know that Mark was in the church with you, and he's only guessing you were there because of finding the cross."

"You saw me with Mark in the church? Have you asked Mark about it?"

Paul could see written over Angela's face, 'what did Paul see us doing?'

"Yes. But I've said nothing about Mark to your dad. I was unhappy about what Mark told me."

Her cheeks flushed. "He probably told you a pack of lies."

"Well, perhaps we'd better ask him together." Paul reached for the telephone. "Would you like me to ring him up and see if he would come down?"

She quickly shook her head. "No!"

Paul thought he'd try a different approach. "Are you still engaged to Mark? Since it seems you've consummated your relationship with him, I hope so."

Obviously embarrassed, she looked down at her left hand with its ringed finger. "He's probably told you something I told him about my mother ages ago, and then said it was what we were doing. But I don't remember anything that happened after the fish and chips."

Paul smiled. She was still sticking to her story. "I won't say what Mark told me because he isn't here to defend himself, apart from which, it's for him to say, not for me to repeat."

"Well, you know what Dad said about me not being his daughter? Mum told me something a little while afterwards. She said, that one morning, she lay down in front of the altar and offered herself to God. Then she prayed for a baby. The vicar prayed over her. She said there was music and singing played on a tape. Everything was beautiful. A stream of sunlight came through the stained glass window and touched her face. She was taken up in a kind of rapture. She had never known such joy — well, that's what she said. It lasted for ages and when she opened her eyes again, she just knew her prayer would be answered. I was her miracle baby. That's why I'm called Angela."

Of course, Paul knew about the so-called miracle baby but it was interesting to hear the story as told to Angela. No wonder Kevin was suspicious. So what was Angela trying to tell him about her lost Saturday evening?

"Are you telling me that Mark might have thought you wanted to pray in the church for some kind of miracle, and that he took advantage of you while you were under the influence of drink?"

"It's a possibility isn't it? Of course, if I'd had too much to drink I might well have cooperated — people do don't they?"

"I dare say it's possible," he agreed, admiring her astuteness.

"So is it okay to go on working for you? I wouldn't want people to think my father was right. If things go on as normal, they'll know what Miss Lee says is true. You were helping me like the Good Samaritan; only you were the one that got beaten up for your efforts. Dad won't do it again. He cried you know. He always does after he loses his temper and does something bad."

Paul thought she was being very wily. "You've made out a good case, Angela, but I need to think about it."

"I won't let you down. I do a good job — you said so."

Some of the things she said did make sense, and there was no doubt that he would be lost without her, but could he trust her not to come on to him again? Since she was denying any knowledge of what happened, he could hardly ask her to refrain from making sexual advances.

After a moment or two, he said to her solemnly, "It would be very unwise for you to do anything but admin from now on. I just can't risk being accused of more hanky-panky. Do I make myself clear, Angela?"

"You just want me to do the typing and so on. That's all I want to do. It's good experience. Working for you got me my present job, but I want to go on to be a PA. You can trust me to be discreet; business relationships are founded on trust."

Obviously, she was on his wavelength. "Okay, Angela, we'll see how it goes. But no more drinking; at least in the vicinity of the church and vicarage."

Her face lit up like a ray of sunshine. "Thank you, Mr Stringer," she said in her best secretarial voice. "You'll see, I'll do a good job, and I'll keep our relationship formal from now on."

He gave her a big smile. "It's quite ridiculous really; I should be thanking you, not you me. Yet here you are pleading to work for nothing. I guess it's the same for all lay people. You work to keep yourselves in house and home, and then give your time and talents freely to the Church — plus your hard-earned cash to run it! Bless you, Angela — you're a good lass."

# Chapter fourteen

It was a magnificent autumn morning; mist was rising from the damp grass in the sun's early rays. In the vicarage orchard, Paul, wearing his new chunky grey jumper knitted by his mother, sat on the child's swing and casually rocked backwards and forwards, thinking about the last three weeks since the incident at the vicarage. He smiled, acknowledging that the pain had been worthwhile just for that week in Glenton rectory. Being his day off, he would soon be seeing Nick and just thinking about it made him feel good. It was a bit of a solitary life at his vicarage but it made his times with Nick all the sweeter.

Was Nick any the better for sharing his home with a wife? At the moment without a doubt, but he knew that Nick suspected Lucy of having an affair with Tony. He'd mentioned it briefly to him while he was staying at the rectory.

"I've seen the way they look at each other. And I've seen the way you react when Tony comes — you know something I don't. But I won't ask, Lucy must tell me herself." He changed the subject and had not mentioned it again.

Paul stopped his gentle swinging. He thought he'd heard a car arriving at the church. His thoughts changed to Kevin Raymond. Things had settled down after the initial speculation and rumour. He'd found Kevin alone in the church and, taking the opportunity to tell him that he was forgiven, had said that he was prepared to let bygones be bygones. The churchwarden had snorted and mumbled something incomprehensible. After being informed that Angela still wanted to help with the administration, and that he had no intention of refusing her offering, Kevin had snorted even louder and walked off muttering, "She does what she bloody-well likes."

A loud raucous voice broke into his thoughts.

"Here you are, skulking in the bloody garden!"

A familiar saying, 'Speak of the Devil and he's bound to turn up', came into Paul's mind. He looked up at his churchwarden. "My day off, Kevin. Is it really important?"

"You might bloody-well think so when you know what I have to tell you," he replied triumphantly.

Paul continued gently swinging, determined not to let his

adversary spoil his day. He smiled pleasantly at Kevin. "Oh, really? You'd better tell me then before I die of curiosity."

The churchwarden looked as if he were about to burst a blood vessel. "Get off that bloody swing! This is serious."

Paul refused to be intimidated. He said amiably, "Better come inside and I'll make us some coffee."

"Forget the bloody coffee, what I have to say can be said here."

Paul stood up. Making sure he was out of reach of Kevin's fists, he leaned against the apple tree that held the swing. "Okay, what's the problem?"

Kevin smirked. "Bob Desmond is back from his holiday."

"Bob Desmond? One of my neighbours from up the lane? I didn't know he'd been away — should I?"

Kevin stood his full height — a few inches past Paul's shoulder. But what he lacked in height was made up by a huge surge of self-confidence. With a look of utter triumph, he declared slowly, relishing every word, "The night my Angela was raped, he was taking his dog a walk."

Paul was puzzled. He didn't like the way Kevin was behaving — he hadn't even sworn during the last two sentences. Surely the whole thing wasn't going to blow up again? "If Angela was indeed raped. So, what does Bob's dog have to do with it?"

Kevin, dressed as usual in his dark suit and white shirt, grinned and puffed out his chest, obviously intending to make the most of his punch line. "He saw you humping a large bundle out of church, not long before midnight."

Paul was beginning to feel sick inside. "A bundle?" he asked warily. "Oh, you mean the bag with the altar cloth and rubbish." He looked at Kevin with concern. "I hope you haven't told him what we found, especially what you picked up later on; Angela could have dropped that cross any time after she showed it to you. I wouldn't want her to be the subject of unsubstantiated rumours."

"I bet you bloody don't, you smarmy devil. Call yourself a man of God?" For a moment he looked as if he were about to resume his bombastic approach but he checked himself. A broad grin appeared on his face. "He saw you before we cleaned up the church."

"Really? If I remember right, it was a dark night and he could have seen anything or anybody. Since it's taken him so long to say anything, how can he be sure of when, what or whom, he saw?"

"It was just before he went off in his caravan — they were travelling overnight."

"Oh, really?"

"Yes, really! He saw you struggling to close the door after you came out of the church. He nearly offered to help, but he heard the door slam and knew you'd managed. That's how Angela got back to the vicarage. She turned up at your door all right — over your bloody shoulder!"

Paul looked at his grinning churchwarden; there was something about his appearance and behaviour that made him think Rita might be right about demonic influences.

"All right. So I saw the light on, went to investigate and found her in the church. For her own good, I thought it best to bring her here until she sobered up and could tell us what happened."

"A feeble excuse. You could have brought her home."

"And have you bully her? I've seen what you do to your womenfolk," Paul responded, ready to dodge if Kevin reacted belligerently.

Kevin's face became contorted. "After what I heard Angela say, who are you to bloody-well talk? Angela didn't rape herself — you bloody swine!"

"There was someone else in the church with Angela. The man ran off when he saw me."

"A likely bloody story," Kevin scoffed.

"Angela had the key. When she's able to remember, she'll be able to say who was with her. Your daughter is well past the age of consent you know. As to how the altar got messed up, perhaps the man cut his finger on a bottle or something."

Kevin laughed derisively. "And pigs might bloody-well fly! You were doing some sort of bloody ritual."

"A bit far-fetched, don't you think?"

"Far-fetched? Like Angela being a miracle baby?" Kevin's fists clenched into hard balls.

Paul automatically flinched — memories of being thumped raw in his mind. "Let's keep ourselves calm," he said composedly, opening his hands so as to show he bore no ill will. "There's probably a simple explanation. Before long, Angela will recall what happened. Until then, we mustn't jump to conclusions."

"You've got her where you bloody-well want her. She won't snitch on you, but I bloody will. I'll give you a choice; either you resign from this parish and the priesthood quietly, or I'll inform the bishop."

"Of what? Looking after a nineteen year old, when she was drunk and incapable?"

"I'll give him all the facts and tell him how you're in league with that witch, Rita Lee, performing hocus-pocus, and God knows what else, in the church."

"Miss Lee is a respectable, highly thought of teacher — be careful what you say about her," Paul certainly didn't want Rita associated with the altar desecration — some people might be inclined to believe it!

"Huh! It's time the bishop knew about the goings on here Bloody drug dealers touting at Penningly church hall when the kids are there. You both encourage youngsters to drive themselves silly with all that bloody rock stuff. I've heard what they get up to at closing time — nothing but drink and bloody sex. What with women forever in the vicarage, you're sex mad and a bloody disgrace."

"Frankly, Mr Raymond, I don't give a toss what you tell the bishop. You must do what you think is right, after all, it's your Christian duty."

"Don't think I'm bluffing. If the bishop fails to act, I'll make sure the whole bloody parish knows what you did. You'll get in the tabloids and your bloody life will be intolerable." He smiled in triumph at his trump card.

"You really must be careful, there are laws against slander and libel you know," Paul said calmly, even though his guts were tying themselves into intricate knots.

"You know as well as I bloody do, it doesn't take much to set a forest fire ablaze — just a dropped fag-end will do it. There are enough facts in this business to cause a fire that will burn for bloody months. Your ministry will be intolerable — I'll make bloody sure of it."

"No doubt," Paul said, anger beginning to show in his voice. "But are you willing for Angela to be dragged through the mud too? I knew you could be cruel but that's sinking to an all time low — even for you."

"She deserves what she bloody gets. She damn well knows what happened all right. She just wants to bloody protect you. You've got her where you bloody want her. You've corrupted an angel — she's nothing but a bloody slut!"

Kevin marched off. Before he left the garden, he turned and bellowed, "You've had your bloody warning. I'll give you to the end of the week to bloody resign. I'm getting the evidence together. Even if you're only tried by the media, your bloody life won't be worth living!"

Paul was shattered. He could but ride out the storm, but he couldn't allow the likes of Kevin Raymond to rule his life. Clearly, he would have to talk to Mark. That he had sex with his fiancée wouldn't lift an eyebrow, but what actually happened in the church should be kept quiet. If he could get Mark to admit his guilt, and apologise for drinking in the church and messing up the altar, perhaps Kevin would drop his vendetta. Would Mark insist on blaming Angela? Possibly not. It wouldn't make any difference to him anyway, he would still be guilty and blaming Angela would only make things worse.

Paul returned inside the vicarage and rang Mark's mother. When he asked her if she would ask Mark to ring him, she said that he was at home. "He's working shifts. He goes in this afternoon. I'll get him."

Mark came on the line. "If you think I'm going to repeat what I said to you, forget it. Shit! Angela's dad would kill me. It was her own fault anyway. She got what she asked for. Angela says her dad thinks you raped her — tough!" He went off line, leaving Paul with only one option. He would have to get Angela to confess to her father that she was with Mark that evening — as much for her own good as for his.

He was about to go out before he had more visitors, when the phone rang. It was Rita.

"I'm on playground duty, so I'll have to be quick. I wanted to warn you that the Desmonds, just up the lane from you, are back from holiday. Their daughter, who's in our dance group, is at this school. She's just told me that her dad saw you carrying a large bundle out of the church — you know when. She says she doesn't know what it's about but her dad told the churchwarden and she thinks they're plotting something."

Paul sighed heavily. It would soon spread around the parish. He could hear the scandalmongers: "Weird goings on at the church, the night the churchwarden knocked out the vicar. Angela was taken to hospital and do you know...."

"Thanks, Rita," he said, trying to sound nonchalant about it. "Kevin's been round already. He's given me an ultimatum. I can't tell you about it over the phone. I'll see you sometime."

"Are you in tonight?" Her tone was urgent. "This is very important, Paul — I must see you."

"Okay. I'll come back for seven. But I'll be out again an hour later."

"To see your lover?" She sounded bitter. "Sorry, Paul; but this is what it's all about you know. Satan looks for a way in. Once you —"

He stopped her. "You're making assumptions again. I so happen to be seeing Nick Palmer. Since he's the rural dean as well as our team rector, I want his advice. If you just want to nag me, Rita, then forget it. I've got enough to cope with at present."

"I'm sorry," she said, sounding genuinely contrite. "But since I was at the vicarage that night, I think we should get our facts straight and be clear as to what happened, just in case things get nasty."

"They already are. I'll tell you about it," he answered more amiably. "See you at seven then."

He didn't particularly want to see Rita but it was as well to find out what was being said in the school playground. He looked out of his window; dark clouds had spread gloom over the garden, matching his own mood. But he would soon be seeing Nick for lunch and then off with him for a three hour drive and walk. He began to smile again. Rain or shine, out in the open air or in his Discovery, problems would melt away. Wise, dependable, staunch, steadfast — Nick wasn't just his lover, he was his support and comforter.

He put on his answerphone, locked his door, threw his walking togs into his car and was about to leave when a car drew up — it was Lucy.

"Hi, Paul," she called as she stepped out of her car. "I'm glad I've caught you."

"Hello, Lucy, nice to see you. Come in and have a coffee."

Inside the vicarage, he put an arm around her and guided her to the kitchen. His cleaner wasn't due for a couple of days and the place was a mess. He put the kettle on while Lucy dried a couple of mugs from the draining basket. She seemed nervous. After nearly dropping one of the mugs, she accidentally poured milk over the table. While she was muttering her apologies, Paul sat her down in a chair by the stove. He mopped up the milk and made their drinks.

He sat himself in front of her. Taking hold of her hands, he tried to look into her eyes, but she kept them lowered. He said tenderly, "What's the matter, Lucy? You didn't come here because you've run out of tea."

"Nick doesn't know I'm here. But I think it right that you should know what's happening." She bit her lip and turned her eyes away from him again. "Bishop Lionel wants him to be the new suffragan bishop when Harold retires."

It wasn't entirely unexpected but why was Lucy and not Nick telling him? She answered his question for him.

"He told Bishop Lionel that he will give it earnest prayer, but I know he's going to refuse it. You can't let him do it, Paul. He's right for the job."

"I agree with you there, but it has to be his decision."

She held on to his hands and looked at him, her face wrinkled with anxiety. "It's because of you that he's rejecting it — no other reason; not because he thinks he can't do it or that he'll make a bad bishop."

"I would never stop him from answering a call, Nick knows that," Paul told her. It was something he'd often thought about but had never been able to plan for.

"Make him see sense, Paul, that's all I ask. Nick works hard and deserves preferment. He'll make an excellent bishop."

Paul had to agree on all points, but how would it affect Lucy? He said, "I can see the possibility of my keeping up a relationship with Nick but what about you and Tony?"

"Tony loves me and wants to marry me and start a family, but it's quite impossible. I'll do nothing to hinder Nick."

"Perhaps that's why Nick wants to stay as he is. He loves you enough to want you to be happy and fulfilled — to let you go and marry Tony."

"Nick knows nothing about me and Tony," she said adamantly.

"I think you'll find he knows more than you think."

"Has he told you something?"

"He's hinted, that's all. Perhaps it's time you told him. Knowing Nick, he won't stand in your way to happiness."

She burst into tears. Producing a hanky from a pocket, she dried her eyes and regained control of her emotions. "But he's the one I really love. Who could not help but love Nick? I've always loved him, but I couldn't tell him so, he would never have married me. I hoped he would learn to love me and want me — you know — as a woman." She sniffed away a tear. "But he never has. Now he has you, he never will."

Paul squeezed her hand. "He couldn't anyway, Lucy. He's like me. It's the way we are. He's very fond of you — you know that for yourself. I dare say he could give you children but he can't love you as a man loves a woman."

"I know. You see, I feel Tony's need to have sex with me; I've never felt that with Nick. Nick's never touched me, and I've never asked him to. I admit I enjoy sex with Tony, but all the time I think of Nick. Neither of them must ever know. Promise me, Paul, you'll not tell Nick. Our relationship would never be the same."

Paul thought what a tangled mess of emotions Lucy had got herself into. He took both her hands in his. "I'll talk to Nick and tell him I heard on the grapevine about the bishopric being offered to him. I'll leave it to him to discuss it."

Over lunch at the rectory, Paul told Nick and Lucy about his confrontation with his churchwarden. He concluded, "I only hope Angela will confess to being in the church and that it wasn't with me."

"Now that Kevin Raymond has a witness placing you at the scene of the alleged crime, the matter could become quite serious," Nick said. He stroked his fingers over his forehead as though trying to release an answer to the problem. "Yes, you're right about Angela. Do you really think she's faking memory loss?"

"Well, I'm certain she wants me to think she has. I must admit I was angry with her for coming on to me when I was asleep. But that bit I'd prefer to forget too. All I want is for her to say I had nothing to do with her losing her virginity."

Lucy said, "If she was drunk at the time, she could only assume you weren't there. It's just as well no one was around to overhear Mark being called Paul."

"Unfortunately, after bringing her back to the vicarage, Kevin heard her saying my name and pleading not to be hurt. It's a mess!" He sighed deeply. "I guess I shouldn't have taken her on again."

"The fact that you did surely shows you have nothing to hide. But the girl is obviously infatuated with you; let's hope she sees sense. As I told you before, when angels lie, all hell is let loose."

Paul was thinking that according to Rita, he'd released the demons himself — the day Nick became his lover!

Once out in the open air, walking deserted footpaths that took them over hills, across fields and through woodland, Paul was again at peace with himself. The rain had cleared and pale sun was breaking through the thinning cloud. They wrapped their arms around each other and kissed under the conifers. Disturbed by a noise above them, they laughed at a squirrel watching them from high in a tree. Looking once more into each other's eyes, they declared their mutual love.

There was so much they wanted to do, and could have done, but they didn't have long for intimacy. Nick had to get back; he had a meeting early evening. Paul was seeing Rita and then returning to the rectory to stay the night. There was plenty of time ahead for them to be alone and make love unhurriedly. Being with Nick for the afternoon, driving and walking, was a thoroughly pleasant build up. But there was far more to their relationship than sexual desire — they enjoyed being in each other's company. There was no doubt about it; Nick made him feel a whole person. And he knew Nick felt the same way about him.

Driving back to the rectory, Paul brought up the subject of Bishop Harold's retirement and of the rumours that were circulating. "Is it true? Are we going to have to call you Bishop Nicholas?"

"Actually, I was going to tell you tonight; I want to include Lucy in the discussion. I don't think I'm meant to take it. A bishop should be beyond reproach. As it is, it's difficult enough for us to keep us in touch without revealing our true relationship. But it's Lucy I'm really concerned about."

"In what way?"

"Tony came to see me. He shouldn't have done so without Lucy knowing but he had to get it off his chest. He wants to marry Lucy. I can understand that. They should be free to live together as man and wife with a clear conscience, and start a family they both want."

"How do you feel about it?" Paul asked him with concern.

"I saw it coming. Of course, there will have to be a divorce. Easier for everyone to turn down preferment, at least for a few years until everything settles. I'll not stand in the way of Lucy's happiness."

Paul nodded in empathy. "I can believe that."

"I sure will miss her though. She's like a daughter to me — the age gap I suppose. I'll always love and cherish her. I think she feels the same about me; the warmth of her love touches me very deeply. But she's capable of running her own parish now and that's what she'll get. It's not unusual for a divorced priest to start afresh in another parish.

"But does Lucy want a divorce?"

"If she wants to continue with Tony, I think he will expect it. We know only too well the problems of secret relationships. It doesn't have to be that way with Lucy. She can be married to Tony and live a normal life."

Knowing the true situation, Paul felt wretched. He drove the rest of the way in near silence. Nick seemed to be lost in his own thoughts. They reached the rectory to find Lucy had been called out to the nursing home where a dying patient had asked for her. Paul was pleased not to have to face her for a while. But Rita did have to be seen. He had a few minutes to get to his vicarage. He found her waiting for him, a worried frown on her face.

"Are you all right?"

"Of course. Come in, I'll make us a drink."

He made her coffee and led her into the warm sitting room. Tired from worry, he dropped on to the cluttered sofa. She pushed aside a pile of his papers and sat next to him.

There was no good news for him. It was now getting around the school that funny things were happening in the church on the night of the vicar's punch-up. Evidently, a couple went to the church for a bit of canoodling in the porch and saw a light was still on. They heard music too. Sightings of all sorts of things were now circulating the school.

Paul told Rita about his churchwarden's visit. "He thinks he has me over a barrel. If Angela sticks to her story I suppose he has. I'm sure that Bishop Lionel will be inclined to believe me, but scandalous gossip could do a lot of harm. If it ever got into the local rag, who knows how it would affect my ministry? If it reached the tabloids under lurid headlines suggesting ritualistic raping of a churchwarden's virgin daughter, everything we've done will be at nought. I'd have no option but to resign."

"Paul, it must never come to that. Angela must be made to tell the truth," Rita said urgently. "She only needs to say that she was with someone else."

"But think, Rita. If Angela genuinely can't remember and she says things to please me, it will be just as bad. She'll be caught out one way or another and then everyone will be convinced of my guilt."

"But she wasn't alone. Mark must be made to give account of himself," Rita replied with conviction. "He's the key to all this."

"Mark's already told me he's no intention of confessing. He could say he was at that party all evening. Or if evidence proved contrary, he could put the full blame on Angela for being in the church, and then say he doesn't know what happened after he left her to me. He could even, with all honesty, say that he heard her pleading for me not to hurt her. Kevin heard the same thing in the vicarage. Our dear churchwarden would believe Mark and make sure everyone else did."

Rita leaned forward to take his hand. "It certainly is a mess. But, eventually, the truth will out."

"Maybe, but by that time, the parish will be split apart and everything will be in tatters; far worse than before I came."

"There are many people here who believe in you; who thank God for you and all you've done since you came here. You are not alone, Paul. This is not just your battle. We all have to unite against the forces of evil. Satan has mustered his demons but we have the power of the Holy Spirit to vanquish them. The battle is the Lord's and you must never forget it. It would be heresy to think otherwise."

Paul looked at her, a very powerful woman indeed, absolutely determined and ready to fight with all the weapons at a Christian's command. She was taking over his cause and he knew she would muster all of her Christian comrades and line them up for battle — in the early hours and on their knees!

"Bless you, Rita," he said, humbled by her faith and spiritual vitality.

She looked at him keenly. "For your own good, and for the good of Christ's kingdom, you know what has to be done. I don't know who he is, but you must give him up and seek to be healed."

Paul put his head in his hands. "Two people are involved. This is no casual affair; we are deeply in love. You don't understand."

"Maybe not, but I can see it would be painful for you," she said sympathetically. "But do you have a choice?"

"This business has nothing to do with my secret affair."

"If you lived a normal life, this could never have happened. You know that. Didn't you say that you're seeing Nick Palmer later on?"

He looked up at Nick's name. "Yes. He knows what's going on of course."

Rita looked him straight in the eye. "If he knew you had a gay lover, I'm sure he'd agree with me. Why don't you talk to him? I know his living alone caused a lot of speculation until he married young Lucy. He would be sympathetic."

Did she suspect Nick of being his lover? Did his face give him away at the mention of his name and when they ministered together? On no account must Nick be compromised. He calmed his nerves. "I don't want to get anyone else involved, unless it becomes very necessary."

"Of course, letting people know you're gay may well solve your problem, at least, in the short run. Sure. There would be some people who would be disgusted and move elsewhere, but most would not object if you were celibate. But you're not, are you? Should your lover be revealed he would suffer too, perhaps more than you, especially if he's in a position of authority."

Paul groaned. "Don't you think I'm aware of that?"

"I'm sure you are."

She drew closer to him. He could smell her perfume, see the

gentle movement of her breathing and sense her vibrant energy. She whispered softly, "Be healed, Paul. Take a step of faith. Come out of the darkness of uncertainty and into the light of Christ. Be the man God created you to be."

He heard the words; they were spinning around in his head. But he couldn't digest them, and didn't want to try. Love for Nick was too strong. God must have brought them together. He wouldn't even be sitting there were it not for his lover. He heard Rita speaking about his present incumbency. Could the woman read his mind?

"God may well have sent you here to be made whole and to find your true calling. You were already priest, pastor and evangelist. Now you're baptised in the Spirit, perhaps the time has arrived for you to become a complete man and a powerful witness to the power of God."

He could see his own reflection in her glasses and it disturbed him. He covered his face again and murmured. "Just leave it for now, Rita. See how things go with Angela. I hear what you say and I'll give it some thought."

She stood up. "There's something I have to do. If I don't see you before, I'll be in the church for Morning Prayer."

She bent over and kissed his forehead. He looked up and she kissed his lips. He made no effort to stop her.

"I love you, Paul. I'll not let anyone destroy you or your work. God is on our side. No one can truly harm you. You must believe that."

She quietly left the vicarage.

Paul took a couple of painkillers and returned to the sitting room to rest on the sofa. But memories of Angela and what she did, overlaid with Rita's dire warnings of satanic influences, kept coming into his mind. After a while, he decided to return to the rectory. As he stood up the phone rang. It was Rita.

"I'm at the Raymond's house. Kevin, Diana, and Mary Jones are here. Angela is too. She's going to try and remember what happened. If you come over, we can witness her statement together."

# Chapter fifteen

"I met Mark. He had some bottles in his car and we had a drink." Angela looked nervously at her dad, before continuing, "It was my birthday and I felt like dancing. Mark wanted to go to a big party in town but I wasn't dressed for it. I didn't want to go there anyway; some people take drugs and behave badly. You know what I mean? Sex and that sort of thing." She looked embarrassed.

Paul was relieved. She was admitting to drinking and to being with Mark. He looked around to see the impression she was making. Apart from her father, they were all giving her encouraging smiles. Kevin was the only one standing up, as though he needed height to give him dominance.

"I've tried hard to remember but part of what happened is just a blur," Angela said, looking at Paul and biting her lip.

"Get on with it, girl," Kevin said impatiently.

"We really must let Angela take her time," said Mary, who was there as an unbiased observer.

Kevin grunted. "We'll be here all bloody night," he mumbled to no one in particular.

"I had the church key," Angela said, giving a quick glance to see her dad's reaction. "We went inside. I put a disc on my player I keep in the church for dancing."

"Not any more, you bloody won't," murmured Kevin under his breath.

Mary gave him a stern look but he merely tightened his beady eyes and fixed his gaze on Paul. Paul had an idea Kevin knew something he didn't and so steeled himself for what was coming next.

"I remember dancing. Well, I sort of remember. I'd had a few drinks you see." She glanced at Paul again. "Everything is sort of patchy. I think something — well someone — was hurting me." She cast her eyes down in embarrassment. "All I remember after that was being in Mr Stringer's arms."

Paul tried to keep his face expressionless but it wasn't easy with Kevin leering at him.

"And what was Mark doing in the church all this time?" asked Rita in her teacher voice.

"I don't know. I don't remember anything from when I was drinking with Mark and dancing, to when I was hurting and being held by Mr Stringer." She glanced at Paul and whispered, "Sorry, Paul, but it's the truth, that's why I didn't want to say anything."

"It's a pity we don't have shotgun weddings any more, or you'd bloody-well marry my daughter, you hypocrite," Kevin snarled at Paul.

Before Paul could answer, Rita put in quickly, "This is ridiculous. It's obvious what happened. The girl had sex with her fiancé before the vicar turned up to clear them out of the church. Paul was merely looking after Angela, like any Good Samaritan would."

Mary Jones nodded, "That must be the logical answer. Mark and Angela were wrong to do such things in the church but we're not here to sit in judgement, merely to ascertain the facts."

Kevin snorted like a wild pig. "You don't know the facts, woman! The vicar was doing something diabolical on the altar with my daughter. It was covered in blood and stuff — you know what I bloody mean. Angela was just the same. Damn it! I saw her bloody starkers in the vicarage, just after he bloody raped her." He pointed at Paul. "It was part of some bloody ritual." He turned to Rita. "And that bloody witch had something to do with it."

Mary Jones was sitting with her mouth open. Diana Raymond started to quietly weep. Angela was weeping too, but far from quietly. Paul, not knowing whether to laugh or to cry, sat speechless. Only Rita was ready with a riposte.

"When you manage to control that temper of yours and start thinking clearly you may wish to reconsider your slanderous remarks. Mark will be able to confirm Angela's story of being in the church and drinking. He will be able to tell us what happened afterwards. The vicar has not denied wrapping Angela's naked body in her coat and taking her into the vicarage. He sent for me to look after her and to clean her up. Hardly the behaviour of a guilty person."

Paul marvelled at Rita's firm control of herself. Then he caught sight of Kevin and knew the battle was not over — the churchwarden was looking at him and grinning from ear to ear.

Kevin said to Rita, "Since you're such a paragon of bloody virtue, you may wish to repeat what you and I heard coming from the lips of my daughter. If I recall correctly, it was, 'Paul don't hurt me.'" He turned to fix his eyes on Paul. "And she was bloody moaning, which is hardly surprising with what he bloody-well did to her." He paused a moment and almost whinnied. "As for bloody Mark, I've spoken to him on the phone. Oh, yes, he admits they went into the church all right, but then our sainted vicar came along and threw him out — and we all know bloody why!"

"And you believe every word that young man says and reject the words of a priest?" Mary Jones asked, looking at Kevin with disgust.

Before a battle commenced on his behalf, Paul said calmly, "Mark spoke the truth but he left things out. Likewise Angela, which is hardly surprising in the circumstances."

Eyes turned to Angela.

"That's all I remember," she wailed.

Her mother went over to her and knelt by her chair. "Are you sure, Angie dear. You've always been such a good girl, why did you go in the church?"

"I wanted to sacrifice myself and pray for a miracle — like you did," she sobbed.

Kevin snorted loudly. "What did I bloody tell you?"

Diana ignored the remark, "I don't understand, Angela. You want a baby?"

Angela shook her head. "I just want someone to love me," she murmured between sobs.

Paul sighed, his heart was full of compassion for his fallen angel, but she wasn't helping matters one bit. He could see Kevin was ready to pounce.

"Well, you bloody-well got what you wanted. Right on the altar, with a randy vicar performing his perverted priestly duty! I bloody knew something was going on — like mother, like daughter." He turned to Paul, his eyes glittering between narrowed lids. "You're finished now. The whole bloody parish will know what you've done. Don't worry, I'll see to that."

"You're being too hasty," said Mary Jones at the same time as Rita commanded, "Stop this at once, you've gone too far!"

But Kevin bellowed, "You're not at bloody school now. Pipe down woman! I'm not one of your bloody kids. I'm the churchwarden here, and it's my sworn and solemn duty to keep order. And believe me, I'm not letting another randy priest turn St Michael's into a bloody brothel!"

Rita and Mary began to protest, Diana and Angela were wailing, Kevin continued his tirade but Paul had had enough — he walked out.

He drove to Glenton. The Palmers were still out. He let himself into the rectory with the key given to him by Nick and drifted to the kitchen to make himself a coffee. Sitting at the table to drink it, his mind was in a whirl. Before long, Kevin would be getting on to Nick to have his vicar removed from the parish. Nick would have no option but to discuss the matter with the bishop, who would already know about it from Kevin. Would Kevin carry out his threat to get the local rag involved? If so, his ministry would be intolerable. At the same time, his mind was trying to come to grips with Rita's explanation of the problems arising from his personal life. His thoughts were also drifting to Lucy and her love for Nick, and to his lover's refusal of preferment. Was it also because of him? Nick, Lucy, Tony Mayhew, Angela, Mark, Rita, and looming over all of them the stocky churchwarden with his glittering eyes — like a demon from hell! It was a tangled up mess and he was tripping up at every turn. Where was the light that had lit up his path? What was God saying to him? Was he so blinded by his love for Nick, that he wouldn't see the answer even if he witnessed the hand of God writing it in laser beams across the evening sky?

He didn't have long to wait before Nick came in. Someone was with him. Paul instantly recognised the robust voice of The Venerable Charles Bowman.

"How's Lucy? Lovely woman — exactly right for a bishop's wife. Couldn't imagine my Geraldine in the job; people would think she was the bishop not me! Pity we never had kids; Gerry's got too much time on her hands."

"I haven't yet accepted my name going forward — it needs much prayer. I'll just get that file for you. I think Paul Stringer's here if you want a word with him. Looks like he's in the kitchen. I won't be a minute."

"I saw his old jalopy in the drive," the archdeacon answered.

There was a sound of footsteps then Charlie Bowman came into the kitchen. "Hello, Paul, what have you been up to then? I received a call just before we came out to say you've raped the churchwarden's daughter. Now that really does make a change, I usually get told the vicar's having it off with the organist or some such."

Paul rose from his chair to greet the archdeacon. "Haven't you heard? That's happening too, and with half the parish according to Kevin Raymond."

Charlie Bowman laughed. "Well, what do you expect when you're a young handsome virile male? You'll have to get yourself a wife," he added, patting Paul on the shoulder and indicating for him to sit down.

Paul liked the man. He was of medium height and build; almost bald, brown-eyed, and blessed with a countenance that was attractively etched with well-worn laughter lines. Although always correctly dressed, he wore his clothes for comfort rather than display. A mature man of fifty-three, he was always good humoured and approachable.

Charles Bowman sat himself opposite to Paul. Leaning back in his chair and resting his hands on the table, he smiled amicably. "Suppose you tell me what this is all about. Nick's given me his version of events but I'd like to hear it from you."

Paul's head was thumping and he had difficulty getting his thoughts together. After a few moments he said, "The churchwarden's daughter, Angela, has fallen for her vicar. I hope I didn't encourage her, but she may have taken things the wrong way. She's been a great help with admin and getting a dance group started."

He stopped speaking as he tried to organise his words amid the thumping going on in his head.

Nick came into the kitchen and put the kettle on. "Mind if I join you since I've been dragged into it as well?"

Charlie Bowman pointed to the chair next to him. "You must. All right with you, Paul?"

"Of course. I welcome Nick's presence"

He took a deep breath to calm himself. "Diana Raymond claims Angela is a miracle baby, and with good reason. You see, in spite of problems concerning Kevin's ability to father a child, she finally conceived. But Angela's dad suspects the real father is the young vicar who ministered in the parish at that time. Hence, he's paranoid as far as his womenfolk are concerned. People gossip and can be most unkind."

His two listeners nodded knowingly.

"He's now convinced I raped his virgin daughter. He believes I took advantage of her affection for me when she was vulnerable. Worse still, he thinks I went through some sort of ritual with her on St Michael's altar."

The archdeacon looked him straight in the eye. "Did you seduce young Angela?"

"No, definitely not."

"Right, Paul, that's good enough for me. But I'd better hear the full story with the sordid details."

Paul explained the circumstances that led up to Kevin's recent accusation.

The two senior men looked at each other soberly and slowly nodded. Charles said, "It's going to be messy. I expect Raymond will soon be on to Bishop Lionel — if he hasn't done so already." He looked at Paul with compassion. "You've been through a rough time and you don't deserve it. You've really turned those parishes around; let's hope they stick by you."

Paul just nodded. It was good to have support but it did nothing to untangle the thoughts in his brain.

After the archdeacon left, Paul asked Nick for painkillers. He swallowed them down with a shot of brandy and sat with his head in his hands. "Sorry, Nick, I'm poor company tonight. Perhaps I'd better go home."

Nick pulled him out of his chair and embraced him lovingly. "Your company can never be poor. Love endures all things remember? We'll get through this together."

Paul could no longer hold back the flood. He wept on Nick's shoulder.

"I must resign; go away from here. If I don't, everything will go to pieces. God has called you to be a bishop, Nick. You must consummate your marriage, give Lucy children and live a normal life."

"We'll discuss these things when you're calmer."

"Maybe Rita's right about me. Perhaps I should give you up and lead a celibate life."

"Forget Rita. You've had a rough time and can't think straight. I'll see Mark myself. He'll tell the full truth; I'll make sure of it. Kevin Raymond is a bitter sick man and I'll deal with him too. I should have done so long ago but I never thought he'd go this far. You will stay here tonight as planned." He sat Paul down. "I'll get you a stiff drink. You'll be all right. Remember what you said before you came here? 'The Christian path isn't meant to be easy' and giving it as a reason not to come? Well, you should be convinced by now that you are on the right path!"

"But you and Lucy—"

"That's up to Lucy. Now she's having an affair, it wouldn't be right for us to start sleeping together. She has to marry Tony if she wants a normal family life."

Paul looked up to see Lucy standing by the kitchen door. Their eyes met in silent communication. She shook her head.

"Hello, what's all this?" she said cheerfully. "Planning to marry me off to Tony Mayhew? I guess it's time we talked about getting a divorce."

"If you don't mind, Lucy, we'll discuss the matter when we're alone. Paul has enough on his plate at the moment."

Paul felt Lucy's pain but there was nothing he could do. She left the room smiling and he wondered at her control. No wonder Nick knew nothing of her deep love for him. She was too afraid of losing him to allow it to escape from her mask of sincere sisterly affection.

In the morning, Paul returned to his vicarage. He felt much better but planned to take things as easy as possible. Before he'd left Glenton, Nick had rung Mark.

Paul heard Nick telling the young man sharply, "Either you meet me before you go on your afternoon shift, or I'll visit you at your place of work — and tell your employers why. I think perhaps you should try and recall what happened on the altar three weeks ago. We still have the white linen cloth; having it analysed might prove very interesting."

Paul had to smile; he'd told Nick that the cloth had been laundered and put back with the other linen, but Mark wouldn't know that. Obviously very worried, Mark said he would drive to the rectory as soon as he was dressed.

Nick had also rung Kevin Raymond, telling him that the matter he was concerned about had been discussed with the archdeacon and was being investigated. Meanwhile he was not to contact his vicar, as this would only hinder matters.

Paul picked up the letters delivered by the postman and then checked his answerphone. The funeral director had rung and so had a mother requesting baptism for her newborn. It was business as usual. He dealt with the calls straight away and then sorted his mail.

He went to his study to do some filing and type his letters. He would do without assistance from anyone, especially Angela. Whether she really thought he'd had sex with her, or was deliberately lying, her presence in the vicarage would now be intolerable.

The phone rang. It was Rita wanting to know if he was all right.

"I'm fine. Don't worry, everything is in hand. Thanks for ringing; I appreciate it. You'd better get back to the kids; I can hear them in the background. No doubt I'll see you later, but it's for Evening Prayer only. Please accept that, Rita. I am what I am." He put the phone down before she could argue.

The phone rang again. This time it was Nick.

"Mark's confessed that he was in the middle of sex when you arrived at the church. Of course, that doesn't let you completely off the hook because he can't say what happened after he left, but at least it pours cold water over Kevin Raymond's theory and that's the main thing."

"What a relief! Thanks, Nick, you're a real friend."

"I'm the rural dean and would assist any clergymen in the deanery, but it does help when I'm certain of the vicar's innocence. Now for your churchwarden. I'm meeting him at two in St Michael's, can you be there?"

"Certainly; is anyone else coming?"

"I would rather this be between us at present. I'm going to give him an ultimatum. If he feels he's been cornered you never know what he might do — the man's unstable. As priests we must be concerned for him too, after all, we have been ordained to cure souls."

"I agree. The whole family are very much in my prayers."

A couple of letters had arrived while he was on the phone. One was unsigned and it told him, in filthy language, that he should be defrocked. The other demanded his resignation. A third letter arrived while he was looking at the other two. This one suggested he make a statement about what really happened and that it should be put on the church notice-board.

He had to laugh at such a proposal. But, since St Michael's other churchwarden had written it he was obliged to write a serious reply.

At five minutes to two, Paul walked the vicarage path to the church. He heard the Mondeo arrive and found Nick waiting for him in the porch. "The church is open. Kevin must be here already. Now leave everything to me. I'm the senior person here and I'll deal with the matter accordingly."

Kevin, dressed in his dark suit and immaculate white shirt, was wearing a grey tie sporting an official-looking tiepin. He was waiting for them in his churchwarden's seat, as though it fortified his position. He stood up. The raised floor of the pew gave him extra height but he was still shorter than they were. Paul thought Kevin's extra bulk made up for that deficiency.

The smirking churchwarden glared at him through narrowed eyelids. "Don't think your pal will get you out of it. I've informed the archdeacon, and the bishop will be receiving my letter tomorrow."

Nick took over. He spoke in such a way that no argument was expected nor would be tolerated. "If you have any complaints at the way I run things, you may indeed pass them on; right now, please remember I am the rural dean as well as the rector of our team ministry."

Kevin's face flushed, his body noticeably stiffened, but he remained silent.

"I have already discussed the matter with both the archdeacon and Bishop Lionel. They have left me to deal with it since the matter is of no consequence."

With eyes bulging, cheeks blazing red and fists forming tight balls, Kevin looked as though he was about to explode. "Of no consequence? What about my daughter's rape!"

Nick continued unperturbed. "I've talked to Mark Brook. He's admitted to having sex with your daughter — they are engaged after all. That they did so in the church, and on the altar, is regrettable, but that is a separate matter and I'll be seeing the two of them about their somewhat shameful behaviour."

Kevin looked totally deflated. He sat down and appeared to sink like a popped balloon.

But Nick hadn't finished with him. "I suggest you apologise to Paul and do your best to make amends for the trouble you've caused in this parish and beyond. I can tell you, Mr Raymond, the bishop is not pleased. You hold an office of responsibility; if you wish to hold on to it, treat it with respect. Because of years of splendid service, the bishop may allow you to remain in office, but you may well find yourself voted out of it next spring."

Kevin had somehow shrunk even smaller and tears were appearing in his eyes. He wiped his hand across his face, and spluttered, "But I heard Angela speak the vicar's name — she told him not to hurt her."

"The girl was drunk, man!" Nick sighed and changed to a softer approach. "I can understand and appreciate your commendable concern for your daughter — and for God's house — but you got it wrong, dreadfully wrong."

"But Angela—"

"I understand Angela is unable to remember details. Mark has told me all I need to know." Nick paused and looked at Kevin quizzically. "Angela's been a great help to Paul and deserves consideration. I'll speak to her myself. I don't want you taking matters into your own hands. I hope you understand me."

Kevin nodded sombrely. He shook his head as if to wake up from a bad dream. "I understand."

Nick went up to him and put a hand on his shoulder. "Let it go man. You'll only destroy yourself if you continue this vendetta. Talk to someone. I'm always willing to listen, but we do have an excellent Diocesan Counsellor if you prefer not to talk to me."

Kevin shook his head.

"Well, the offer is always open. Give me a ring any time. Meanwhile, I think you have something to say to your vicar."

Paul could see Kevin's muscles tighten in his neck and face, and his hands beginning to form fists. Undaunted, Paul walked up to him, offering a hand of friendship. "I hope we can pull together in the future."

Kevin looked up, a mixture of hatred and bewilderment in his eyes. "Pull together? I wouldn't want this church to go where you're bloody dragging it. Someone has to pick up the bloody pieces when your eager beavers have torn it apart."

Nick cleared his throat.

Kevin, looking sheepish, took hold of Paul's outstretched hand and grasped it firmly. "But I'm sorry about all this business," he mumbled.

"Perhaps we could have a drink together at the local sometime," said Paul affably. He expected to hear Kevin's choice statement about flying pigs but he was pleasantly surprised when Kevin said, "Maybe, if you're paying."

Back in the vicarage, Nick shared a pot of tea with Paul while they discussed events. Nick went into details of his discussion with Bishop Lionel. Then he told Paul some surprising news.

"Lucy is applying for a chaplaincy at Riggington General Hospital. The present chaplain is about to retire. I mentioned it to Bishop Lionel this morning. I told him it was time for her to move out of my shadow. I said the chaplaincy would be ideal for her. He agreed wholeheartedly. So she's in for a good chance."

"How do you feel about it?"

"It will be an excellent career move for her, and will give her some space to decide if she really does want a divorce. She can resign from her present position, but still live at the rectory until she gets settled in her new job. No doubt there will be gossip, but the gradual move will be less sensational, especially as she's willing to help out occasionally until she moves away."

"Is this what Lucy really wants?" Paul asked him, knowing how she felt about Nick.

"It was her idea. She'll be free to see Tony away from this place, and get a better idea if she really does want to marry and have children. We should never have married, but she was utterly convinced she wanted a celibate life. Our marriage was her idea you know. I guess her biological urges are stronger than she realised. It seemed like a good thing for both of us at the time, especially with all the gossip about us being together so much. I was used to speculation about my personal life, but it was hard on Lucy. Being a women priest was difficult enough, but her youth and good looks made it difficult for people to take her seriously. Now, with few exceptions, she is greatly loved and admired."

"I'm sorry, Nick, I've ruined things for both of you. You should be accepting the preferment and Lucy should be by your side."

"Supporting me? No, Paul, Lucy deserves better than that. This would have happened sooner or later; you have nothing to do with it." He sighed deeply. "Dear God, I'm going to miss her."

"Me too." Although genuinely concerned at losing Lucy, both as a colleague and a dear friend, he was also thinking of the changes that would have to be made in the way he met up with Nick.

Nick pulled himself together. He drank his now cold cup of tea. "I have to go now — duty calls. We'll get our heads together sometime over Lucy's replacement. It's just as well Penningly hung on to the new vicarage; it's an ideal spot between Longdale and Glenton. Should be very suitable for our new curate."

Nick left, leaving Paul with a great deal to think about. But he had much to do and no time for speculating on the future.

After visiting a couple of sick parishioners in the hospital and making a bereavement visit, he was back in time for Evening Prayer. Rita was waiting for him. The Petersons and Mary Jones were with her. He remembered that he was supposed to be seeing Mary about her training programme. Her ministry was certainly going to be needed.

"Hi, Paul, I hope you're okay," said Mary. She gave him a knowing look that told him she wasn't going to discuss anything in front of others. "Are you still able to see me after prayers?"

"Of course," Paul said, relieved that Rita wouldn't be able to start on him again. There was a deanery meeting that evening as well, so he couldn't afford to waste time and energy in theological debate over his sexuality.

"Bill Smith wants to see you sometime. He wants to be a reader too," Mary said smiling.

The news lifted Paul's flagging spirit. Someone from Bradmire had also approached him about the same thing. Requests for formal training were signs of a lively parish. They would have to be interviewed and accepted but Paul saw no reason for their being rejected.

The Petersons wanted a quick word with him after the service. Paul gave Mary his key so she could let herself into the vicarage.

"There's a wall plan in my study, look to see which services you would like to help with; time you tried a bit of preaching." He gave her an encouraging smile.

The Petersons didn't take long. They had definitely decided to go ahead and seek ordination and told Paul they would be seeing Nick about it at the deanery meeting.

Paul found himself alone with Rita. He told her what had happened when Canon Palmer talked to Mark. She nodded her head, smiling. But their meeting with Kevin in the church brought an instant triumphant comment.

"Thank God! It's what we've all prayed for."

"Yes, indeed. Thank you for your support, Rita."

She looked at him with sorrow in her eyes. "You think it's all over don't you? It never will be, and you know why."

She walked out of the church leaving him sick at heart.

# Chapter sixteen

Work kept Paul too busy to dwell on Rita's warning. His mother rang him the next day to say his father was to have major surgery and they would like to spend a little time with him. Although he was overworked already, he said he would be very pleased to have them.

In spite of putting some things off until later, his ministry kept him fully occupied most of the time during the week his parents were with him, so when his father suggested they go to a pub before they went back home, Paul was very willing. At his father's suggestion, they went to the local, a pseudo Tudor building with interior to match, very popular among quite a few of his parishioners. Although it was early evening, there were no tables free.

"There's your churchwarden over there; I'll go see if we can join them," said his father and was gone before Paul could object.

Kevin looked up when he was being spoken to and nodded at Paul. He waved for them to go over and join them, pointing to some hefty wooden stools that needed pulling over to his chunky dark oak table. Paul was unhappy to see Bradmire's scandalmongers, George Hadley and his wife Elsie, sitting at the table. His parents already knew Kevin so he just introduced them to George and Elsie. Paul said he owed Kevin a drink and went off to buy a round for everyone.

While he was waiting at the bar, he heard odd bits of the conversation taking place at Kevin's table.

"What do you think of the new archbishop then?" It was his father speaking.

Kevin responded, "Bloody awful! He'll turn the Church into a club for gays."

Elsie said, "But didn't he say he'll not ordain a gay man if he's practising — at least, knowingly?"

All the men burst out laughing. "Shouldn't think they need to bloody practice what they get up to," Kevin said. "What do you think, Jack?"

"Like I always say, it's a 'don't ask and don't tell' get out. There's only one way to be sure they're celibate — chop 'em off!"

Amid muffled guffaws, the worried voice of his mother drifted to his ears. "Jack, really, not here please."

George joined in. "Jack's right. Queers can't be priests."

"Nick Palmer says different. He's a very wise person." It was his mother trying to be even-handed.

"I sometimes wonder about him. Good job he's married. Don't trust bloody liberals," Kevin told her in his usual blunt manner.

"Canon Palmer is a lovely man," she protested.

"Your Paul seems to think so — he spends most of his bloody time at Glenton."

Paul's father jumped in, "I must admit, I rather like the man. But are you suggesting—"

Noisy customers came in and Paul could no longer hear what was being said. He bought the drinks and took them to the table on a tray. The conversation had turned to politics but, much to his relief, the barman announced the pub quiz was about to start. That would keep them all occupied and in good humour for the rest of the evening.

Paul was sad at heart. A huge emotional divide separated him from those who gave him birth and there was no way it could be bridged. On the way back to the vicarage his father spoke to him in a concerned voice. "You should get married, Paul. Single men in your position cause gossip. I'll say no more." And he didn't.

Back at the vicarage, his mother insisted on making him a cup of chocolate. She gave it to him with tears in her eyes but refused to say what had upset her. What had been said at the pub? Or was it concern for his father — worried that she might lose him and be left alone? Somehow, he didn't think so. She had mentioned "lovely Rita" again, saying what a grand wife she would make some lucky man. What joy it would give her to see him married to his organist and making sweet music together, producing grandchildren for her old age.

The following morning, after his parents had gone home, Paul was deeply depressed. He hadn't slept well. He was exceedingly tired. Running around trying to get his work done with frequent interruptions from his parents had been frustrating. Trying not to get irritable and feeling guilty for even having to try only caused him further stress. His mother had asked why "that nice young lady" wasn't helping him any more. The fact that Angela was no longer helping him was bad enough, he didn't want to have to find excuses or be reminded of why she was absent from the vicarage. The constant mention of both Angela and Rita, and his father's camaraderie with Kevin Raymond, increased the pressure he was under with his parents living in both his home and workplace. He was living a lie and felt alienated from all of his family.

What's more, he'd convinced himself that he was the cause of Nick's marriage break up. Was it sinful lust that drew him to Nick? Was Lucy's infidelity entirely his fault? Should he have pursued the evangelical road of ministry, sublimating his sexual energy as he'd done previously? Nick would have made a perfect bishop. Had Nick refused God's call rather than let him down? Not having had chance to be with Nick in private to discuss his doubts, he couldn't cope with his self-questioning so he threw himself into his work. He had a lot of catching up to do anyway. But his heart was heavy and his ministry was becoming more of a strain than a joy.

The Petersons, Rita and Angela joined him for Evening Prayer that evening. Angela kept giving him sorrowful looks. He knew she wanted her job back but he couldn't allow it. The Petersons were on their own wavelength but Rita was definitely on his.

After the others had gone, she said to him bluntly, "You're ready for healing prayer. I can feel it."

Paul could no longer resist Rita's powerful personality. Terribly depressed, weary, full of self-doubt and guilt, with his body aching and his head pounding, he knew he couldn't go on as he was doing. He put his head in his trembling hands and whispered, "Yes."

Rita locked the church door. The church descended into a pregnant silence. In the chapel, Paul knelt down in front of the altar and clasped his hands together — as much to stop them from shaking as for reverent prayer. He sensed, rather than saw, Rita come up behind him. He made no resistance; he was too tired with lack of sleep and the constant giving of himself in pastoral ministry. He wanted to be healed, strengthened and made new. For that, he needed prayer. Nick would pray with him but he didn't want to worry him, neither did he want him to stop what must be done for both their sakes, and for the happiness of those they loved.

As soon as she began praying, his emotions welled up within him like a powerful force. He began to shake and he heard himself moaning. As her voice rose in power commanding the demon to depart, he found himself groaning. Rita's prayers increased in power and he began struggling within himself and moaning Nick's name. He was in agony of spirit - love and duty tearing him apart. He fell from his knees on to the floor rolling and shouting, "Oh, Nick! No! No!" He heard his voice change to a pathetic whimper: "I can't do this. I can't, I can't. God help me, I can't do it. I love him."

Through bleary eyes he saw a ghostly face moving beyond the panes of the window. The statue of Mary seemed to be swaying towards him. Caught in a spotlight, a fiery St Michael with his Holy Angels loomed ready to war with Satan and his demonic host. Over all was the deep commanding voice of Rita. Only it didn't sound like Rita — surely it must be St Michael himself! He began to violently shake with his heels drumming on the floor. Rita was more forcefully praying and commanding the deceiving demon to depart. He had no control over his body. He writhed as if in torment and retched repeatedly. Suddenly, "Aughhhhhhhhhhhh...." echoed around the church.

The next thing he knew was Rita holding him in her arms, wiping the tears from his cheeks and cleaning round his mouth.

"You must rest, Paul," she said tenderly. "I'll go back with you and make sure you're all right. Go to bed — you need to sleep."

In a daze he went with her, through the churchyard and garden and into the vicarage. He realised he'd wet himself and it embarrassed him.

Rita helped him remove his clothes. "Don't worry, my darling, I'll help you,"

She ran the shower for him while he sat on the bathroom stool watching her in bewilderment. She was taking off her clothes too. Even through his blurred vision his mind registered her body as being slim and beautifully proportioned. She took hold of his hand and drew him over to the shower. "It's all right, don't worry, I'm going to help you wash. You might fall over on your own."

The needles of water were delightfully refreshing and helped clear his brain. Rita was standing just behind him, smoothing lather over his shoulders and back in a massaging motion; it was very pleasant.

"Mmm, that's nice," he murmured.

She put her arms around him and pulled him up to her naked

body.

"I'll support you while you wash your front," she said, "unless you would like me to do it for you?"

While he was trying to get his brain around the implications of her suggestion, he felt her hands move over his chest, her fingers gently pressing into his flesh in a circular motion. He took hold of her hands and pushed himself backwards — holding her in a back-to-front embrace, as he'd often done with Nick. Was he with Nick? He couldn't quite grasp the situation. The hands were now moving downwards — he must be with Nick. The washing was a pleasant soothing ritual. But he was so tired, so very, very tired.

As he staggered naked to his bedroom, he thought he heard the phone ringing but he had no urge to answer it. He fell across his bed — the sheets were pulled back ready to receive him.

He was awakened by the sound of voices. He opened his eyes and pulled himself together. It was Rita and Nick arguing. Then he heard heavy footsteps on the stairs and Rita yelling, "Leave him alone, you've done enough damage to him already. Go back to your wife. He's free of you — free I tell you!"

Then Nick was there, standing by his bedside with Rita clawing at his shoulders.

"Nick?" Paul couldn't get his thoughts together. Then the noise of voices began hammering at his brain.

"What have you done to him?"

"You ask me that? What the hell did you do to him? He was a God-fearing priest until you got hold of him."

"Paul is still a God-fearing priest. Treat him with respect."

"Me treat him with respect? You led his soul astray."

"You don't know what you're talking about, woman."

"Lying demons! That's what I'm talking about."

"Superstitious nonsense. Get out of here!"

"I'll not leave him with you, Canon Palmer. You've brought chaos into the Church with your sinful lust."

"Rubbish, woman! Get out!"

"No! Go away and leave him alone before you do more damage."

Paul could see scuffling, and voices were now deafening him.

"Get out of the way, Rita."

"Get back to your wife, you fornicating devil!"

"I'm taking Paul with me. You don't know what you're doing."

"Leave Paul alone, he needs to rest."

"With you in his bed? You're fooling yourself, Rita. You've been after Paul ever since he arrived here."

"God brought us together, for me to free him."

"Rubbish!"

"He needs a woman — you've perverted his mind."

"Get out of this vicarage — or I'll throw you out!"

"Just try it and you'll get what I gave the churchwarden."

Paul groaned and put his hands over his ears. The muffled voice of Rita reached his brain.

"He's awake — thanks to you. Ask him yourself what he wants — know the truth if you can stand it."

"Go away — go away — go away," Paul heard himself moaning. Then a new but familiar voice shrieked into his brain.

"What are you doing to him? Leave him alone, Rita."

Rita yelled, "Angela? What are you doing here? Get out!"

"Stay, Angela — until Rita leaves." It was the authoritative voice of Nick.

"She has no business here." Rita argued.

"Angela rang me, thank God! She saw Paul staggering out of the church with you. I phoned here several times but there was no answer...."

Nick's voice was drowned by yelling and crying — three voices in a frightful cacophony of passionate venting of feelings. Paul crept under the bedclothes, curled himself up and pressed his hands over his ears. He felt hot tears running down his face but he was too weary to care. Then silence fell and all he could hear was his own sobbing.

The clothes were pulled back from his face and a cool damp cloth wiped his brow and cheeks. A voice he loved spoke to him gently. "Come on, Paul, it's over now. I'll stay with you until morning." Secure in Nick's all-embracing presence, he drifted into a peaceful sleep.

He awoke to find a cup of tea being placed on his bedside table.

"How are you, Paul?" Nick asked him. "I'll have to be going soon; it's half past eight and I have a Eucharist at ten. Can I get you anything?"

"I'm a bit groggy but otherwise I'm okay. Gosh, I must have been asleep ages. I'll have a quick shower and get dressed. I have to talk to you, Nick — seriously I mean."

Within ten minutes Paul was sitting eating toast with Nick. He was trying to put into words what he knew he must say to him.

"I want you and Lucy to stay together, Nick. She loves you. You must know that by now."

"She told me, but it makes no difference."

"You're completely devoted to her. If I hadn't come on the scene, she wouldn't have gone with Tony and you would soon be a bishop. It isn't too late is it?"

"The offer has been withdrawn. Don't worry about it. We've already had this discussion, Paul. Nothing has changed as far as I'm concerned."

"Why did Bishop Lionel change his mind? Were there objections from the others?"

"Just Bishop Lionel being cautious. He'd been informed of rumours and didn't want the new archbishop being dragged into a difficult position. I totally agree with him. I had turned it down anyway, it was the bishop who insisted on giving me time to pray about it."

"Rumours? Something's been going on hasn't it? Things were said to my parents out of my hearing. Dad was sort of quiet and mother had been crying. Rita probably thought I'd heard the rumours, that's why she knew I was ready to be delivered."

Nick sighed. "Just gossip. Kevin's been looking to get his own back — that's all. Try to put what happened with Rita behind you, she was completely out of order. I've told her she is not to repeat any of that nonsense in any of the churches again. I hope she got the message."

Paul didn't want to talk about the previous evening. He knew Nick was angry about it. He only had vague memories of much that had happened anyway. But he knew there was something he had to do. A lump came up in his throat but he took a deep breath and came out with it.

"I have to let you go, Nick. I have to exercise faith and accept that I've been delivered and live accordingly. I'm sorry — really sorry. I must leave the area. Find somewhere like my last place. Let you get on with your life and your ministry. What you do is too important for your position here to be compromised by your association with me."

Nick pulled his chair closer to him and took hold of his hand.

"I'll not stop you doing anything you feel called to do, but I think you're wrong about this deliverance business."

"It was real, Nick — it bowled me over."

"I know. Angela told me what she saw and I have to say, Paul, I was most disturbed by it."

"Angela wasn't there, it was just the two of us."

"She was waiting outside to see you — thank God. She heard the door being locked and wondered why. She was worried about you and with good cause."

Paul's head was beginning to spin again. He was trying to recall the details of what happened and Angela didn't fit into the scene.

"Angela wasn't there, Nick. I was alone with Rita. That much I do remember."

Nick gave him a reassuring smile. "Now keep calm and I'll explain."

But Paul felt far from calm — what had Angela seen?

"Angela went round to the window of the side chapel and climbed on a broken gravestone leaning against the wall. She could only see through the odd panes of clear glass but since the light was on in the chapel she could make out what was happening. The deliverance business was bad enough, it's what happened afterwards that makes it even more questionable."

"Afterwards? I have little memory of what happened."

"Angela says Rita was all over you. Then she helped you to the vicarage where she saw you both silhouetted against the bathroom window. Angela rang me on her mobile but I was out. The second time she rang, the archdeacon was with me. I phoned the vicarage but there was no answer. I came as soon as I could get away. Angela kept watch over the house and was waiting for me."

"You know you can't trust what Angela says. Rita was only helping me clean up and get into bed."

"I'm certain she was in bed with you. It took her ages to answer the doorbell. The only light that came on was in your room, and I could tell you'd had a companion in your bed. Long reddish hairs were on your pillow and her scent was on your sheets. Apart from which, it was obvious that someone had got out the other side of your bed."

"I expect she was looking after me."

"You always think the best of people, that's what I love about you, but you're blind to the wiles of women. Rita intended being there when you woke up. She would reinforce the belief, which she had put into your head, that you're no longer gay. Without doubt she would help you prove it. When she hurriedly dressed to answer the doorbell, she left off her undies — I found them in the bathroom. I'm absolutely certain the two of you were naked in bed together. She was furious when I insisted on going upstairs to see you."

Paul put his head in his hands and groaned. "But even if that's true, it doesn't mean the deliverance was invalid."

"If I'd have known what you two were planning, I most certainly would have stopped it. There is to be no more such practices within this deanery. We have someone within the diocese to advise on such serious matters, and it isn't your organist."

"I'm sorry, Nick. I guess I've let you down. It's just that—"

"Don't apologise. I should have sensed how you were feeling. Look, Paul, you're overworking and under a lot of stress. I want you to take a break. I've phoned the Diocesan Retreat Centre up in the Lake District and they can put you up for as long as you like. Go, Paul; get away from me and your parish. Walk the hills and be alone with God for a while. When you return, I'll accept whatever you decide to do."

"I can't do that, Nick. There's too much to do, especially in the run up to Christmas. So many things are being planned and I have to — no, want to — see them through. Apart from which, I have to work at being healed and I can't do that if I'm away from you. I'm sorry, I don't want to hurt you, but that's the way it is."

Nick looked at him with a pained expression. "Work at being healed?" He slowly nodded in resignation. "Do it your way, but the offer stays open." Rising from his chair, he sighed wearily. "I must go now."

Paul stood up with him, expecting Nick to embrace him. But Nick walked straight out of the kitchen, his face a mask of composure. Only a tear escaping an eye to sparkle on his cheek, betrayed Nick's true feelings. Paul watched him with a heavy heart.

Nick made his way through the hall to the front door. "I'll be seeing you at the Clergy Meeting at eleven. Don't worry if you can't make it." As he was about to go outside, he turned, his face now strained from controlling his emotions. "God be with you, Paul. Take care. I'll always be here for you."

Paul wanted to call him back; tell him he loved him and couldn't do without him. He fought back the tears that threatened to swamp his eyes. He fell on his knees, and with a painful throat prayed for strength to overcome his lustful desires and to be able to love Nick as a brother. Suddenly he was overwhelmed by guilt. His prayers had been for himself — what of Nick? His lover had already lost one partner to God, now he was being deserted again. Full of sorrow, he cried out to his Lord. Determined to control his emotions, he took some deep breaths and then prayed earnestly for Nick: his happiness, his ministry and his marriage to Lucy.

The telephone rang. Paul pulled himself together and went to answer it. It was Angela.

"Paul? I'm just ringing to see if you're okay."

"Thanks, I'm fine."

"I didn't know about — well — you know. Now I do, can I work for you again? Please? I'm free tonight, can I come round?"

Paul had missed her presence as well as her secretarial skills. He made a quick decision. "Yes please; I've got some notes of a meeting still waiting to be typed up."

An excited voice replied, "Thanks, you won't regret it. Seven okay?"

He'd only just put down the phone when the doorbell rang. It was Rita. She made her way in before Paul could invite her.

She was looking anxious. "I slipped out of school — free period. Can't stop long. How are you? You've been weeping — I can see it. Oh, Paul, are you so unhappy?"

"I'm okay, Rita — truly. I've told Nick we're finished. I've hurt him badly."

He fought back the threatening tears and walked to the kitchen to get them both coffee. Rita trailed after him.

"Oh, Paul, you're so brave. And poor Nick." She sighed with deep feeling. "We must pray for his deliverance too. I said bad things to him. I must apologise."

Paul nodded. "I should have told him first. My fault it turned out as it did."

"No, Paul, he would have stopped you. But you're free now. You do believe that don't you?"

"I'm assuming it to be so. I have to accept it by faith. But I have to be honest with you, Rita, my feelings are the same."

She threw off her tailored brown checked jacket, revealing a soft figure-hugging cream jumper and short brown skirt. Her slender legs were looking even longer and shapelier in high-heeled shoes. She put her arms around his neck. Her face felt soft against his and her delicate perfume drifted sweetly to his nostrils. She moved her warm, fragrant body close to his and whispered in his ear, "You've never had a woman in your life. Woman was made for man — she's God's gift to you. Just give it a chance. You were happy with me in the shower last night. You enjoyed my body close to yours — I could tell."

He pulled her arms away from his neck. As much as he needed comforting, the sexual connotations of the embrace embarrassed him. "I've decided to be celibate," he said solemnly.

She looked at him, her eyes flashing. "It won't do, Paul. You're acting like a petulant child. Can't have what you want, so you won't have what you're given." It was the voice of Miss Lee, the schoolteacher!

Paul felt the rebuke keenly, but he knew she was right. He would have to give the matter earnest prayer. "I'm sorry," he said meekly.

"You know, Paul, God has blessed you with many gifts but you throw them back at him. Rejoice and be thankful — let yourself go!"

He made an effort to smile. She was so right. What had happened to that wonderful joy — that sense of liberty — which had been so much part of his ministry? He had allowed things to get on top of him and was shouldering unsustainable burdens. Time for the curer of souls, to cure himself.

"Can you give me half an hour? We could go into church, lock the door, and have a praise session."

"Let's do it!"

She picked up her things, Paul threw on a jacket against the bitter cold wind, and they set off half-running to the church. Once inside, Rita climbed the steps to the organ loft and started playing the hymn Paul had sung that first day he visited the church — "How great thou art."

Paul joined in singing lustily. The gloom lifted and his spirit began to rise. Rita went on to play "Shine Jesus shine" and Paul started dancing for joy — his heart on fire. She changed the mood to "Our God reigns" and once more Paul was singing, his arms raised in praise. Yes! He'd said his "Yes" to God and he was back on track. He had 'good news' to proclaim and God was with him. Rita played for another five minutes then she came down to join him in the dance. She pulled off her shoes and slipped off her jacket. They put on a disc and danced together.

Dancing with Rita was perfect. They anticipated each other's movements and they flowed as one to the rhythm of the music. As the melodic notes came to an end, they wrapped their arms around each other. Paul sighed deeply, content that he was back on his path.

"Thanks, Rita. I guess you'd better get back to work. I have much to do myself. It's been great — just what I needed."

She pulled away from him and gazed deeply into his eyes. Was she trying to penetrate his soul? She came forward and kissed his lips, opening her mouth to touch him with the tip of her tongue. He opened his lips and fully responded. She pulled her body tight against his and clung to him in desperate desire. Knowing what she wanted, he moved his hands over her buttocks and pulled her hips hard against his own.

The sound of the church door being rattled broke the spell. Paul let go of her and she stood back looking at him adoringly.

"I must go, Paul. The kids will be in the classroom in fifteen minutes, causing chaos if I'm not there. I'll see you for prayers at five."

"Yes, I look forward to it." The door was rattling again, with thumping to add to the racket. "I'd better unlock the door before it gets battered down."

"Why is the door locked with the bloody key inside? It's bloody freezing outside," Kevin Raymond thundered as he bulldozed his way past Paul. He saw Rita putting on her shoes, and gave her and Paul a look of disdain. "Bloody disgusting," he mumbled to himself.

"If you have something to say, say it, man, and be done with it," said Paul.

"I said it's bloody disgusting what you two get up to. Door locked indeed!"

"I didn't think you'd enjoy dancing with us, but I'll give you a buzz next time."

"You can come over and join in," said Rita, who was now putting on her jacket. She came up to Paul, kissed him on his cheek and said goodbye.

Paul smiled. "I'll see you later."

She picked up her things and left the church.

Kevin glowered at Paul. "Did our Angie have a word with you last night?"

Paul felt his muscles tighten and made an effort to relax them. "About what? Typing for me again? She did that this morning over the phone."

"Well, what the bloody hell was she doing here last night then? She was out long enough. Didn't she tell you 'er and Mark are getting bloody married?" Kevin fixed him with his beady eyes. "She's bloody pregnant!"

Paul was taken by surprise but he tried not to show it. "Oh, really? She's coming to the vicarage tonight, perhaps she'll tell me then."

Just as Paul was going through the door, Kevin called after him, "If we need to get in touch with Canon Palmer tonight, Vicar, will he be here same as last night?"

"Meaning what?"

"Just asking. From what Bob Desmond told me, Palmer's car was here all night. He says funny things were going on in the church earlier on. You staggered out with arms around our obliging organist. When he took his dog out later on, and again this morning, a certain blue Mondeo was parked at the vicarage." Kevin grinned. "He thought maybe you were poorly but you look bloody good to me. Maybe our rector's a bit of a healer, eh?"

Paul contained his agitation. "Why don't you ask him? I'm sure our rural dean will give you a copy of his diary too, that is, if you ask him nicely."

Whatever was now being circulated around the parish, Paul was determined not to let it disturb his equilibrium. He returned to the vicarage and prepared to go out. He wanted to pop in at the hospital before the Deanery Clergy Meeting at Nick's. It was going to be a tight squeeze but he wanted to fill his day and not have time to ponder his relationships.

It had been all right kissing Rita. Maybe he did have to push away imaginative thoughts that it was Nick's tongue thrusting with his own, but it was a step in the right direction. He was wrong to think he could ever be celibate. Nick had aroused his sexuality from slumber and he couldn't see how he could put it permanently to rest. But he must continue to accept his deliverance. Perhaps he should marry Rita and make his parents happy. Nick would surely come to realise it was for his good too.

Nick was acting his normal self at the meeting — circulating until introducing the speaker, and chatting with fellow clergy while the buffet lunch was being served and eaten. Occasionally their eyes met but Nick gave no indication of whatever pain he might be suffering.

At the end of the meeting, Lucy cornered him and whispered angrily, "Nick's told me. How could you do it to him? Isn't it enough that he's losing me? You'll be back, Paul. Don't be surprised if he turns you away."

Paul was cut to the heart but he refused to give way to his emotional impulses. As the clerics left, some jovially shaking hands, others quietly nodding or smiling, Paul went forward and offered Nick his hand.

"Thanks for everything. I'll see you tomorrow then; perhaps we can get the Christmas services planned," he said cheerfully — too cheerfully.

"That's what I had in mind. I'll be taking Friday off; I'm going with Lucy to Riggington. I'll be back Saturday afternoon. Can you hold the fort?"

"Of course."

Finding a lump coming into his throat, Paul let go of Nick's hand and hurried to his Discovery. Words that he'd said to his therapist so long ago echoed in his brain; "I'm emotional; Nick's the strong one."

# Chapter seventeen

Apart from the extra workload in the run up to Christmas, Paul spent much time visiting his parents after his father's operation. It was only made possible because of Angela's help with administration. Although she suffered slightly from morning sickness, pregnancy added that extra bloom to her looks and a certain maturity to her personality. Not once did she give Paul cause to worry over her previous infatuation. Her capacity to love was now directed towards her growing foetus. Mark, if indeed she did love him, barely made second in line — or so it seemed to Paul.

He saw Rita daily for prayers and occasionally they kissed — she always taking the initiative. He knew Rita wanted more but he felt no desire to experiment, or in any way encourage her expectations of a deeper relationship — certainly not marriage — until his life was more settled. Nick was not yet out of his system and he wasn't sure if he ever would be.

The busiest time of the year was soon over. There was now a slack period until the run up to Easter — unless they had bad weather or a 'flu' epidemic to cause extra funerals. But Paul didn't want time on his hands; he wanted to keep active. He'd even given up his meditation because thoughts of Nick clawed at his heart. Nick was on his mind before he went to bed and again on waking. He came to realise that being in love was more than sexual attraction; he missed Nick's personal presence in his life. Seeing so much of him formally only increased his yearning for him. He told himself repeatedly that he was being tempted, and that he must have faith in his deliverance and not give in.

Rita had a whole week before she was back at school and was expecting to spend much of it with him. Secretly, he was dreading it.

Tonight would be the first time alone together in the vicarage since she'd helped him to shower, and it worried him. He had no excuses to make to put her off coming. Rita would have him to herself. Kissing was one thing, would she want to go further? Worse, would she push him into marriage?

The doorbell rang. It was Angela. He sighed with relief and let her in.

"I hope you don't mind me coming; I wanted to ask you something."

"Not at all, Angela. Come into the kitchen." The sitting room was out-of-bounds as far as Angela was concerned. "Want a drink?"

"No thanks."

Paul put the kettle on in case she changed her mind. He sat down opposite her. "Would you like to take your coat off, or aren't you stopping?"

"Thanks, I will take it off," she said, getting up. "And I will have a coffee since you asked."

Paul smiled and helped her with her coat. He made them both coffee and sat at the table with her again. She seemed to be a little nervous and it rather disconcerted him.

"Well, Angela, what brought you here on such a cold dark night? Have you walked?"

"No, Mark dropped me off. He's waiting for me in his car."

Paul stood up and walked towards the door. "I'll get him in, poor lad."

"No!" she almost shouted. "Please don't. He wouldn't come anyway."

Paul was intrigued. He sat down again and picked up his coffee mug. "What is it, Angela? Something to do with the wedding? Too soon for you?"

"It's sort of to do with the wedding." Keeping her eyes down, she started stirring more sugar into her coffee. "Mark's not convinced it's his baby."

Paul was mystified. "Well, only you two can know that."

"I haven't been with anyone else."

"Then what's the problem? Doesn't he believe you?"

She shook her head and bit her lip. "It had to be that time in the church."

Paul couldn't understand what she was getting at. "Since I witnessed the event, I would say that it was highly likely. Is Mark trying to deny it now?"

She dropped her eyes. "He says he withdrew before — you know. He says he always does. Doesn't like using — you know. Other girls haven't got pregnant, he says."

"Perhaps other girls use the Pill. Really, Angela, Mark is rather stupid if he thinks he can get away with it. He might get out of marriage, but he can't get out of supporting his child."

She gave him a brief look and then dropped her eyes again. "He says it must be your baby."

Paul sighed heavily. "Oh, Angela — we've been over all this. You both know it isn't."

"That isn't what Mark says. He thinks you took over where he left off."

Paul put his elbows on the table and head in his hands. "I can't comment on what Mark thinks happened. All I know is what I saw and that you're pregnant. Perhaps you conceived soon after the church business."

"Not possible, I knew I was pregnant before we did it again."

Giving himself time to think, Paul drank the rest of his coffee. He looked her in the eye. "Whatever you may or may not remember, I can assure you, Angela, I have not touched you. As lovely as you are, I have no desire to sleep with a woman. You know I'm gay and always have been."

He suddenly realised he'd openly admitted to what he truly was — gay! In his heart he knew there had been no deliverance from demons — he was what he'd always been and there was no getting away from it.

She stared at him with big open eyes. "You're gay?"

"You know I am. You were around when Rita—" But why should he go into details? "Oh, never mind about that, just accept my word for it. When the child is born, you'll both know for certain that Mark is the father."

"But I thought that business in the church was Rita casting a spell on you. My dad says she's a witch. I knew she wanted you, and now she's got you. So how can you be gay?"

"I was born that way. Rita is not my lover — if that's what you're thinking."

"But your mother seems to think you'll soon be married. She said so when she was over at Christmas."

"Wishful thinking on my mother's part," he told her, wondering what else his mother had been saying. Anyway, Angela, I am not the father of your child. If Mark is trying to get out of marrying you, perhaps you should reconsider what you're doing. Marriage is for life you know."

She stood up, put on her coat and walked pensively to the door. She turned and said, "I guess all that talk about Rita being a witch is kind of stupid. I had no idea about the other thing though — you know, what you said about being gay and all that. What was Rita up to then?"

"Just helping me with one of my little turns. Don't get it around though. Please don't repeat anything I've told you, Angela. I couldn't let you help out here if I can't trust you."

"I won't — who'd believe me anyway? Goodnight, Paul, I'll see you Saturday," she said with a little smile on her face. As she went outside, she gave him a knowing look and murmured softly, "Your secret is safe with me, Mr Stringer."

Paul watched her run down the drive to Mark's waiting car. He sighed, so that's why she hadn't told anyone he was gay — she hadn't known about it after all.

Headlights of another car approached. It was Rita coming for the evening.

A few minutes later, he was helping her remove her coat. She looked absolutely stunning. She was wearing contact lenses instead of her heavy-rimmed glasses. Her hazel eyes and strong facial features were highlighted by her lightly applied make-up. Her hair was tinted a rich chestnut and it fell slightly over one eye and down to her bare shoulders in quite an alluring manner. Thin straps held up her shimmering black dress, which was cut low enough to reveal large portions of unfettered breasts. The short skirt not only enhanced her long shapely legs, but the slit in the side was an open invitation to insert an exploring hand. He knew the magnificent sight should have turned him on — that was clearly the intention. But it did no such thing, and that was enough to convince him, beyond any possible doubt, that he was still gay.

"You look beautiful," he said, trying to make the right noises.

She smiled at him and said sexily, "I want to please you. Am I succeeding?"

He walked with her to the sitting room. "You always please me, Rita, especially when you play the organ."

She gave him a puzzled look. "Is that an invitation of some

kind?" She put her hands on his shoulders and looked into his eyes. "Mm. Perhaps later we can take another shower together. I'd like that," she added in a sexy voice.

"What? Oh, no, you got me wrong. How about you play the piano and I'll get my guitar?"

"What's the matter with you, Paul? We can make music together any time. Come and sit with me on the sofa. It will be easier to talk."

"Rita, I have to tell you something."

"Then sit here and tell me," she insisted. "Mm, nice fire. Put another log on, we might need it later."

He did as she asked. With that dress, she certainly needed to be kept warm and he didn't want excuses for her wanting to cuddle. He used his trouser legs to rub a bit of sawdust off his hands. Although a little nervous, he sat by her side. After all, he was going to let her down and he ought to be decent about it. But she moved up closer to him and put a hand on his knee. He took hold of the straying hand before it reached its target. He had to tell her before she made a fool of herself.

"Rita, I'm sorry. I've probably led you to believe we're an item, but it isn't possible — I'm as gay as I have ever been. You can't change the way I was born. I can't love you as a woman; only as a friend."

She looked at him wild-eyed. "That's rubbish! The way you kiss me? Not possible and you know it."

She threw herself at him and tried desperately to get him to share her erotic kissing, but he refused to oblige her. With her weight holding him down, she reached for his zip and managed to get a hand inside his pants. "I'll prove it to you, like I did in the shower."

He was nauseated by her touch. She tried again to get her tongue past his lips but he refused to cooperate. He pushed her away. "I can't, Rita. I'm already in love and he's the only one I'll kiss that way again."

She stood up, one of her breasts now completely exposed by the struggle. The split in her skirt had torn up to her waist, revealing a shapely thigh and hip. A curious thin black string crossed over the revealed white flesh. Thongs? With hands on hips and legs apart, she looked at him in fury. As he tried to stand up, she swung back her right arm and, with all the force she could muster, slapped him across his face. He reeled over and fell to the floor. She stood astride over him, hands again on hips. Through a painful haze he saw where her legs divided and a small black triangle hiding what he had not the slightest desire to see.

"You're filth, Paul Stringer. Your mother will weep for you when she finds out the truth. It will just about kill your father. You're finished here - you know that. And that lover of yours will be thrown out with you. No church will want either of you defiling their parish. The sooner you go the better!"

Paul lay floored by the powerful blow she'd given him. He couldn't stop her leaving even he wanted to, and he most certainly did not. He heard the front door slam. A burning log shifted, the fire crackled, sparks flew up the chimney and then everything settled in the grate.

He struggled to his feet, poured himself a stiff drink, and staggered to the kitchen for a couple of painkillers. He had some thinking to do. There was no telling what Rita would do in her fit of anger. He must warn Nick.

Lucy answered the phone.

"Hi, Lucy, I must speak to Nick. Is he there?"

"What do you want, Paul? Is it ministry or personal?"

He didn't like the way she was monitoring Nick's calls — it wasn't the first time.

"I need to speak to him, Lucy. Is he there or not?"

"He's had a hospital visit this morning and a midweek service, plus two funerals this afternoon. Did you know the police have been to the youth club again? Now he's just had the archdeacon on to him. Can't it wait until he's had chance to get a meal in peace? He's put in extra hours to cover for you while you've been visiting your parents. You're so selfish, Paul — can't you think of Nick occasionally?"

Paul was hurt by Lucy's rebuke, but he understood her feelings. "You're quite right, Lucy, but—"

Nick came on the phone. "What is it, Paul?"

"I'm sorry to disturb you, Nick. Lucy says—"

"Never mind Lucy, you wouldn't ring unless it was necessary."

Nick sounded tired and yet his voice was full of concern. The warmth of his love for him bridged the distance and entered his heart. He wanted him so very badly it hurt.

"Nick, I think we have a problem."

"We?"

"My fault I know. I should have listened to you and gone away to think things through. Now I've hurt you and Rita — my parents too when they find out. God alone knows what will happen to our ministry. I'm so very sorry, Nick. I've ruined your life too. Oh, Nick I need you—" The words had been spilling out of him and he wanted to say more, but his throat, tight with tearful emotion, had suddenly seized up.

"Perhaps you'd better come over and we'll talk about it. Lucy's going out any time and we'll be on our own." Nick said calmly, as though talking to an overwrought child. There was a pause and then he added, "Are you all right for driving? Do you want me to fetch you?"

"Thanks, Nick, but I'm okay to drive." He put down the glass he had in his hand; he had no need for liquid comfort now. "I'll come straight away, if that's okay with you."

"Sure, sounds urgent. Look, I've a big meal here. Suppose we share it? Put your phone through to here, you might want to stay over."

There had been nothing suggestive in the way Nick had spoken, but the thought of an intimate night with him dispelled the gloom that had descended on his soul. Whatever the consequences of the whole parish knowing their secret, Nick would deal with it — of that he was certain.

"Thanks, I'll be there soon."

Within minutes Paul was getting into his Discovery. As he turned up the lane, he caught sight of Bob Desmond returning home with his dog. Had he seen the shimmering figure of Rita dashing to her car — half-naked on a cold night and dragging her coat behind her? If he hadn't seen her, he would have heard her car take off — along with half the gravel from his drive!

Nick had heard his vehicle arriving and was standing by the open door to welcome him. He smiled warmly but was holding back from embracing him.

"Nice to see you, Paul. Take off your coat and come through to the lounge. How about a drink? I'll put the food in the microwave when you're ready."

"Thanks. A brandy — neat would be great."

Sitting in front of a roaring fire with glass in hand, Paul began to relax. But how could he tell Nick what had happened between him and Rita? He'd tried to let a woman take his lover's place — even considered marrying her — to prove what? That he was 'normal'? What then did that make Nick? He'd been an idiot. He looked across at Nick who was smiling at him benignly.

"I've been a fool, Nick."

"Yes."

"I've hurt you badly."

"Yes."

"Will you forgive me?"

"Yes," Nick answered softly, his eyes beaming with good humour.

"There's something I have to tell you. I'm not sure how to say it."

"Let me help you," Nick said cheerfully. "Miss Lee rang just before you arrived. You no longer have an organist; that's something we'll have to sort out for Sunday. You don't wish to hear what she said about you, and certainly not what she said about me, but I gather you led the poor woman up the garden path and dumped her on the compost heap!"

"I didn't exactly do much of the leading but that's no excuse. I'm so sorry."

Nick sat back in his chair, thoughtfully sipping his brandy. "Actually, Paul, Rita isn't our main concern; it's what she does with her knowledge about us that we must prepare for."

"Surely she wouldn't open herself up to ridicule?"

"There's more than one way of defrocking a priest."

Paul sat up straight. "What on earth did Rita say to you?"

"That she was informing the bishop about your dishonesty concerning your sexuality, especially your relationship to me, and that you spend too much time with the teenage boys. Apparently, you've been seen with your arms around them. And she said that she would tell the bishop what she knew about the altar incident — that she'd heard Angela telling you not to hurt her."

"That's ridiculous! She hasn't a leg to stand on. It's true I used to spend time with the local lads before we had the youth group going — I taught a couple of them to play the guitar and we all played football. I dare say I might have put an arm around the odd shoulder, but you might as well accuse football players of indecency — hugging and jumping on each other in public! As for Angela, that's been sorted out."

"Not quite, Paul. According to Rita, Angela had anal sex with someone that night. Obviously, Mark was making the most of his opportunity, but I'll be surprised if he'll admit to it. Evidently, Rita has thought all along that you took advantage of the girl. She equates anal sex entirely with homosexuality."

"But that's stupid, we—"

"That's not the point," Nick cut in. "What happens between us in private is no one else's business. But, I can't see the bishop listening to Rita's speculations anyway. To have everything dragged up again would not be fair to Angela."

"Oh, no!" Paul suddenly remembered his visit from Angela. "I suppose Angela is now thinking it was me who did that to her." He told Nick what had happened earlier that evening.

Nick laughed. "Sorry, Paul, but with foxy women around you'd better wear an armoured cod piece!"

Paul frowned. "Do you think Mark's trying to deny his preferred sexual activities, as well as saying the baby can't be his?"

"I have no idea. But if he tries it again, and he probably will, she'll know it was him that night, so don't worry. As for the baby, perhaps it isn't Mark's. Like I said before, you always want to think the best of people — perhaps Angela isn't the little angel you think she is. There will be no problem revealing who is not the father — if it comes to that."

"Apart from revenge, what does Rita hope to gain from her wild accusations?"

Swigging down the last of his brandy, Nick told him, "She wants both of us to repent and leave the priesthood. I've told her I won't give in to blackmail."

Paul sighed deeply. "What am I to do, Nick? If I give up the priesthood will she leave you alone?"

"You'll do the same as me — pray and carry on. Priests have had worse charges thrown at them. It will all blow over. Rita's an unhappy woman and needs our prayers. She'll simmer down when she's had time to think about what her actions will do to her own public standing."

Nick's strength of character, his trust in God and forgiving nature were reasons enough for Paul to love him, but there was far more about Nick that drew him like a magnet. They were soul mates, fitting together like two pieces of a jigsaw puzzle — each complementing and fulfilling the other.

Paul looked at the flickering flames. "Lovely fire — getting a bit hot in here." He looked at Nick, yearning for his closeness. "I've missed our times together."

"Yes, I know. So have I."

"I know you love me. Why didn't you stop me, Nick? Why did you let me go my own way? Why did you risk losing me?"

Nick closed his eyes a moment and then looked at him closely. "Do you remember the first time we met at the conference? I recited from Paul's letter to the Corinthians that wonderful hymn of love: 'Love is patient and kind; love is not jealous or boastful; it is not arrogant or rude. Love does not insist on its own way; it is not irritable or resentful...'"

Paul smiled at the remembrance of that fateful day and picked up the quotation. "'Love bears all things, believes all things, hopes all things endures all things...'"

Nick stood up, pulled off his jumper and started unbuttoning his shirt. "God brought us together," he said softly. "Let no man part us."

"Amen to that," said Paul, smiling as he pulled off his shoes and jumper. "Shame to waste that lovely fire. When is Lucy back?"

"Early hours. I'll put on the answerphone."

"What about your supper?"

Nick grinned. "Exercise on a full stomach is bad for you. We'll eat later."

Paul walked over to the tall windows facing the rectory garden and looked out into the dark cold night. Smiling serenely, he closed the shutters against the world and its problems. He was now completely free to embrace the fire of Nick's passion in a celebration of their mutual love.

Don't miss
page 238 ⟶

# Epilogue

Paul picked up his keys and walked out to his car. Nick had already left; his first lecture that morning was at nine-thirty and there were students to see first. As for himself, he had a number of very sick young men to visit at the AIDS clinic. Being a chaplain was emotionally wearing but it was a ministry he loved — he truly believed he was taking the light of Christ's love into the dark places of man's soul. What's more, living in relationship with Nick was everything he'd prayed for. No longer alone and divided within himself, he was now complete.

To be living so close to sunny Californian beaches was a bonus he'd never ever dreamed about. To have his parents visit, accepting his situation even if they could never approve of him living with another man in a gay partnership, had made him even happier. They couldn't help but love and admire Nick; they always had. It saddened him that his sister refused to acknowledge she had a brother, but Ann was top of his prayer list, and one day his love for her would win her over. "Love believes all things, hopes all things," he constantly told himself.

One day, they would be back in England, but not until they could live together without causing controversy and divisions. Meanwhile, Nick had found being Professor of Ethics and Religion at the local University very fulfilling, especially as he served as an assistant priest in the huge church close by.

Before getting into his car, Paul collected their mail from the box at the bottom of their drive. There was a letter from England. He opened it and smiled; it was from Angela Brook. When he read the contents, he burst out laughing. Angela and Mark's little boy was celebrating his second birthday and, according to Angela, although he had Mark's ears and hair, he was now the image of his beady-eyed, short and stocky granddad. His little angel had been a 'miracle baby' after all — how ironic!

# Also from Magpies Nest Publishing

**Red Boxes** – When Phones Were Immobile and Lived in Red Boxes

Gladys Hobson, fully illustrated by Gladys Hobson and Gary Lyons, ISBN 0-9548885-0-2

"the author reminisces about her childhood years between 1939 & 1953. ... She covers a multitude of things she experienced (or not) from the NHS , WWII, Sex Education, Boys, Family Affairs ... The book has some very funny anecdotes, but it also shows how people had to 'make do & mend', and how life was much simpler then. It shows a different way of life, but it is a very entertaining book, I could not put it down."

Gwen Green, Westmorland Gazette, Sept 2004

# Coming in 2004/5 from Magpies Nest Publishing

**Blazing Embers**

Angela Ashley, ISBN 0-9548885-2-9

"Love, laughter, passion and poignancy are found in the struggles of an elderly woman to find and put into her marriage, orgasmic sexual experience so far denied her."

**Designer Love**

Angela Ashley, ISBN 0-9548885-3-7

"A tale of passionate love conflicting with burning ambition, set in the Midlands of post-war Britain."